Holly's Christmas Secret

Holly's Christmas Secret

Kirsty Ferry

Where heroes are like chocolate – irresistible!

Published 2022 by Choc Lit Limited

Penrose House, Crawley Drive, Camberley, Surrey GU15 2AB, UK

www.choc-lit.com

A CIP catalogue record for this book is available
from the British Library

ISBN 978-1-78189-467-5

Printed and bound in Great Britain
by Clays Ltd, Elcograf S.p.A.

To everyone who loves a good fairy tale,
especially at Christmas.

Acknowledgements

Welcome to this new edition of *Holly's Christmas Secret*!
It's book three in the 'Cornish Secrets' series and has
practically doubled from its original beginnings as a
novella. If you've read the original eBook, you might
see a few things have altered slightly in this version, and
I do hope you like them. I also took the opportunity
to put a little more in about Biscuit the dog, as he was
a bit of a fan favourite in *Lily's Secret* and I'd hate
people to think he wasn't around any more in this lovely
Christmas story – as Christmas is, of course, a time for
all members of the family, be they fur babies or human.

A few years ago, I bought a book at Barter Books
in Alnwick, Northumberland. It was called *Princess
Mary's Gift Book* and was published in 1914.
Princess Mary, Princess Royal, later Countess of
Harewood, was heavily involved in charitable
works and nursing during the First World War, and
this book was published to raise money for The
Queen's Work for Women Fund. The fund was set
up in August 1914 and intended to initiate and
subsidise projects for employing women during
World War One. *The Gift Book* contains a treasury
of children's stories by the likes of J.M. Barrie,
Sir Arthur Conan Doyle and Rudyard Kipling,
along with some gorgeous illustrations from well-
known artists like Arthur Rackham. The illustrations
are literally coloured pages, stuck with glue down
one side, onto a pre-printed box on a page – very

precious indeed. It is an incredibly beautiful book, and one of my favourite parts of it is the poem 'A Spell for a Fairy' by Alfred Noyes (you might know he's one of my favourite poets if you've read *Watch for Me by Moonlight*), which is illustrated with a delicate picture from Claude A. Shepperson.

I've always loved fairy tales, and my grandma bought me a wonderful hardcover book of Hans Christian Andersen tales when I was very small, but I didn't quite appreciate how dark these things could be until I studied them for my degree! The books I've read, and the pictures I've seen by these amazing illustrators, almost demanded that I be inspired by them to do my own version of a fairy tale. And when I decided to do a Christmas book based at the fabulous Pencradoc, where all sorts of weird and wonderful things go on, I knew I could bring them all together in Sorcha and Locryn's story, which is also, by default, Holly and Noel's story.

Like the suffragettes and the ladies who were empowered by Princess Mary and her fund, Holly is not your standard historical heroine – she's got a bit more of the modern woman about her, and I like her very much. I do hope you enjoy this particular Cinderella story, and come back to see what happens to Elsie in book number four of the 'Cornish Secrets' series, *Summer's Secret Marigold*!

As always, thanks must go to the fabulous team at Choc Lit for bringing this fairy tale to life in the modern world – thanks to my editor, my cover designer and my fellow authors at Choc Lit and Ruby Fiction. Also to the

Stars who chose this gorgeous cover, and to the Panel who agreed this book could stand a chance in the real world (Gill Leivers, Sharon Dobson, Gillian Cox, Sharon Walsh, Erin Thorn, Bee Master, Kate Doyle, Alma Hough and Fran Stevens) – but it is awfully nice to escape the real world at times, and I hope you manage to do that by reading and enjoying *Holly's Christmas Secret*.

Huge thanks to my family too – I edited this in a hot and sticky July through to August, and they helpfully plied me with tea, coffee, cold drinks and alcohol where and when necessary in order to stop me dehydrating and gasping for sustenance. Thank you, I love you all!

The king's son soon came up to her, and took her by the hand and danced with her and no one else; and he never left her hand ... But she slipped away from him unawares, and ran off towards home, and the prince followed her.

Cinderella, The Brothers Grimm

Prologue

Once upon a time, about twenty years or so ago, there was a little girl called Sorcha Davies. Sorcha lived in a village near Bodmin Moor in Cornwall, and that village was called Pencradoc.

Pencradoc was also the name of a big old stately home in the village, and a very old lady called Miss Loveday lived in the house.

Well, she seemed very old to Sorcha, who was only a little girl, and quite enjoyed climbing, unseen, over the old, rusty wrought iron gate to get into the grounds of Pencradoc, but Miss Loveday probably wasn't that old really. And to a little girl from a rather standard three-bedroom family home on a nice little estate, who quite liked to disappear from her annoying, much older sister at times, Pencradoc was magical. It had a foreboding grey gatehouse, and lawns and gardens that stretched way into the distance. The house itself was also built out of grey stone and had high roofs and lots of windows. In the summer, the gardens were a riot of colour and the scent of roses drifted along the boundary wall, and Sorcha would sniff, taking in big breaths of the lovely scent as she crept along very close to the trees that lined the estate next to the wall.

Once or twice, she thought she'd been spotted when Miss Loveday was out in the gardens with a basket that she was filling with flowers, presumably to take indoors to decorate her house.

Once or twice, Sorcha had to squeeze right behind the trees and shuffle sideways through the bushes, holding her breath for a dreadfully long time until she popped out the other side; then she'd run as fast as she could towards the big tower that stood apart from Pencradoc.

Once or twice, she maybe even spotted a secret smile twitching at Miss Loveday's lips as she snipped carefully at the blooms and definitely did *not* look in Sorcha's direction. Instead, Miss Loveday concentrated enormously hard on cutting her flowers, and then said in a very loud voice to nobody in particular: 'Dearie me, what a shame I have so many strawberries and raspberries ready to eat just along by the potting shed. If only there was someone who would take a few handfuls of them to help me out. They really are rather delicious.'

Sorcha could confirm, even years later, that they were very delicious indeed.

But it was that tower, set away from the house in the middle of some more gardens, that she always liked to run up to and look at best. It was rather tumbledown, but her father told her it was what was called a "folly", and for some reason people in the old-fashioned times used to like building new things that looked old – which didn't make much sense at all to Sorcha. But the tower, tumbledown or not – and it wasn't really, it was actually quite sturdy, as she eventually found out – always seemed as if it would be more at home in *Rapunzel* or *Sleeping Beauty*, and Sorcha studied the building carefully to see if there was any hint of a secret princess trapped inside it. She usually studied it whilst she was chomping on a mouthful of sweet, red fruits she'd collected on the way, depending on the season.

There never had been any princesses waving back at her from the tower, much to her chagrin, but that had never stopped her from daydreaming about it.

'One day,' she told herself, 'I will get inside that tower and it will be just as pretty inside. And if it's not pretty inside, I will *make* it pretty so people can come and visit me in it.'

And then, on one occasion when she'd clambered over the gate on a sunny Saturday afternoon, she'd seen a group of children playing, dressed up in what looked like their best clothes – although their clothes *did* look a little odd to Sorcha, because all the girls wore frilly dresses and big hats. Even the boys were wearing straw hats along with short trousers. She knew two boys sometimes came to visit Miss Loveday, and they'd run around outside or kick a ball around until tea time, but they dressed like the boys at school did, in jeans and T-shirts; she'd never seen any little girls there until now and the boys that were there today were definitely not the boys she had seen before.

Sorcha had watched for a while, peering out of her shady hideaway and wishing she was one of the children who were playing out there at that moment. Four little blonde-haired girls and one dark-haired girl, who was a little bigger than the rest, were running around the lawn outside the house. A few smaller children were nearer to the French doors, one or two clearly desperate to join in.

She'd continued to observe, looking out from the shrubs she was hidden in. She'd wondered if it was a birthday party and imagined what the cake might be like if it was. Sorcha liked baking cakes, and had helped make a dozen fairy cakes that very morning before she'd sneaked away to Pencradoc. As her tummy rumbled at the thought of birthday cake, she wished she'd brought some of those cakes with her. She'd stayed watching for a while longer, hugging the idea of her secret hiding place to herself, but then she'd continued her exploration, and when she'd come back, it seemed they'd all gone in.

And still there were no princesses in the fairy tale tower ...

Chapter One

Sorcha had had enough. Martin was getting more and more on her nerves; in fact, she was rapidly running out of nerve for him to get on.

'So you've *definitely* decided to go for it?' he'd asked her again incredulously, as they'd been prepping veg together. Well, *she'd* been prepping veg. He'd been blustering around yelling orders as he always did, and occasionally standing next to her and jabbing his finger at her carrot batons saying they were the wrong size, and dismissing the lovely carrot-flowers she'd been making to show him what he could try to do differently.

She often wondered why she bothered suggesting things to him.

'We'll talk about it later, Martin,' she said. It was busy enough in the hotel kitchen without him deciding to have another shout at her about her plans, and they both had the evening off, anyway.

Although, she had to acknowledge, he'd been pretty shouty all day, actually. 'You could make Christmas roses out of white carrots,' she'd suggested earlier. 'They'd look really pretty on the Christmas lunches. I'll help—'

'Don't be so ridiculous!' he'd yelled, and she'd rolled her eyes heavenwards yet again. *See? What is the point?* It seemed that her suggestions were always being knocked back and it was starting to get to her.

Martin was a good chef – in fact, he was a great chef

– but Sorcha was also a great chef, although her skills lay more in patisseries and cakes. So she'd not pursued the conversation and made a mental note to bring it up later instead – because outside of Martin's kitchen, he was also her boyfriend. They'd been together around a year, and she had initially been attracted to his passion and his drive, as well as his dark, brooding good looks … but sometimes she had the uncomfortable feeling that she might have made a mistake in dating someone she worked with.

Martin himself didn't always find it easy to separate "work" Martin from "home" Martin. And since he'd had a promotion, he was even worse. Now he couldn't seem to separate "boss" Martin from "boyfriend" Martin, and she'd started to think they'd be better off working in two different places.

As she'd hoped, he had been more than happy to pick the subject up at a wine bar after work. But unfortunately, part of the way through their conversation, she'd twigged by the look in his eyes as to why he *might* be more interested, and alarm bells immediately started ringing.

'So – tell me more about your business plan again,' he said. 'We've never really properly discussed it, have we? I mean, would it be just *your* business? Or would you want a partner? Someone with a bit more experience behind them?'

That was the look she'd recognised – the glint of ambition. She'd seen it in bucketloads when the senior post had come up in the hotel, and immediately she felt irritated. Again. Because she knew what was coming.

'It's just me, Martin.' She smiled, trying to take the sting of rejection out of her words. 'You've known for ages that I want to specialise in baking. I've done all the training, done all the hotel work, and I know what I want to do next. And that is set up my own tea room, and now I've got the perfect place to do it. Alone.'

A little squiggle of excitement jittered through her tummy. The fairy tale tower at Pencradoc had come up as a possible location. The place was now an Arts Centre, as Miss Loveday, God rest her, had passed away, and the two boys Sorcha remembered from so long ago had inherited the place – the boys were, she knew now, Loveday's great-nephews, Kit and Coren Penhaligon. Sorcha had finally been able to visit Pencradoc legally and had loved what she'd seen … although the tower was still empty and she hadn't been able to go inside, which had frustrated her slightly.

Then, a couple of months ago, her mum had rung her excitedly to tell her they'd been advertising for someone to set up a tea room in that very same tower, and within a few hours, Sorcha had contacted Coren and had an informal chat with Merryn – whose partner was the other brother, Kit.

Before she knew it, and even before setting foot in the place, she'd provisionally agreed terms and conditions, spoken to the bank, and fully intended to move back to Pencradoc village with a bright, exciting future before her. She had her eye on a small rented flat and the shiny new premises beckoned. She should be in before Christmas, all being well. Merryn had told her they were getting some work done to the tower to make it fit for purpose. Although she had seen photos and detailed plans, she'd still never actually been inside, and sometimes she wondered if she was being wise agreeing to it so readily, but apparently it was being done out as a fully fitted tea room, and if Sorcha didn't take it, someone else was bound to snap it up.

Sorcha was nothing if not determined, and had already set her heart on it, sight unseen. It just felt right. Pre-destined almost – well, it would have done *if* she was given to flights of fancy, which she was not, unless it involved random secret princesses in ramshackle, tumbledown towers, of course.

The only fly in the ointment was Martin.

Sorcha had talked to Martin about her plans, and not once had she considered asking him to work with her. Or even offered that as an option. They didn't live together and it should really have been quite simple.

This was one occasion when she didn't need to make enthusiastic suggestions to someone only to be told to rein it in. It was *her* project, *her* tea room, *her* future.

Besides, Pencradoc was only about ten miles from the hotel Sorcha and Martin worked at, and it would be quite easy for them to continue seeing each other, so to Sorcha a move back to Pencradoc was quite manageable.

But Martin, despite being brilliant, was also quite lazy at work these days; he rarely did much in the kitchen except shout at people, always seemed to miss himself off the rota for weekends, and moaned if he ended up doing extra-long shifts to cover events.

Sorcha knew it wasn't a career where you expected weekends, high-days and holidays off, but Martin, drunk with power now, thought differently. And it also seemed he felt differently about Sorcha's decision to go it alone with her new tea room.

'I disagree. You'll be needing a partner,' he said to her. '*I* could come in with you and then we could run the place together. You've got no real business experience and I can help you there. I mean, I could be a consultant and take on the odd weekday shift for you to get a feel for it. How does that sound? You could keep weekend working for yourself so you feel more in control.'

'That sounds appalling!' Sorcha stared at him in horror. The offer of "one shift during the week" didn't really go with the idea of Martin "being a partner". He clearly wasn't thinking about being an equal partner, was he?

'What do you mean, "appalling"?' Martin seemed genuinely shocked. 'It's a great plan. You have the value of my expertise and experience, I can advise you on what to do to draw in and maintain customers. And I'm even volunteering to cover shifts for you, so I can offer the best advice. I'd be a great partner.'

'You would not.' Sorcha stared at him. She'd once known a girl who'd said she wanted to run a tea room but didn't seem to grasp that unless she took a chance on midweek trade being stellar, she'd be responsible for working every weekend – potentially the busiest time for trade. 'You've turned all lazy, and you shout at people, and there'd only be me working there, so you'd end up shouting at *me* all the time. Trying to tell me what to do! And *you* don't like it when I suggest things to you for your kitchen – so why would I want to take advice from you, Martin?'

'Because *you* don't know what you're talking about in *my* kitchen, Sorcha. It's my kitchen – my rules. And to be honest, you need to stay out of it. The difference is, I'd be helping *you*! Your ideas are so far-fetched that you'd never make them work. I mean – babyccinos? Mini-mochas? Lunch boxes for kids? Dog-friendly seating and Waggy Walkies groups?' He shook his head and folded his arms. 'If you encourage young families and dog-walking groups in, you'll never get them to leave. They'll take root there all day long and paying customers won't be able to get a seat. You'll be losing trade.'

Sorcha could sense her cheeks flaming with temper and mortification. *I don't know what I'm talking about, do I? Rot!* She knew *exactly* what she wanted and what would work. 'You can't not have things for young children, Martin! Parents won't come in if the kids aren't going to be catered for. And the dog walking group will be a summer thing and will only happen once I'm established, and there'll eventually be seats outside for them anyway.'

She was embarrassed to see that they were attracting curious looks from the other customers, although Martin seemed pompously oblivious to it all. 'No. You should discourage that. Sell items at a premium. Make it seem exclusive. Boutique. Upmarket. Encourage the quick turnaround of customers. If they look like they're chatting, clear the table they're sitting at *whilst* they're sitting at it. They'll soon get the message.'

'No! No, Martin. This is the village I grew up in and the people I know. I won't start doing that to them! I want them to have a great experience and recommend me by word of mouth. I—'

'You have no idea, Sorcha! If you want to be successful, you need to be ruthless. I can help you. I mean, like I say, we'll work as partners, you set it up, run it as you see fit. I take the odd shift to see what it's like – then I advise you on the best model, the way *I* see fit, for a fifty per cent cut. You know it makes sense.'

Sorcha wasn't sure whether it was the fifty per cent cut, or the downright arrogance of the man, but she was beginning to feel her temper bubbling up. She made a great effort to keep her voice down as she leaned forwards and hissed a response.

'Martin, this is *my* dream. It's *my* tea room in a location that I've loved for years. If there are any mistakes to be made, I want to make them myself. For the final time, I'm not inviting you in as a business partner. I don't want a business partner. And if you think you can do one shift every week and get fifty per cent of the profits by telling me what to do, you have so many other thinks coming!'

'I'd quite like a new challenge too!' he said, scowling. 'I've always wanted to run my own place as well. I can *do* that if we go in as partners.'

'No! We cannot. I don't want a partner! I just want my tea room! Mine!'

It had sounded a little petulant and entitled when Sorcha thought about it later – but it was the way she felt, and she had to try to make it work on her own.

Locryn had had enough. Laura sat opposite him, arms folded, her mouth set into a thin little line.

'I can't understand what your problem is,' she said. 'We've got the chance to do something really exciting for Christmas and you're not even interested. I've already told them we're going, and I said I'd give them the money for the deposit this week. Patsy's going to sort it out.'

"Them" was a gaggle of Laura's friends who had nothing in common with Locryn and everything in common with one another. The "really exciting" thing was going skiing for Christmas and sharing a log cabin *á la* Wham's 'Last Christmas' video. It was Locryn's idea of hell. He was an antiques dealer, a little older than his girlfriend Laura, and generally liked a fairly calm existence where he didn't spend a great deal of time with people who shrieked nonsense and squealed at each other.

He'd gone along last year, sure that a lovely break in a romantic log cabin halfway up a snowy mountain would be the perfect way to spend his and Laura's first Christmas together. What Laura had omitted to tell him was that they were the only couple in the whole crowd, and the few days they spent there had consisted of him sitting on the outside of everything, chatting to Charlie and Nick, the only other two guys there – and he was pretty sure Charlie fancied Nick anyway. Locryn also suspected that Nick had a tally-sheet of how many of the girls he could manage to flirt with and seduce before the holiday was over; even though Nick, apparently, had a girlfriend back home, who hadn't been invited along.

Laura had shrieked and screamed and got drunk every day, and they all seemed to revert back to their student personas and had so much shared history that Locryn wondered on more than one occasion why he'd come. Even the "fun" snowball fight had ended up with Nick pinning Laura to the ground while he shoved snow down the front of her pink ski-jacket as she writhed beneath him in a rather uncomfortable-to-witness manner.

Christmas Day had consisted of everyone getting up at lunchtime with hangovers while Locyrn somehow ended up in sole charge of cooking a turkey the size of a Shetland pony, only for most of the party to announce they "felt too rubbish to eat", and one quiet, pale girl, who had mostly sat in the hot tub draining Prosecco the whole time, muttering that she was a vegan now anyway, and hadn't anyone remembered that?

They had lurched through Boxing Day in a similar vein, and then on the twenty-seventh, Locryn decided that he had never been so pleased to board a plane home. He'd missed spending time with his family and hadn't liked waving to them all via FaceTime on Christmas Day instead of actually seeing them in person. Even his favourite aunt, Aunt Susie, had joined the rest of his family for Christmas lunch and brought her homemade Christmas cake with her, so he had missed seeing her too. And he'd missed the cake, of course. It never seemed so festive eating it after the twenty-fifth.

'Laura,' he said now. 'I think we said we'd have Christmas at home this year? It's the first year we've lived together, and I thought we'd said that your parents, my parents and Susie could come over for lunch? I said I'd cook it. So you can just relax.'

Laura pulled a face. 'Well, yes, I know we *said* that back in September when I moved in, but I've been thinking that it's more fun to go away with our friends again. I mean, we're only young once, right? So we talked about it on the WhatsApp group and Nick posted some pics from last year and we all thought it would be great to go again. Which is why Patsy is on the case. I just said to tell us how much we owed her and we'd fall in with the plans.'

'I'd rather not, to be honest.' Locryn did feel bad. He didn't want to be a spoilsport or a stick-in-the-mud, but it *was* their first Christmas in the house and he just ... well, wanted them to have it together at home. 'It would just be nice to have it here.'

'But I don't want to spend it with a whole load of old people!' Laura's face was thunder. She was four years younger than Locryn, and he hadn't felt that was particularly an issue, but clearly she had now decided he fell into the "old" category. 'I had years and years of family Christmases when I was a kid and I want something different. I want to spend it with my *friends*!'

'Don't you want to spend it with me?' Locryn's voice was mild, but alarm bells were ringing in the back of his mind. *Again*. The latest in a long line of alarm bells.

'You're a friend as well,' tried Laura. 'But I've known these guys so long. I love the very bones of them. I mean me and Nick go back to the first flat we shared at uni—'

Locryn didn't really want to hear any more. He knew all about how wonderful Nick was and how much fun they'd had. He let her talk and wondered, not for the first time, why they were still together.

Chapter Two

Christmas, 1905

Holly sat on her bed, legs tucked under her, watching her friend, Elsie Pencradoc, rummage through a travelling trunk.

'It's here somewhere,' muttered Elsie. 'I know it is.'

'Remind me again what you're searching for?'

'Photograph. Of. Lily. Ah!' She stood up and waved an envelope at Holly. 'Knew it. Jolly good.'

Holly uncurled herself and shuffled across the bed. The girls studied together at the Liberal College of the Arts and shared rooms in a rather nice townhouse, given over to the young ladies who studied there. Elsie was already searching for her own private accommodation and quite fancied a house in Bloomsbury. Holly knew that her friend would get her dream London home eventually – Elsie was the "posthumous daughter of a Duke of Trecarrow" after all, as her friend was fond of intoning darkly, and her full title was Lady Elsie Pencradoc. She didn't throw her full title around to all and sundry though – but if you knew Elsie, you'd know she came from Society without having to be told. She just had a sort of air to her that was confident and slightly wild and rather driven.

She was also one of the nicest people Holly knew – when she'd first discovered she was sharing a room with someone with a title, she was unsure of what to expect.

But Elsie had swept in, shook her hand firmly and

smiled widely. 'Good morning. I'm Elsie. Which bed would you prefer? I'm easy.'

And from that moment, the girls had clicked. Holly, nervous and unsure of her talent now she was at college, compared herself unfavourably to everyone else, but was unfailingly bolstered up by Elsie, who was absolutely incredible at art. Elsie looked after her, almost nurtured her, and they explored London together. Elsie knew the place well and they spent many a happy hour wandering around companionably, arm-in-arm.

And here they were, a few months after starting college, living in a rather cluttered space full of sketchbooks and paintboxes, and looking forward to Christmas. They'd looped garlands around the fireplace and had strange, untidy bunting up at the windows – pine cones, and paper chains and paint brushes, interlinked with ribbons and lace – and Elsie had been on a mission to find this one particular item in her trunk for a good fifteen minutes.

'My sister, Isolde, posted this photograph to me *aeons* ago,' explained Elsie, slipping the picture out of the envelope. 'I kept it safe in my trunk until they needed it for *The Tattle-Tale*.'

'*The Tattle-Tale* is just full of student gossip!' said Holly with a laugh. 'Who on earth writes the thing? Nothing is sacred in that college!'

'No. You have to be *so* careful of what you say and to whom.' Elsie was indignant. 'I casually mentioned Louis over lunch one day, and the next issue was full of "Lady E— admits her love for the mysterious Mr L— A—". Poor Louis. And also, I think Leonard Atkinson thought he was the mysterious man. I couldn't shake him off for days!'

'And anyone worth their salt *knows* it was you and

Louis Ashby!' Holly crowed. Then she started to sing her own take on a Music Hall tune: 'I'm a smart and stylish girl you see, belle of good society. Not too strict, but rather free, yet as right as right can be! Never forward, never bold – not too hot and not too cold! But the very thing I'm told, that in your arms you'd like to hold ...'

'*Ta ra ra BOOM de ay*!' The girls sung together, then laughed.

'Rascal!' said Elsie, grinning. 'You're no Lottie Collins, Miss Sawyer.' She referred to the Music Hall star who had made the slightly risqué and flirtatious song her own. Elsie adored anything to do with performing and the theatre, and her young life had been greatly influenced by the famous actress Lily Valentine, who had visited her family home of Pencradoc when she was a child. 'And chance would be a fine thing, to have Louis sweep me up in those arms. Oh Louis, Louis. One day, one day.' She clasped her hands together and looked soulfully up to a make-believe gallery.

'One day, darling heart, one day.' Holly reached out and patted her arm. '*The Tattle-Tale is* good fun to read though. What's so special about the photograph, anyway?'

Elsie looked at it and smiled, then held it up for Holly to see. It showed a stunningly beautiful woman dangling by her feet from some rigging, and a rather dashing man standing grinning beside her. The woman was dressed as a pirate, with bare feet and a fetching spotted kerchief tied around her long, wavy hair, and the man was dressed quite similarly, complete with an eye-patch. Just peeking into the picture was the snout and face of a dog, which was some unidentifiable mix of breeds but looked very sweet.

'Well, it's irrefutable proof that I know Lily Valentine and her husband, Edwin. Look. It's my dog, Biscuit. It's incontrovertible.' Elsie smiled at the photo. 'I took it when I was a little girl. Lily and Edwin came to visit me for my birthday, and they brought along Albert, who was just a baby then. I took more than one picture, and this is my least favourite, because it doesn't have all of Biscuit in, and Albert isn't in it – but it does the job. That dreadful Diana Jenkins was saying there was no way could I possibly know Lily, and this is my proof. So there.'

'You absolutely *do* know Lily!' Holly was shocked. She'd even visited Lily with Elsie on a couple of occasions.

'I know that and you know that, but they don't know that. I'll submit it to the magazine through the usual channels, and it will appear in the next issue and my reputation will be boosted.'

There was a post box at the college where students submitted notes, articles and pictures for the magazine. At some point, and Holly swore it must be at the dead of night, the bits and pieces were collected and then they appeared in the next issue of *The Tattle-Tale*.

'Super.' Holly slid off the bed and stretched. She walked over to the window and peered outside. It was a grey day and the sky was full of what might have been snow. She shivered, grateful for the warm fire that burned in their room. 'When are you leaving for Christmas, Elsie?' she asked.

'Probably next Thursday after classes end.' Elsie came over and stood next to her. She leaned into the glass and blew a soft breath on it, misting up almost a perfect circle. She lifted her hand and, with her forefinger, drew two little robins sitting on a branch. She surrounded them with a heart and studied them. 'Not too bad,' she judged and threw herself onto the window seat, pulling a sketch book and a pencil over. Then she must have realised it was almost time to go to class, because she cursed under her breath, which made Holly hide a smile, and stood up again.

'When do you leave?' asked Elsie.

'Probably Friday morning,' Holly replied. 'I'd rather get the train to Cornwall in daylight. And not wait until Saturday to travel on Christmas Eve.'

'True. I'm going home with my brother, Laurie. He's coming into town Thursday on his way back from school, so we'll travel together and he can protect me from footpads and highwaymen. Or train robbers. Then I suspect he'll wassail when we return, and I won't see much of him until the day itself. He thinks he's ever so grown up, and he's not! But I could be partial to some wassailing myself. Shall we do it, Holly-Dolly? *Shall* we?'

Holly laughed. 'I think we need to get to college first. Come on. Let's get ready.'

'I suppose you're correct. Holly, you really ought to come to Pencradoc for a visit. You'd love it. You really would. And it's practically on the way to your home, so we could make a thing of it.'

'What a splendid idea.' Holly pulled her shoulders back, stood up straight and held her hand out to Elsie. 'Let's agree to that for the New Year.'

'Yes. Let's.'

And the girls shook hands on it.

Noel was trying to be polite. He really was. But Emma, his cousin, was quite frankly irritating him.

Emma and her parents had come to visit Noel's family in the run up to Christmas, and Emma, who had annoyed him greatly ever since she was a little girl having tantrums in the nursery, did very little to endear herself to him. There had been some vague dinner-table talk of his grandfather's courtesy title, and how he very rarely used it – being quite a down-to-earth gentleman – and Grandfather had laughed over his dessert, and said, 'Well now, Noel, my boy. I wonder if you'll be the next Honourable chap in the family? Shall we see about that then. Eh? Eh?'

Noel's younger sister, Marion, had snorted into her own dessert and quipped that there was nothing honourable about Noel.

Everyone had found that highly amusing, especially Noel, but Emma now seemed to be completely obsessed by the idea of her cousin potentially inheriting a title, and had taken to following him around questioning him in a very irritating manner.

'Noel, do you think you *will* be an Honourable one day? The Honourable Noel Andrews. It has a certain ring to it, does it not?'

'I have no idea, Emma,' Noel said patiently. 'Grandfather only got that title because his father was a member of the House of Lords and he was the younger son. My father hasn't inherited it. I don't suppose I will either, as I can't see the King singling me out to give me special dispensation.'

'But wouldn't it be wonderful? To be known by a title in Society?' Emma's eyes had gone dreamy and Noel forced himself not to roll his own eyes up to the heavens.

'I'm not particularly sure that would be quite at the top of my agenda.'

'But your wife would like it.' Emma stared at him, almost appraisingly. 'The Honourable Noel Andrews and

Mrs Andrews. It's not ideal, obviously, that your wife wouldn't automatically get a title, but it would be quite nice to be introduced as such, and then one would feel quite at home at events. "Good evening, yes, my husband is the Honourable Noel Andrews." I suppose one wouldn't need to introduce oneself as just "Mrs" because the person to whom one is speaking would possibly assume one was a Lady in one's own right—'

'And who, pray tell, is this mythical "one"?' Noel interrupted. He didn't really want to know the answer.

'Nobody in particular. It's simply a generalisation.' She glowered at him. Emma had grown up near Bodmin Moor, and Noel had heard her talk, on more than one occasion, about Lady Elsie Pencradoc who lived nearby, and Lady Elsie's cousins, Lady Clara, Lady Mabel, Lady Lucy and Lady Nancy. It seemed to be a thorn in Emma's side that she hadn't been born a Lady, and as she grew older and attended more of the Society events the other girls were going to, the more she seemed to resent being introduced as plain "Miss Emma Carew".

According to Marion, one of the chaps in Emma's set had inherited a title and a vast estate not so long ago. And for a while, Emma had obsessed over this poor fellow – Ernie, that was his name – and chattered incessantly about him. It seemed Ernie had managed to repel Emma's attentions though, and swiftly married some wealthy American girl. Noel desperately hoped that Emma would find herself another Earl or a Count or someone to fixate on soon, as she was now beginning to wear *him* down with her attention, and he wasn't enjoying it one jot.

'I see,' he responded now. 'Because I don't intend on marrying any time soon, so the mythical "one" is just that – mythical.'

'I'm sure if you had a title there'd be many a girl willing to marry you.'

It was such a ludicrous comment that Noel had to bite his lip to stop himself laughing. 'Perhaps, but *I'm* not sure what kind of girl would just be interested in a title. Surely I have more to offer a person than just a courtesy title – which, by the way, I haven't got and don't expect to get? Actually, Emma, don't you think that I've got enough to interest a girl as it is?' He was deliberately goading her and stood politely whilst she opened and closed her mouth and stared at him, clearly desperately trying to assess what other good points he might have that didn't involve a title.

'I couldn't say,' she said eventually. 'All I know is that if I was to marry, I'd certainly prefer to wed a man with a title than a man without. My parents keep trying to introduce me to young men, but for me to make a match and eventually a betrothal, I have to say that I have already discovered the young men *with* a title are far more interesting that the ones *without* a title.'

At that, Noel did laugh. 'Emma, you sound as if you've been born a century too late! A match! And a betrothal! Goodness me.' Then, because he couldn't resist teasing her due to the absurdity of the conversation, and because she looked exactly like the spoiled little madam she'd been for the last eighteen years, he laid his hands on her shoulders and looked into her eyes with what he hoped was an intense, smouldering and attractive stare.

He knew such things existed, because he also teased Marion about the dreadful novels and stories she read; as a writer himself, he had been churning out trite pieces for magazines and newspapers for some time now, scribbling Penny Dreadful tales that he cringed over, and commercial, serialised Gothic tales that were the high end of ridiculous. Some had even been read by an unwitting Marion, and exclaimed and sighed over – but he made sure he used a pen name when he did those ones. He really didn't want to be associated with work like that, but it paid his bills. He wanted to write a book, a sort of fairy tale book which was a cross between *Alice's Adventures in Wonderland* and Grimms' Fairy Tales, and he had started and stopped so many times now that he was quite irritated with the whole thing.

Almost as irritated as he was with Emma.

'Emma,' he said now, lowering his voice and maintaining the smouldering stare. 'If I were an Honourable, instead of plain old Noel Andrews, do you think a young lady in your position would find me more attractive?'

'Get off me!' she squawked and slapped his hands away.

He laughed and held them up. 'Sorry, Ems. But if you think having a title might make me marriageable fodder, I think I have to speak to Grandfather and see what we can do.'

Then he put his hands in his pockets, turned around and headed back to the house whistling, where he had no intention at all of speaking to Grandfather about inheriting some ancient title that none of them really cared about anyway.

Chapter Three

The first time she'd set foot in her beloved fairy tale tower, she knew that it was going to be the ideal place for her. Martin had insisted that he go with her of course, and they'd stood outside the building with Merryn Burton, the woman who had chatted to Sorcha on the day that she'd simply intended to "make enquiries".

It was late autumn at that point, and the trees that Sorcha used to lurk in when she was a child were dressed in burnished brown, orange, red and yellow leaves which crunched satisfyingly underfoot as they fell.

'We've been getting some work done inside, as you know, just to bring it up to spec because we knew we wanted a tea room and exhibition centre in the tower. We've sorted out power, heating, lighting, that sort of thing,' Merryn told her. 'The kitchen's been fitted, there are tables and chairs and units in there already, and it's all been painted, but obviously if it's not to your taste, you can redecorate. There'll be exhibitions upstairs, but you'll be in charge of downstairs, and access to the exhibitions will be using the staircase at the side of your tea room. Basically, we won't meddle in the tea room, and we don't expect you to get involved with upstairs. Rather, we'd be working alongside one another.'

'Sorcha, did you know all this before you signed up?' asked Martin. 'Because you do realise that if you've only got the downstairs, you're limited in space?' He turned to Merryn, frowning. 'If we wanted to expand, could we build an extension at the back? Glass cube, bifold doors, straight out onto the lawns, kind of thing?'

'Martin ...' Sorcha hadn't missed the possessive pronoun coming in, subtle though it was.

'No, we have to ask the question, Sorcha. You've got to future-proof it. There's no margin for increased footfall if we can't build out. I mean, it's a prime location, so once it's up and running, there could be quite a *bit* of footfall.'

'I'm afraid the tower is listed,' said Merryn with a professional smile. 'We won't be adding to the footprint.'

'Hmmm.' Martin stared up at the building, hands in pockets, clearly thoughtful. 'Hmmm.'

'I'm so sorry,' said Sorcha, feeling her cheeks flame. 'I never mentioned expansion to him – and he's not actually part of the decision-making process, and he's also not part of the business, so it's all going to be down to me and my decisions.'

'Sorcha, I think you'll see sense eventually. I mean, this is a huge undertaking – something you will have to do on your own if you don't appoint me as partner. I'm not sure you're ready for it. Some of your ideas and suggestions are a little outlandish, and you know we always have that conversation about you reining it in and being realistic. I know you haven't confirmed things fully yet, so I recommend we go away and discuss it a little more.'

Sorcha cast a glance at Merryn, who now looked more than a little uncomfortable and was still standing with the key poised ready to open the door. 'Do *you* want to go away and think about it some more?' Merryn asked. 'Just to be sure it's what you want. I mean it's fairly large inside to me, but it might not be what you would consider viable.'

'No! No, I mean I don't want to go away and think

about it.' She glared at Martin, feeling utterly foolish and humiliated and, yes, furious at him and his comments. 'The very least I can do is come inside now – and honestly, I'll know the moment I set foot in it whether it will work. Whether it will match my vision, sort of thing.' She prayed Martin wouldn't respond to that one – she didn't need him trampling on her visions and dreams in public any more than he had already, but thankfully he seemed distracted and was now peering around the corner of the building, scowling.

'Great. I mean, we're here now anyway, so you might as well.' Merryn smiled and slid the key into the lock. It turned beautifully and smoothly, and the door opened.

Sorcha stepped inside and the first thing she noticed was the smell of fresh paint and cut wood. The second thing she noticed was the circular space which already had some tables and chairs set out on it, just as Merryn had said. The room was bright, white and friendly. It may have been too clinical and bland for some people, but Sorcha saw past that. She saw, in her mind's eye, old-fashioned units with vintage tea sets on; mismatched plates; big, welcoming mugs of coffee and a cheerful barista-style machine behind the counter. She saw dainty, three-tiered cake stands piled high with treats, and glass-domes covering cream gateaux, and traditional sponges, and rainbow layered cakes covered in buttercream and sprinkles. She could almost smell the savoury tang of freshly baked cheese scones with a hint of paprika and mustard, the buttery scent of sugar-dusted shortbread, and the warm, homely smell of toasted teacakes …

'I'll take it,' she said. 'Definitely.'

'Sorcha! Don't you think you should see the kitchen first?' snapped Martin, looming up behind her.

Dammit!

She had to concede that he had a point there – so, reluctantly, she nodded her agreement and walked behind the counter into a lovely, but small, well-appointed kitchen. She cast a professional eye around it, mentally filling it with her equipment. Yes, it was big enough for her purposes – and she had worked in tinier kitchens anyway, to be fair.

'Still a definite yes,' Sorcha said. She turned to Merryn and grinned. 'I'll not be doing banquets in here, but it'll be perfect for what I need.'

'Great! Would you like to see upstairs as well?' Merryn grinned back. 'Just before you fully commit – or totally fall in love with the place? One of the two!'

'Am I that obvious?' Sorcha laughed. 'Honestly, I've wanted to be in here since I was a child. It's much harder guessing what it's like by peering through a grimy window covered in green algae than one might suspect.'

'I can imagine! Come on.'

Merryn led the way, and Sorcha determinedly avoided looking at Martin, whom she left poking around in the kitchen.

They went up the stairs and emerged into a bright, airy circular room with whitewashed walls, and Sorcha could immediately see what a bonus it would be to hold exhibitions in the space. On the far wall was a piece of Perspex and she walked over to it, curious. Behind it was some writing in heavy pencil at about chest height, as if a child had scrawled it there.

Rose Morwenna Hammett.
Rose Morwenna Pencradoc.
Mrs Jago Pencradoc.

'Our legacy from Duchess Rose, who set out the Gothic rose garden,' explained Merryn, coming up beside her and looking at it. 'It seems as if she had a bit of a crush on her future husband's younger brother at some point. We wanted to preserve it for her.'

'So the tower *did* have something like a princess in it then – at some point, as you say, anyway.' Merryn was ridiculously pleased with that.

'I guess so. Yes.'

Then Sorcha suddenly had an idea. An idea she, at least, thought was brilliant.

'Would I perhaps be able to display some pictures leading up the staircase?' she asked. 'I've got some perfect prints that would look great on the walls there.'

'Sure.' Merryn nodded. 'Just run it by us first if you decide to do that, but I can't see it being a problem.'

'Fantastic.' Sorcha had some prints depicting scenes from fairy tales that she knew would look stunning on the staircase walls. They would fit perfectly with the theme she had in her head about vintage chic and the whole storybook atmosphere of the place.

Then there was a clumping of polished shoes on the steps, and her heart sank a little as she recognised the purposeful tread of Martin.

'Hey – I'm not sure the kitchen area will be big enough if more than two people are working here,' he said. 'I'm used to much bigger areas. More staff.'

'I don't anticipate there being more than two people in the kitchen on a regular basis,' replied Sorcha, turning away from the intriguing graffiti and facing him. She could hear the tightness in her own voice and flushed, wondering what Merryn must be thinking of her.

'You've got to consider expansion,' persisted Martin.

'I just need to get it up and running.'

'I've told you, it needs to be future-proofed.'

'And I've told you, that's not a concern for now.' She was trying to stay calm and not show herself up in front of Merryn as someone who didn't have a clue what she was doing and needed to be told how to handle it all from a pompous man. 'Look, let's go back downstairs and Merryn can lock it all back up. I think we still need to iron some things out between us.'

'Good idea.' He nodded, and looked around the room. He perked up slightly. 'We could expand up here,' he suggested. 'That might work.'

Patsy had failed to find a Wham! style log cabin and Laura was furious. For some reason, she decided to fall out with Locryn as if it was his fault that there were frolicking holidaymakers in all the log cabins Patsy located, and the run-up to Christmas was therefore pretty miserable.

Work wasn't much better. His antiques shop was part of an old townhouse in Newquay. Well, "shop" was putting it loosely. He rented space in the house, the whole building of which was dedicated to antiques and collectables, and he had used that as his outlet for the last few years. However, the guy who owned the building obviously wanted a cut of the profits, which was fair enough, but he kept putting the percentage up as well as the rent, and it was getting to the point where it just wasn't going to be cost-effective.

Locryn now had to reassess what he wanted to do with the business – he was tempted to leave the rented space and set up on his own, but that seemed like a huge step. He'd have loved to have been able to discuss it with Laura, but she was still unhappy about being "forced to spend Christmas at home" as she put it: 'And if I have to stay here, I do *not* want to be entertaining anyone.'

To save any further arguments, and to make her feel better, Locryn hadn't pushed to have their families over. He was fine with it just being the two of them, and he hoped she'd cheer up as the preparation got underway. He took her Christmas tree shopping and suggested they get a whole new set of decorations that would be "theirs", which they could use instead of using "his" old, shabby ones – but even this didn't seem to make her feel better.

'Nick says he's going minimal this year. He's as cross as I am that we can't celebrate together,' she said, fingering a silver-winged angel whilst looking bored. 'Perhaps *we* should go minimal?'

'Perhaps we shouldn't.'

'It's going to be a fairly miserable Christmas anyway,' she commented. 'Who wants to be stuck in Cornwall over the festive period? There's nothing to *do*.'

Privately, Locryn thought there was plenty to do. She could drink Prosecco until it came out of her ears just as well in Cornwall as she could abroad. She could run around outside in the countryside here just as well as she could tramp through pine forests overseas. But yes, it might be harder to do all that from a Cornish two-bedroom terrace than it would from a log cabin in Switzerland. And there would be fewer people to do it with, because with the best will in the world – and some thinly veiled hints from Laura – he couldn't put up ten of her friends with only two bedrooms.

'Having said that,' she continued, as if just remembering something, 'Nick said he'd be hosting a Twixtmas Party at his new place.' Nick was renting a penthouse flat near the Royal William Quay in Plymouth – all open plan living and chrome and glass and balconies. It was lovely, and no doubt suited Nick's bachelor lifestyle perfectly, but if Laura had shown Locryn the photos once, she'd shown him them a dozen times. 'We could go there and have some fun.'

'Laura,' he said, stopping suddenly in the middle of the rows of Christmas trees. 'What's your problem?'

'What?' She looked at him, stunned. 'I don't *have* a problem. Well, I do – I mean, we're stuck *here* for Christmas, aren't we? That's a *big* problem.'

'Not for me.'

'Oh, come on. It's dull.'

'I don't find Christmas in Cornwall dull at all. My family is here. My friends are here. Why can't we get together with my friends instead of yours, for instance? We could do something with Bella and Dev between Christmas and New Year. Or Carrie and Tom. Or Trudy and Finn—'

'But they're all … *boring*!' Laura seemed shocked at his suggestion. 'I mean, they're all coupled up, and isn't one of them pregnant? And who's got the toddler? It'd be like spending Christmas with a hellish middle-aged Saga Holiday crowd.'

Locryn was torn between snorting with laughter at the simile, and pointing out that being in your late twenties/early thirties was rarely classed as middle-aged in this day and age. And none of them were really old enough for a Saga Holiday.

'So you don't like my friends?' he asked instead.

'No! I bloody hate your friends!'

'Okay.' He nodded. 'I don't really like yours. So if you refuse to spend time with my friends, why should I

31

spend time with your friends? At Christmas, as well. And, actually, newsflash, aren't *we* supposed to be a couple?'

Laura stared at him as if processing that. 'Yes. We are. I guess. But that's different.'

'How? How is it different?'

'Because we still have fun.'

'No, Laura, I don't think we do have fun. I think you complain a lot of the time, and, actually, I think you only moved in with me because your lease expired in September.'

Laura flushed and Locryn's stomach sank. He'd suspected it for a while, to be honest. But he hadn't wanted to face the facts. She'd been funny and outgoing, and that's what he'd been attracted to at the beginning. They'd not been together long when they'd had the first Wham! Holiday, and he had managed to convince himself that it was just a case of being a bit awkward with a group of people who he didn't know very well.

Once they'd come back to real life and her friends had been diluted a little with distance and space, he had been happy to continue the relationship. They didn't live together at that point, so she did her thing and he did his, and it worked. At a distance.

The problems had really started when she'd moved in, and had organised a birthday party for Minty-the-Vegan without telling him. He'd been away at an antiques fair for work and had come home on the Sunday lunchtime to carnage.

Charlie was on the sofa, and Minty and Patsy were in the spare bedroom. Nick was making brunch dressed only in boxer shorts with a cigarette hanging out of his mouth – Locryn didn't really want to know where *he'd* slept, although Laura swore he'd been on the lounge floor.

There'd been a blazing row after they'd all gone, and Laura had yelled that it was her home too now, and if she wanted to invite friends round she could, and Locryn had said he didn't have a problem with that, but it would have been nice to know ...

It really seemed that Laura couldn't leave the student lifestyle behind, and she was chatting away on that WhatsApp group more than she ever talked to him these days.

And, as he helped a truculent and hungover Laura to tidy the place up after that party, Locryn had begun to suspect that he was being treated more as a landlord than a boyfriend.

The current situation, where a similarly truculent and also apparently petulant Laura was now staring with disgust at a glittery silver reindeer and pulling her mobile out of her pocket to respond to a series of loud WhatsApp notifications, did nothing to dissuade him from that idea.

Her face briefly lit up and a smile flickered on her lips as she read the messages. 'Ha! It's Nick. I'm going to take a photo of this horrible tat and send it, so he knows he's doing better with going minimal and stuff. God, I *so* wish I was going to a log cabin with them all this year instead of staying here ...'

Her voice petered out as she snapped a photograph of the poor defenceless glittery reindeer, and her fingers flew across the keys as she typed the message.

And Locryn unhappily came to the conclusion that, yes, this romance was pretty much doomed, unless things changed dramatically over the next few weeks and they experienced some sort of Christmas miracle.

Chapter Four

When the girls returned to college after the festive season, Elsie was highly excited to be back studying, but highly miserable to be leaving her Pencradoc Christmas back at – well – Pencradoc.

'Medora was simply adorable,' she told Holly, pulling out one of her ever-present sketchbooks. Holly knew Medora was the youngest sister. She thought she was around fourteen or fifteen, but Elsie had so many brothers and sisters and cousins – there might have been three more brothers all younger than Medora, as far as Holly knew – that she often wondered how they all remembered each other's names. In her own family, there was only Holly and her much older sister Anna, who had already married, moved into her own home and had three children.

Holly sometimes wished she came from a big, noisy family, but her upbringing had been loving, despite the feeling, at times, that she was practically an only child. She'd filled the quiet times in with drawing and painting, and her talents had gone on to develop as she got older, ultimately leading her to the Liberal College of Arts. Her ambition was to be a book illustrator – that seemed like a lovely profession, she thought. Not only would she get to draw pictures for a living, she would be able to read all the books they related to as well.

It all seemed like it would be a desperately perfect life, and she'd often be full of confidence and enthusiasm as she imagined her future career; but then she'd inevitably see something Elsie had drawn, compare it with her own work, and feel the things that she drew were really rather inadequate next to her friend's. What made her feel even worse was that this year, the students had to start thinking about a portfolio to submit for their final assessments, and Elsie was confident enough to know exactly what she was planning – 'it'll be based on the stage,' she'd said blithely. But Holly felt a little embarrassed at what she wanted to create – 'something perhaps based on fairy tales and mythology,' she'd muttered vaguely, and that was as far as she had got.

She *really* needed to work on her confidence and be her own person! Honestly, she could sometimes do with giving herself a good shake …

She often felt like Cinderella; just grubbing around, usually stained with paints and pastels, waiting for a handsome prince to burst into her life. She wasn't like Elsie at all; instinctively confident that life and love would work out for her, and she'd live happily ever after with a prince of her choosing – Louis Ashby in her friend's case, obviously.

But Elsie was still talking about Medora, so Holly tried to forget about her self-doubt and turned her attention back to her friend.

'Medora decided she would quite like to get dressed up as a Christmas Fairy, so we had fun making over some of Mama's old dresses and creating her some wings and pinning her hair up, and we got Biscuit to pull a makeshift sleigh to precede her through the house so she could deliver her gifts herself rather than putting them beneath the tree on Christmas Eve.'

'Biscuit?' Holly was shocked. Surely Biscuit must be

the oldest dog in the world as he seemed to have been in Elsie's life forever?

'Yes. Biscuit. We didn't overload the sleigh, in fact it was very light and he looked happy, so it was all jolly good fun.' Elsie thrust the sketchbook under Holly's nose. 'So this was Medora on Christmas Eve, and can you see Biscuit? The way he's smiling at her? So lovable.'

There was a perfect pen and ink sketch of a young girl, with a fair resemblance to a slightly curvier Elsie, dressed in a gorgeous gown that, even in the picture, looked as if it was made of gossamer threads. Biscuit the dog was highly recognisable from the Lily Valentine photograph, and he was indeed smiling, which made Holly smile back at him and tickle the inked nose.

'I simply love Biscuit,' she said. 'Even from this picture.'

'Then you simply *must* come to see him at Pencradoc. How about two weeks' time? Do you think you can squeeze a Saturday-to-Monday in before we start to get desperately busy in class?'

'A Saturday-to-Monday?' Holly laughed. 'Don't you mean a weekend? I know Society hates that term – isn't it a "vulgar Americanism"?' She spoke the last two words in an exaggeratedly hoity-toity style of voice which made Elsie laugh. 'But it is, Lady Elsie Pencradoc, intrinsically a weekend! Gracious me.'

'All right.' Elsie was still smiling. 'I agree. A weekend. But really – do you want to come? *Do* you? And you can meet my family and my cousins and we can see Biscuit. He'd adore you, I know he would. He's an excellent judge of character.'

Holly looked outside at the damp January greyness of a wet and miserable London, and then glanced at the picture of Medora and Biscuit. Even if it was a damp and grey January in Cornwall, it was still probably a better place to be. 'I'd love to come,' she said. 'And do you think I can meet Louis properly as well? I know you've seen him when he's been in town, but all I've managed is a brief wave to him out of our window when you've been off on a jaunt. And I'm not about to fall for him like your cousin Clara has – so he's quite safe from my attentions.'

Elsie had the grace to flush, but then she grinned. 'Damn Clara. If she wasn't so golden and pretty, I wouldn't be so worried.'

'From what I understand, he prefers the slightly wild, dark-haired variety of girl.'

'Minx!' said Elsie and nudged her friend, 'But yes. Yes – you can meet Louis too.' Her eyes sparkled at the thought, and she suddenly got a very faraway, day-dreamy look in them.

Holly hid a smile. Elsie was clearly in love. It was as simple as that.

A couple of months into the new year, Noel was regretting joking with Emma about being the kind of man she might want to marry if he happened to inherit his grandfather's title.

'She's got it into her head,' said Marion, 'that you are definitely inheriting Grandfather's "Honourable", and she's started dropping enormous hints to her friends that she knows a young man who is due such a title, and that their families are very keen for a match to happen.'

'That's the most ridiculous thing I've heard in a long time!' Noel was shocked. 'And do you think she really means *me*? Dear Lord.'

Marion shrugged and resettled herself on the sofa in the morning room with a book and her cup of tea. It was a dreary, grey day outside and Noel had taken himself off to the study to write, but the smell of hot buttered crumpets had him prowling into his sister's lair next door, and now he had his own cup of tea and a plate piled high with crumpets to boot.

'I'm not certain, to be honest, Noel – but it does seem quite a coincidence, doesn't it? After that conversation at Christmas, she's started asking about you a lot more in her letters.'

Marion and Emma were fond of writing letters to one another. They were about the same age and had more in common than Noel and Emma did – Noel couldn't think of one good reason why he and Emma should keep up a correspondence, but understood that was what girls "did". He was a keen observer though, and many of his sister's habits ended up in his stories.

Wryly, he considered the fact that Marion was blissfully aware that she was the catalyst for many of the heroines that appeared in his serialisations, and instead, just as she was doing now, munched her way through crumpets, sweets and cakes and read avidly about girls she could "most *definitely* understand".

Noel appreciated the anonymity of his pen name when she passed comments like that and had made a vow to himself that he would never ever let any of his family read his work in progress.

But still the idea of his fairy tale book nagged at him, and still he wanted to write it – but the biggest spark of all, the inspiration for his main character for that particular story, was absolutely lacking.

He pushed the thought of his non-existent book to one side and raised the question of Emma again – not that he was sure he wanted to hear the answer.

'You haven't given her any false expectations of me, have you, Marion?'

Marion glanced up at him and frowned. 'No! Of course not. But when she asks if you have any attachments, I have to be honest.'

'Attachments. Good grief. Can't you make up a love interest for me, Marion? Just in case she is imagining herself into such a role?'

'Again. Of course not. And to be frank, I personally can't imagine *who* would want to attach themselves to you, Noel.' There was a beat. 'Except Cousin Emma, of course.'

Noel had great satisfaction in hearing the soft *thud* of the cushion he threw across the room as it connected with the side of his sister's face.

'Do that again, Noel,' she said, tossing the cushion back to him, 'and I'll write the marriage notice myself and submit it to the newspapers.'

Chapter Five

Last Christmas

In the end, Martin got the message. He got the message in no uncertain terms, and it hadn't been a pleasant discussion. Especially not at Christmastime.

Suffice it to say, there were no white carrot Christmas roses on Martin's Christmas lunches – and by that point, Sorcha couldn't care less whether his turkey was under-basted, over-cooked or served with a garnish of reindeer droppings. She was just glad he was no longer going to be a "partner" in either her romantic life or her business life.

And on a positive note, three days before Christmas, Sorcha moved into her shiny new flat in Pencradoc; then, on the day before Christmas Eve, she collected the keys for her shiny new Tower Tea Room.

On Christmas Eve itself, she let herself into the tower and shut the door behind her. Leaning against it, she looked around in delight and imagined the place bustling with customers in the New Year, filled with the scent of freshly brewed coffee and home-baking. She went over to the counter and placed the first personal object in her new premises – a fat, red teapot in the shape of Father Christmas. She thought it was appropriate somehow and, anyway, it made her smile.

Then she climbed the stairs, mentally filled the wall with her beloved fairy tale prints, and walked slowly around the exhibition space, trailing her fingers across the Perspex. Then she quickly wiped the smeary fingerprints off the pristine surface.

Eventually, Sorcha went up to the window and leaned

on the windowsill, chin in hand, and stared out across the estate.

From her vantage point, she could look across the treetops and over the village, tracing well-known landmarks with her eyes. There was the church, where Duchess Rose was buried. There was The White Lady pub, named after that unfortunate lady – she knew now that Rose had died following a fall down the steps in the tower she was in at this very moment. But oddly, tragic though that was, Sorcha knew Rose hadn't actually died *in* the tower, so she wasn't worried that her wraith would appear and torment her customers.

She didn't believe in ghosts anyway.

And, continuing her visual journey across the landscape, over *there*, just beyond the formal gardens was the waterfall which ran through the Pencradoc estate. A little further along the river was the Mill House, the old waterwheel frozen in time, and the place now a sweet little holiday let for visitors.

Sorcha wasn't aware of it at all, but there in the window, with her dark hair loose and the furry hood of her coat resting on her shoulders, she was the very image of a pensive, wintery fairy tale princess.

But rather than being trapped in the tower, it was all hers to enjoy.

Christmas Day was one of the most miserable days Locryn could remember. Yet again, it was another FaceTime session with his family as Laura had point-blank refused to see anyone on the day itself, and once again Locryn got up early and was in sole charge of the turkey. At least it was less Shetland pony-sized and more average turkey-sized this year though.

More than once, he felt as if he should just leave Laura stewing in her sullen misery and drive to his parents – but then, he reasoned, he couldn't just leave her alone on Christmas Day, miserable as they both were. She spent most of the day WhatsApping her friends after pushing the turkey lunch around her plate, and he spent most of the day watching Christmas television, munching desultorily on dry-roasted peanuts and a deconstructed selection box from Aunt Susie, and wishing the day was over.

He needed to do something about this relationship, and he resolved he needed to do it soon. It wasn't good to break up over Christmas, but he didn't want to go into the New Year hanging onto it. That much he knew for sure.

Fortunately, in some respects, the decision was taken out of his hands.

Nick had his Twixtmas Party.

Locryn made an excuse not to go.

And Laura came back late the next day, wearing the same clothes she'd been out in, and packed her belongings.

'I'm moving in with Nick,' she announced. 'His rent is almost two grand a month and he's got two huge bedrooms. I'm going to stay there for a bit to help him out. I can't stand being herded into middle-age here with you. I hate your lifestyle. I hate your friends. And I hate living with you.'

'Ditto,' said Locryn. 'But you're not fooling anyone.' He held his phone up. 'Charlie messaged me. He's totally upset because Nick and you disappeared into the bedroom and didn't emerge until this morning. He says he felt I needed to know but, to be honest, I think it's more a case of him being upset that Nick isn't interested in him. But you know what? I don't really care any more. I just hope you find someone else's house to move into when Nick's lease is up, because I can't see him sticking to you, or you being happy when he sleeps with the next person on his list.'

She didn't deny any of it. 'At least Nick and I have *fun* together!' she yelled as she slammed the door.

And Locryn quickly locked it shut behind her.

He was relieved. Very relieved.

But he didn't realise how relieved he actually was until a couple of weeks later when he took stock of the situation and looked around his house. None of Laura's possessions were anywhere to be seen, and none of her friends were anywhere to be seen either, which had to be a bonus. He found that he was happier to go home in the evenings again, rather than making excuses to work late. But the "feel" of his house had subtly changed and he wasn't sure how. It was different, and not necessarily in a good way. Perhaps there was still too much of Laura there – too many memories and too much bad feeling hanging around.

It was true, though, that he didn't have that sense of dread every Friday that the weekend would involve spontaneous get-togethers, or forty-eight hours of watching Laura text her friends whilst she laughed at the in-jokes and relayed information to him that made no sense. Without Laura, he could now see his own friends and family without fear of his girlfriend looking miserable and bored in their presence.

But, of course, as is often the case after a break-up, it wasn't all joyful relief. They'd been together over a year after all. They'd lived together for a few months, and before that Laura had been a frequent overnight visitor. It did feel a little odd at times that she was no longer there.

He missed the company of another human if he was honest – someone to chat to and share a bottle of wine with over a takeaway. Or even having someone around to make a cup of tea for ... although latterly, he had to acknowledge, there hadn't been much chatting or sharing with Laura. There'd been a lot of arguments and a lot of shouting, and not much fun. It had been a strain at times – and Christmas had been dreadful, of course.

Then one day, Locryn looked around his house again and suddenly felt like a stranger. In a peculiar fashion, it no longer seemed like his home at all. The memories of the arguments were still there, colouring every room. The image of Nick in his underwear in the kitchen wasn't something he could ever unsee. There were red wine stains splattered across the cream carpet and ground into the pile – remnants of one of Laura's get-togethers, when Minty and Patsy had come over for a pamper evening and they made him stay out of the lounge while they put face-packs on one another and painted each other's toenails.

No. The house felt very different indeed – and he wasn't a saint, and he did find himself resenting the fact that he and Laura had clearly made each other so miserable that it had come to this.

A little while after the break-up, once the dust had largely settled, Locryn bumped into Charlie in a restaurant. Locryn was with Bella and Dev, who were trying to matchmake him with a girl called Roberta. It wasn't going well – she was a nice enough girl but the spark just wasn't there, and Locryn could tell by the polite smiles, the long silences and the way Roberta kept checking her watch that she couldn't wait to leave. He'd escaped to the bathroom and seen Charlie washing his hands in there. They'd said hello, slightly awkwardly, and then Charlie looked up at Locryn glumly.

'They've gone to Barbados,' Charlie informed Locryn. 'Fun, sun, sea and sex. Apparently.'

'Lovely.' Locryn didn't really know what else to say.

'I'm sick of seeing the photos on WhatsApp. They're both topless in one of them. He looks pretty good.' Charlie frowned, lost in thought. Again, the image of Nick cooking brunch semi-naked floated hideously into Locryn's mind. Charlie blinked, seeming to remember he was talking to Locryn and continued. 'We're heading to Switzerland again at Christmas. Not sure how I feel about that. It's not like you're going to be there to chat to this time.'

'Then don't go.' The answer seemed logical to Locryn. 'If it's going to upset you.'

Charlie looked at him oddly. 'But we've *always* done stuff together. I can't really say no.'

'Hmmm.' Locryn definitely had no answer to that one. But he wasn't going to lie to himself – he was awfully glad he wasn't going to be part of the Wham! Trip that year …

A month or so later, fed up of spending evenings staring at the red wine stains and visualising Nick in his underwear yet again, he'd taken himself off to Aunt Susie's in Pencradoc.

Pencradoc was a perfect little village, balanced right on the edge of Bodmin Moor. Aunt Susie had lived there for years, and had always maintained that she'd come home as soon as she'd moved there.

'I've been here for two decades,' she told Locryn once. 'Some of the older people still tell me I'm not a local. But little do they know I can play the "family card" just as well as they can.' There was an impish twinkle in her eye as she told him that, and Locryn had laughed. They'd had connections there apparently, a few generations ago – and Susie and his mum were descended directly from that branch of the family.

'I was always sad that we weren't part of the proper Pencradoc family,' she said today, as they drifted on to the familiar topic, and Locryn walked with her along the high street towards the Pencradoc estate. 'The story goes that our lot were good friends with the family though, and spent a lot of time around here – I'd have loved to have seen the place in its heyday. Apparently it was like a fairy tale castle at Christmas. The family had some of the best Christmas parties in the area – the joke was that some of them went on for days. You hear something like that, and you just want to be part of it, don't you? So, like I said before, my argument is that we've got as much right to be here as any of the locals, and that's definitely what encouraged me to settle here. Pencradoc's reputation has always been a good one in our family, and I do feel exceptionally at home here.'

'Maybe I should think about coming here then,' he said, only half-joking. 'It's weird ... but Newquay's just not home any more.'

'Hmmm – well, dear nephew, come along here.' She pointed to a building a little way off. 'I think there's something that might just tempt you to think about that properly. See that sign? I do believe we have a premises for sale in the village. Worth a look?'

Locryn opened his mouth to reply, automatically

preparing to shrug Susie's suggestion off – but then he saw it.

He saw the most perfect premises – and with it, a perfect opportunity. He couldn't deny it, he absolutely couldn't. He was finding himself disliking his house more and more, and things were also reaching breaking point at his shop in Newquay.

From a distance, the building they were approaching had looked like a small cottage, but the downstairs had been converted into a shop and the upstairs appeared to be a flat. It was just begging for someone to take it on.

When Locryn got close enough, he stopped, stood in front of the place and stared up at it.

'It's perfect.' The words were almost a whisper, his heart suddenly hammering in his chest.

Aunt Susie took his hand and squeezed it. 'I thought you'd like it,' she said quietly. 'Definitely worth thinking about, yes?'

'Definitely … yes.'

It all happened quite quickly after that. Locryn went home, thought about it a bit more, made plans and ultimately put his house up for sale. He soon sold the two-bedroom terrace – red wine stains and all – without a moment's regret, and everything went through in November.

And, suddenly, there he was, almost a year after breaking up with Laura, hurtling towards December and Christmas with a shiny new shop, a flat still in disarray and a head full of ideas.

Chapter Six

Almost Christmas 1906

It soon became a pattern that whenever Elsie travelled to Pencradoc for a weekend that Holly joined her. Holly loved Elsie's family and they loved her. On one or two occasions, Holly even used Pencradoc as a stopping off point when she was travelling to her own home, such was the friendly welcome she was given.

Biscuit, as decreed, was indeed a wonderful dog. And, although he was quite elderly, that was only evident by the grey hairs on his muzzle and his tendency to flop down and sleep in inappropriate places before getting up and playing like a puppy again with anyone who was available.

Louis was similarly deemed "wonderful", and Holly could see how well-matched he and Elsie would be – where Elsie was dark and spirited and inclined to passionate fancies, fair-haired, grey-eyed Louis was a little older than her friend – she and Holly were both nineteen that year – and far calmer and, overall, a good balance for Elsie. They clearly adored one another and the relationship was that indescribable blend of love born out of a friendship formed in childhood; a love which had deepened over the years – but wasn't quite at the point where the pair of them could comfortably give into it. Maybe neither of them were ready for it yet? It was clear that Elsie had too much living to do, whereas Louis had his feet firmly on the ground and was concentrating on securing his future in the family business.

Holly could see why Elsie had pinned her hopes on the

young man, and was confident it would all work out for them eventually – and she had delighted Elsie by telling her she thought this.

Holly even ended up spending a portion of the long hot summer break at Pencradoc; although, fortunately, in her mind at least, she wasn't around for any of the Society events that were planned so meticulously by the local families. There'd been a wedding the previous year between a couple called Ernie and Pearl which, according to Elsie, had been stunning. The formalities she'd described had made Holly shudder though, despite the fact that her confidence had grown greatly over the last year or so at college with Elsie. The pair of them enjoyed a rather delinquent social life at times with fellow art students, but Holly still felt ill-equipped to blend in with Elsie's group of home friends.

She had no desire to shine at any of the grand balls Elsie talked about, and even though she loved helping her friend look at large, airy houses in London with a view to buying one for when their course ended, she knew that house would be bought using family money – Elsie was the daughter of a deceased Duke after all, and had a healthy inheritance from him. Her step-father was the acclaimed artist Ruan Teague, and he too was quite wealthy – hence the fact the family could still live in comfort in a place like Pencradoc. And much as Holly would also have loved a nice house with a studio of her own, it was, for the moment, a dream.

Much better than the Society balls, though, were the Pencradoc birthday parties Holly was now always invited to. They were largely centred around birthday teas and party games, and were greatly beloved events for Elsie's three smaller brothers and two youngest cousins.

It was thus a "done thing, Holly-Dolly", that when Elsie decided to host a Christmas party, Holly would be invited.

'I have to square it all with the family first,' Elsie said, 'but if I promise to be quite sensible then hopefully they will allow it. And if you come, you'll stop me from getting into mischief, won't you?'

'I can stop you from drinking champagne, if that's what you mean?'

'Oh, don't remind me.' Elsie pulled a face. Two days after a pre-festive get-together with their classmates, Elsie was still suffering a little. 'I actually don't think champagne likes me very much. I certainly don't like *it* at the minute.'

Holly laughed. 'Next time, I'm taking your camera. So I can prove how utterly mad you are when you're blotto.'

'Fiend. I shall refuse to show you how to use it.'

'Fair do's.' Holly shrugged good-naturedly. 'But are you sure you want me there? I'm guessing that a lot of your friends from home will be with their families, and that the mere fact you are planning on evicting your siblings means that it's more of a grown-up party?' She raised her eyebrows quizzically.

'Maybe a *little* bit more of a grown-up party.' Elsie grinned mischievously. 'But there *will* be games, and we know how much everyone loves my games.'

'Oh, we simply *adore* them at the birthday teas!' Holly rolled her eyes dramatically. 'But tell me, aren't your friends, well … dreadfully *grown-up* and too clever and important for games? Wouldn't they just be happier with you hosting a nice fancy Society winter ball? Because if they are, I can't dance that well, and I'm not sure I'd be the sort of person they'd take too kindly to tolerating—'

'Rot. If I say we're playing games, we'll be paying

games. And you, dearest Holly-Dolly, have too low an opinion of yourself. They have no more right to visit Pencradoc than you do.' She grinned. 'And Biscuit loves *you* best of all.'

'I love Biscuit *too*.'

'Excellent. Of *course* you do. Super.' Elsie clapped her hands. 'So, once Mama and Teague agree, you can stop saying such silly things about winter balls and not dancing and things, and I can start planning.'

'Jolly good. Well, if you're certain, I'll make Pencradoc my first stop, and then I can go home for Christmas. How splendid.' Holly clapped her hands in delight too and they both laughed.

And Holly had a sudden feeling that Christmas 1906 was going to be superb.

Noel's family were heading to the continent to visit his great aunt. The old dear lived in faded Bohemian glory in a villa in Italy, and had decided to return to England and set up home with her brother: his "Honourable" grandfather.

Marion had sighed and opined how marvellous it would be to visit Italy, and somehow the original arrangement, which was for his father and grandfather to travel there and bring Great Aunt Rachel back, had grown to include Marion and his mother and an extended family trip abroad.

Noel had declined to go – he genuinely had commitments at home, and would see Great Aunt Rachel when she was back anyway. However, there had been some fussing about Emma's family, because his mother and father were overdue a visit there and the dates had clashed.

'Would you be an absolute darling and visit Aunt

Elizabeth and Uncle Percy when we are away?' his mother had begged. 'Take the Christmas gifts to them, that sort of thing?'

'Of course,' said Noel. 'And when do you anticipate coming back?'

And that had been *another* headache because they couldn't get passage before Christmas – then Marion had thrown a tantrum as she didn't want to miss out on Italy. If they continued with the plans, it looked highly likely that Noel would miss his family Christmas which upset his mother greatly – but then nobody wanted to tolerate a maudlin, hysterical Marion if the Italy trip didn't go to plan. His mother had been torn as to which child to disappoint and had sobbed that she also wanted to help relocate Great Aunt Rachel, so Aunt Elizabeth had stepped up and said of *course* Marion had to have her trip, and of *course* Noel had to spend Christmas with them …

This had caused an even bigger headache, as far as Noel was concerned, because Emma had begun to write him long letters speaking of the plans she had in place for the pair of them over the festive season.

The biggest horror was talk of a Christmas party at Pencradoc, the home of Emma's friend, Lady Elsie Pencradoc. But it seemed it was a sacrifice Noel would have to make to keep everyone else happy.

So he sighed and packed his notebooks along with the Christmas gifts, hoping he would get some time to himself to write and that the miracle of inspiration would strike. Then he bid farewell to his family and braced himself for Christmas with Emma.

Christmas 1906 was *absolutely* going to be superb …

He wished he could make himself believe it.

Chapter Seven

One Year Later, Christmas Present

'There's me, myself and I. So I hope they're not expecting a four-course Christmas dinner.' Sorcha stared in horror at Coren Penhaligon. Coren had caught Sorcha just as she was deciding how much like Santa's Grotto she could make the place look this year. Apparently, someone had been making enquiries as to whether they could use the upstairs space for an event near Christmas, and whether the Arts Centre might be able to cater for the opening night. Sorcha had helped out with a few events throughout the year, and had loved them all – but trade was really building up towards Christmas, and feeding visitors a veritable feast at a festive event was a bit too much to take on right now.

'Nobody's expecting a four-course Christmas dinner. They're wanting to run a Victorian Christmas Exhibition – or an Edwardian one, I'm not quite sure – and they asked if there was any chance of food afterwards. Like a buffet, or some tea and cakes on the first night.' Coren moved smartly to the side and put his hands in his pockets as Sorcha approached him with an armful of tinsel. He was out of luck.

'Here – you're taller than me. Pin that end up there please, will you, Coren?' Sorcha brandished a silver garland at him. 'Then we can trail it across there, and it'll drape over the counter quite nicely. See? It's pretty, isn't it, when it's stretched out? Anyway. I can do tea and cakes. I can even do a buffet. I just can't do a four-course Christmas dinner.' She pulled a face, the tinsel half-trailed. 'Well, I can. But not here.' Space was definitely at a premium in the tea room, although she would never admit that to anyone – and, as everything was freshly baked on the premises, she'd meet herself coming backwards with a pile of sprouts if she tried to do anything quite so ambitious. 'Who's it for, anyway?' She tugged the tinsel straight and gestured for Coren to tack it up at the other end as well.

'A guy called Locryn Dyer.' Coren moved over towards her and reached up, sticking the drawing pin into the ceiling firmly. 'He's just moved into the area – he's a collector of some sort – opening up a shop. Maybe it's an antique shop. Maybe not. Merryn was the one talking to him about it.' Coren frowned. If there wasn't a clear, logical sort of spreadsheet or business plan attached to a concept, he couldn't always visualise the idea. It was the way his brain worked – sharp as the tacks Sorcha was making him use, and always on a sensible, focused trajectory. He would want to know what Locryn was selling and how he anticipated growing a business. The vague idea of a man who collected stuff and was possibly opening a shop was alien to poor Coren.

Sorcha hid a smile and lifted an ice-blue garland out of the box next to her. She knew all about vague concepts of businesses. After all, hadn't she moved away from Pencradoc when she was eighteen? It had worked in her favour though – all those years studying catering and working her way around the country in various hospitality places had definitely made her realise that her idea of heaven was a tea room she could call her own.

And now she was back, running her own café in her beloved nineteenth-century folly! The café had done extremely well over the last year – even without Martin's tips and suggestions for clearing tables and making people leave quickly. In fact, in Sorcha's experience, customers often bought a second or third drink, and perhaps even an extra snack as well, if she just left them to it. She'd had her appendix out in the summer and it had been downright hideous leaving the poor tea room in the hands of her friends and relations. She hadn't been able to wait to get back.

She still had to pinch herself sometimes though – the fact that it had all worked out for her so perfectly was amazing. She absolutely felt that tea room was right where she should be; as if it was exactly what she should be doing.

Her childhood ambition to get inside the tower had officially been fulfilled, and now that her tinsel was up securely, she thought that providing a selection of Christmas nibbles was quite a nice thing to be thinking about, to be perfectly honest. Especially if there was going to be an exhibition to go alongside them. She loved the history of Pencradoc and the thought of seeing some festive-themed photographs or paintings, hopefully related to Pencradoc in some way, would be lovely. She'd also always been a huge fan of Christmas and putting the decorations up today was making her feel particularly jolly.

Sorcha was also notorious for baking monstrous quantities of goodies for everybody, especially at this time of year, and that was not in any small way related to the delectable scent of Christmas spices, mixed fruit and warmed rum or brandy that tickled her nose pleasantly as she baked, of course.

'Leave it with me,' she told Coren as he frowned at

a bunch of mistletoe she waved around jokingly before winking, teasing him. Everyone knew Coren was not a mistletoe type of person, reserved and business-like as he was. He never took offence though, and really did seem to enjoy Christmas in his own quiet way, even if that way was not quite as exuberant as Sorcha's way. 'If you can tell me how many people to expect,' she continued, 'I can get it all organised. Just a little higher with that bit of red tinsel please – look, you've put it on a wonk.'

'Sorry – is that better? Good. Okay. I'll get Merryn to sort it all out,' he replied, shoving his hands back in his pockets and attempting to back away as Sorcha pulled an all-singing, all-dancing Santa out of the box and looked eagerly up at a high shelf on the dresser which held the crockery. There was a perfect spot for it next to the Santa teapot she had put out again from last year – her own little festive talisman. 'And then Locryn can let you both know what he's planning,' added Coren.

Sorcha nodded, her mind already flying ahead with what she could make. She was looking forward to this one. 'Lovely. Look – won't an extra Santa be splendid up there? Honestly, if you put him there, I'll love you forever.' She grinned at her boss and thrust Santa out at him. 'Or maybe I'll let you have a gingerbread muffin for tea break?'

Coren, at last, smiled. 'A gingerbread muffin is fine, thank you. Merryn'll be in touch soon.' And Sorcha clapped her hands as Coren slotted the decoration into place for her.

Locryn had quite a collection of things already. He'd brought his stock with him from his old antiques shop in Newquay and was beginning to sort things out.

He was elated that he was now moving on, well away from his old house – a place which held the energy of all the arguments and disagreements between him and Laura.

Locryn shuddered, remembering it all again. Yes, he had been more than ready to sell up and make a fresh start. Yet if anyone had told him last Christmas, when the atmosphere had been heavy with the impending doom of his ending relationship, that he'd be living in a new place, in a pretty little Cornish village – that apparently, according to Aunt Susie, meant something to his family in a peculiar, roundabout way – he wouldn't have believed them.

But goodness, he was very pleased he'd made that break and was extra pleased to be here and planning this cheerful exhibition, rather than planning how many extra hours he could put in at work before he had to go home and face Laura again.

With Aunt Susie being a local and always very interested in what was happening community-wise, Locryn had followed the news keenly about Pencradoc Arts Centre with her for ages; how the centre had become quite a successful enterprise within the last couple of years and, from the first time he had read about it in an arts and culture magazine Susie had posted to him, he had been drawn to the whole ethos of it. The chance of living and working so close to the place was also exciting. He had honestly never thought such a thing would have been possible until his aunt had shown him that empty building. Good grief, he'd never even visited the Arts Centre! Something he was pretty embarrassed about, now he thought about it.

He even had his Christmas tree decorated, which was

something – and his favourite pictures were already up on the wall. His *most* favourite picture – a delicate watercolour of a fictional, and truly magical, woodland scene that Aunt Susie had given him – was in pride of place on the chimney breast. The picture seemed very much at home here, he thought, more than it had done in the fairly modern place he'd lived in before, when it had been presented to him as his Newquay housewarming gift. Laura, of course, hadn't liked the watercolour – she'd said it was old-fashioned and didn't fit in with anything. She definitely hadn't liked the finely-detailed figures in the foreground either, branding them "awfully twee".

'Can we not replace it with a huge collage of photographs of us having fun with our friends?' he remembered her moaning one day.

'I don't think so,' Locryn had replied mildly and, fortunately, she hadn't pressed the point. But that was one thing he wouldn't have budged on, regardless.

That painting had been in the family for many years, and he knew exactly as much as Susie did about it – he'd loved hearing the story about its creation when he was little, and now, as an adult, he could appreciate its history even more. Susie's grandfather had given it to her when she'd bought her first home, and it was one of *her* most treasured possessions as well. 'There's a whole world of magic attached to that painting,' Susie had told Locryn. 'It's an original, and, as far as we know, unique. I haven't got children and I'm not likely to have any now, so you may as well have it – you'd get it when I died, anyway! It always goes to the favoured child – it's part of the story,' she'd said it with a huge grin on her face, and he hoped his sister and brother hadn't been told that tale, or it would lead to some *very* awkward conversations next time they were all together ...

However, despite having his pictures on the wall, he seemed to have lost his favourite books, most of his mugs and his frying pan in the packing boxes.

But, on a positive note, he was already displaying a vast array of festive things in the shop window, like antique decorations and fine china decorated with hand-painted robins. He even had a box full of vintage *cartes de visite*, some of which were Christmas themed. He'd placed a few of the cheerful cards in the display as well. It didn't look too bad.

Locryn had a pile of things to one side though – the items he felt were particularly special and deserved a place in his Christmas exhibition. He'd tentatively approached the owners of Pencradoc and had been delighted when they'd agreed to allow him to use the Tower Tea Room to showcase it. They were going to cater it too – so the idea was he'd raise awareness of his shop and spread a little festive cheer amongst the community if he could. So far, the people he'd met had all been friendly and enthusiastic. He wasn't quite sure how the lady who ran the tea room would be though. It was a big request at quite short notice but, amazingly, she'd apparently agreed to do it. So here he was today, striding through the chilly, frost-covered streets to meet her for the first time, in the company of Merryn Burton, who worked at the Arts Centre and was helping him to arrange things.

There was a fair-haired woman standing at the gatehouse when he arrived who he guessed was Merryn. The house was bedecked with big contemporary festive wreaths, but the decorations still managed to look traditional against the grey stonework. He was impressed.

The woman he assumed was Merryn appeared well wrapped up in a winter coat, scarf, boots and a bobble hat, and she walked forward to meet him, a smile on her face and her gloved hand held out in greeting.

'Locryn?' She came to a stop in front of him.

'That's right – you must be Merryn?' He took her proffered hand and shook it.

'I am indeed. It's a pleasure to meet you in person. How are you finding the village?'

'It's great.' Locryn grinned. 'I was worried that they wouldn't take kindly to a stranger – some places are like that, but Pencradoc has been fine. I guess it helps that my Aunt Susie is pretty well-known around here though!'

'Yes. Imagine how I felt – a Londoner in their midst! But you're right, it's all good. Now, I'm going to take you over to the folly – you've probably guessed it's that big tower over there. Sorcha said she'd be in there with the kettle on and, if I'm not mistaken, she did promise mince pies as well.'

'Fantastic.' A hot drink and a mince pie was always a good option, especially after a chilly walk, Locryn always thought.

Together, they made their way through the wintry grounds, the skeletal trees looking somewhat elegant as the branches criss-crossed in lacy, woody tracery. The evergreen shrubs were undefeated by the cold snap, but the gravel paths crunched loudly beneath their feet, echoing weirdly across the gardens.

Merryn must have noticed Locryn looking in astonishment around him – he'd never been in a garden this big and this empty in his life – and she laughed. 'It's really not as desolate as this normally. The gardens are beautiful and, to be honest, sometimes it's good just to wander around and see nobody. The waterfall over there froze one year a very long time ago, apparently, and I think that would have been weird – the sound of that is always here. Without it, Pencradoc just wouldn't be the same.'

Locryn looked across at where she was indicating, and he knew that in summer it must be a lovely place to be. 'You could have a picnic on that flat rock overlooking it, couldn't you? Must be beautiful in the summer,' he commented. 'I haven't been to the Arts Centre, I must confess, but I'm pretty familiar with the village.'

'Pencradoc has its own special feeling all year round, whatever the season. We're busy with setting up a Christmas Winter Wonderland Walk around the grounds at the minute – willow reindeers and robins made out of clockwork stuff. Pretty light shows in the trees, that sort of thing. Should be fun.'

'Should be.' Locryn nodded. 'Years ago, I had relatives from near here, and apparently they always said that the place was like a fairy tale castle at Christmas. My aunt says there are stories about the Pencradoc Christmas parties going on for days. Aunt Susie persuaded me to think about moving here, and when I saw that building up for sale, the opportunity was just too good to miss.'

'I know what you mean.' It was Merryn's turn to nod. 'It *is* like a fairy tale at times. When the snow covers everything, it's simply magical. Oh, and here we are – at the tea room. Sorcha! It's only me.' She raised her voice as they approached the tower and pushed open the door. 'I've brought Locryn with me.'

An extremely pretty dark-haired, brown-eyed woman popped her head around a door that Locryn presumed led to the kitchen and smiled at them. A dimple appeared in her cheek, and Locryn couldn't help smiling back.

'Oh! Hi. Sorry, I'm just taking the mince pies out of the oven. I've only made a dozen or so. What we don't eat, you can take back with you.'

'Works out at four each,' said Merryn. She shook her head. 'There won't be any left.'

'I second that. Mince pies are my favourite,' added Locryn.

'Fabulous.' Sorcha smiled again and indicated that they take a seat. 'What would everyone like to drink? Might as well get comfortable before we start on the details.'

'Latte please,' said Merryn with a smile.

'Same for me, if that's okay?' said Locryn.

Sorcha nodded. 'That's three then. Great. I won't be a minute.'

While Sorcha bustled around getting drinks and mince pies ready, Locryn sat down and looked around the place. It was lovely circular space. There were a dozen tables or so, nicely set out. A staircase to the left of the counter wound its way upstairs, and a hand-painted sign in the shape of an arrow advised visitors that the exhibition space was "This Way". Someone – probably Sorcha, he reckoned – had put tinsel on the sign, and fairy lights decorated the tea room, along with a small Christmas tree in an alcove and a jolly Santa on a shelf next to what looked like a bright red Father Christmas teapot. The whole place smelled of warmth and baking and Christmas spices. He couldn't help smiling again.

'We'll show you upstairs after this,' Merryn told him.

'Can't wait,' he replied. 'Those pies smell amazing.'

'They'll taste amazing as well.' Merryn winked. 'Four each may not be quite enough at all.'

Locryn decided he'd be happy to test that theory out.

Chapter Eight

Christmas, 1906

'There's no need to be afraid at all.' Elsie linked arms with Holly and pulled her closer. 'My parents – sorry, Mummy and Teague – have told me that they're honestly very happy for us to take over the house for a party. Anyway, it'll just be a small party, like we said. Only a handful of us.'

They were walking through the grounds of Pencradoc, Elsie confidently striding around a route that was as familiar to her as anything. They wandered around the network of little paths which snaked through the wintry gardens, amongst the bare-limbed trees of the woodland, the eerie old folly-tower Holly loved jutting out of the landscape – but suddenly, as Holly looked across at the vast expanse of the estate, it all seemed a bit overwhelming to a girl who came from an unassuming little village in the south of Cornwall.

'Yes, but it's that handful I'm afraid of.' She pulled her arm out of Elsie's and drew her coat closer to her. 'I've had time to ponder it all again, and I do actually feel a little daunted, Elsie – let's be honest. I mean, I don't *know* any of your home friends, do I, except for Louis? They might think I'm just a strange, arty Bohemian-type with no conversation or anything. I suppose I do know your cousins and your sisters, and I love them dearly – but what if your friends are all …?' She hesitated to say it, but she knew what she meant. She knew the word she was reluctant to say was "rich". Elsie was technically a

"Lady" after all. And she was just plain old Holly Sawyer. It didn't matter usually, but the enormity of the event she had so happily agreed to attend was slowly nibbling away at her confidence the closer the time got. She now wasn't sure if this *had* been such a wonderful idea!

To be honest, the number of people she already knew at Pencradoc was quite enough. Elsie had one of the strongest personalities Holly had ever encountered, but she was also fiercely loyal and Holly knew she was the best friend she could have hoped for at college. Where Elsie was dark-haired, dark-eyed and had skin the colour of wholesome country cream, Holly was silvery-blonde, grey-eyed and as pale as a bucket of milk. They both drew admiring glances from the young men at college, but Holly was certain it was Elsie they looked at first, and their attention only landed on her as the pallid, uninteresting friend.

She felt that being pallid and uninteresting and in Elsie's shadow here at Pencradoc this evening would not be to her advantage. There wasn't really anywhere she could lurk to get away from them all, was there? Apart from maybe one spot she could think off if luck was on her side, thanks to Elsie's smallest brother ...

'All what?' Elsie turned and smiled at her friend, bringing Holly's attention back to the present moment. 'All from the set I grew up with? Well, yes, some of them are. And actually, *I'm* a strange, arty Bohemian-type when you think about it, and I say to hell with anyone who dismisses me on that basis.' She winked at Holly, teasing. 'But as far as my guests for this party go, even *I* don't know Emma's cousin, Noel, that well. Noel Andrews, he's called. I know *that* much. He's here for the holidays, and as such I wanted to invite him – it would have been dreadfully impolite not to. I know he writes. But I don't know what. His grandfather has some sort of courtesy title, I think, and I'm not sure if he would be entitled to inherit it. Emma seems to think he would be, but I'm not sure of the situation. As I say, I don't know him very well.'

'Noel.' Holly gave a short laugh. 'An appropriate name for someone to meet at Christmas, I suppose. But it doesn't make me feel much better – that's one single, solitary person out of the lot of them!'

'Don't be miserable,' scolded Elsie. 'And you're a fine one to talk with a name like yours! You're both very festive indeed. You should get along quite well with one another. What else were you going to do this weekend?' It was Saturday the twenty-second of December. Holly was planning on going back to South Cornwall on the Sunday lunchtime, so she'd be back at home and settled in for Christmas Eve.

'I don't know.' Holly shrugged and pulled her scarf tighter. Despite it being Cornwall, it was still Cornwall in the dead of winter and it was jolly chilly. 'Work on my portfolio?'

'Your portfolio can wait. Mine's waiting.' Elsie raised her chin, like a small, pointed-chinned animal sniffing for familiar scents as Pencradoc came into view from the edges of the old Gothic rose garden. 'Two days isn't going to change much.'

'You'd get top marks even if you just slapped paint onto the canvas in the half hour before we handed it in!'

'I would.' Elsie had full confidence in her talent and, with Ruan Teague in her life, that wasn't surprising. Elsie had confided once, after they'd made the huge mistake of trying absinthe at a party held by one of the wilder students, that she thought Teague was her actual father, but Holly had wisely never pursued that line of discussion. 'But that's beside the point,' Elsie finished now.

Holly sighed. Elsie's portfolio was, as she'd decreed months ago, based on the stage and already had a definite hint of the Impressionists – her work wouldn't look out of place in an exhibition of Monet's or Renoir's, or perhaps Degas' ballet dancers. Holly knew she'd always loved that aspect of things anyway, and it didn't hurt that the famous actress Lily Valentine was a family friend and, thanks to that silly magazine, everybody knew now that Elsie was particularly close to her. Holly's own portfolio was based on her beloved fairy tales and mythology as she'd originally planned, but she couldn't help but feel that all her work seemed rather trite and controlled against Elsie's confident, sweeping strokes.

If she was honest, she was quite glad she'd decided to abandon it this weekend, although she had packed her art materials and most of her completed work, just in case the party got too hideous.

'It might be, but all I'm saying is some of us are blessed with natural talent, and some of us have to work at it.'

'And some of us have natural beauty, decorum and grace, and some of us need a little more work in that area.' Elsie grinned at Holly. 'Look at you – you're the perfect ice maiden. I'm like a feral thing.' She shook her head and her dark curls bounced around wildly. 'I hate being contained. Hence, I'm striding around Pencradoc when I know for a fact that I should be in there getting ready to receive my guests.' She laughed and took Holly's hand. 'And you'll be all delightful and show me up terribly.'

Holly couldn't help laughing. 'Show *you* up, Lady Elsie Pencradoc? Never. Look – is that a visitor?' She raised her free arm and pointed towards the house. 'My God! They have a *car*!'

A green vehicle stood outside the big house, and a figure – a man – alighted and went around to the other side to help a woman down.

'Oh! Yes. That's Pearl and Ernie.'

'The ones from that "Society wedding" you went to?'

'Yes. And as I mentioned, Pearl's still struggling to fit in a little. But one must accept her. She's here for keeps. She probably feels a little like you do – you both need to have a great deal more confidence in yourselves. She *does* lack it a little, poor thing, even though she was a *very* beautiful bride and half the county attended.'

'Very well. Point taken. So remind me – who else is coming?'

'Emma and Noel, of course, and my cousins, Clara and Mabel. They don't realise how lucky they are to be invited, I can tell you.' She scowled. Clara and Mabel were, Holly knew, still her annoying little cousins, despite one being eighteen and one being seventeen and both being "out" in Society – not that their free-thinking parents had pushed that. But the girls had wanted to experience the parties and the fancy frocks. 'My sisters aren't coming. Isolde is just a little too young, and Medora would only have a fit of the vapours if Isolde came and she didn't. They said they'll take good care of Biscuit for me, because I know he will miss me dreadfully. Laurie is otherwise engaged with his wassailing – not surprisingly – and then there's also Louis, of course. So *he'd* better watch out if Clara is on the prowl again.' The scowl turned into a glower and

Holly hid a smile. Elsie was very possessive of Louis and wasn't going to let him be snapped up by just anyone, even her cousin, if she could help it.

It was sad, Holly thought, that the group of young people at the party tonight might not have that much choice in their relationships if they were expected to marry for a particular purpose – like to shore up a struggling estate with a nice dowry. She knew how much Elsie yearned for Louis and it was so obvious that she was already half in love with him. For a moment, Holly felt quite pleased she had a bit more freedom of choice. Not that she had ever met anyone she wanted to marry, of course. But the thing was, she could, if she wished, be in control of her destiny and marry someone for love; not privilege, or money, or titles, or for what was "expected". She could make her *own* choices, and she suddenly felt that it was actually quite wonderful to be able to do that as a woman.

Pearl and Ernie were, of course, a shining example of what was "expected" and demonstrated perhaps the lack of choice people of Elsie's rank in Society had in their relationships. Pearl was, apparently, what was scathingly known as a "Dollar Princess"; one of the many young women, heiresses of industry perhaps, who flocked from America to snap up titled young heirs and inject the floundering estates with Papa's fortunes. Ernie's estate had floundered after his father's death – yet here the young man was now, driving to Pencradoc in a car.

'No. I don't know *any* of them except your cousins and Louis. But I know *of* them, I suppose, from what you've told me.' It was Holly's turn to frown. 'I just hope I don't make myself look ridiculous.'

'You won't. They're all delightful, really.'

'Even Pearl?'

'Yes. Even Pearl. Emma's a bit of a handful at times, but I find it best just to ignore her.'

The girls looked at one another and suddenly laughed. 'Oh dear! I actually *do* feel sorry for Pearl!' Holly shook her head. 'She's miles away from home and probably feels as out of place as me.'

'Hmmmm.' Elsie tried to make her grumble sound stern, then gave up and laughed. 'Come on. Race you to the house. Before we have to be decorous.' And she shot off in front of her friend in a flurry of winter coat, sturdy boots and ankle-length skirts. Holly shouted with laughter and hurried after her, even as the first flakes of snow began to fall.

The snow spurred Holly on to run faster – it might have been cold and miserable outside, but a warm house awaited her and, to all intents and purposes, a weekend of fun with her best friend.

And it's almost Christmas! What in the world is there to be so negative about?

Noel was lurking at the bottom of the grand staircase, trying to hide behind an extraordinarily large Christmas tree, very conscious of the glowering Ellory, Duke of Trecarrow, staring down at him – indeed at everyone – with a sense of disapproval.

That "everyone" included the irritating Emma who was busy shrieking as she greeted a couple who had just swanned in. He had caught a glimpse of a green car outside when they had been granted entry and, from the awkward way the young man accepted the enthusiastic greeting from Emma, and the tight-lipped disapproval the man's companion gave his cousin, he thought that he might just as well stick pins in his eyes and throw himself off the top of that folly in the garden.

Bloody awful.

He turned his attention back to the portrait and shivered as the man's cool gaze seemed to disapprove even more. It was hard to believe that Elsie had sprung from that parentage. She definitely took more after her mother, Zennor. Noel had only met Elsie and her mother once and had barely said a word. He *couldn't* say a word – there was no space for words once Emma began entertaining.

It was damn annoying that he'd come to this area simply to visit his aunt and uncle – and bring Christmas gifts to keep the family happy – and ended up, somehow, escorting his cousin to a party. But he hadn't really had an excuse, seeing as he was spending Christmas with them all and had nowhere else to go.

Just as he was pondering his misfortune, the front doors swung open and a girl burst in, looking over her shoulder and laughing. She had silvery-blonde hair that was escaping from a long plait down her back, and her navy serge coat and hat were dusted with snowflakes. Her cheeks were flushed, apparently from running, and hot on her heels was Elsie Pencradoc. Elsie hadn't even bothered to try and tame her hair, which was flying out around her head in a cloud of dark curls, and she was similarly attired, but her coat was scarlet and her beret half falling off her head.

'Slow coach!' cried the fair-haired girl, then suddenly brought herself up short as she realised she had burst right into a social gathering. 'Oh! Lord help me! I am *so* sorry …' She stared around her and the colour faded from her cheeks, then beamed even brighter as the embarrassment clearly set in.

'Top hole,' murmured Noel, trying to hide a smile. He thought he liked this girl already.

'Oh! You're here. You're all here!' Elsie clapped her hands, not embarrassed in the slightest. 'Please accept our apologies. We were walking in the garden, and I saw Mr and Mrs Ernie arrive.' She held her hands out to Ernie, the awkward-looking young man, and strode across to him, ready to receive a kiss on the cheek.

Emma, however, pounced in between them, blocking off the pinched-faced woman, who stood ramrod straight next to Ernie. 'Isn't it simply *wonderful* to see Ernie? I haven't seen him for *eons*. But Ernie! It's so *wonderful* to see you.' She turned her back on the woman, presumably Ernie's wife, Pearl, who Emma had been so dismissive of at home, and practically pushed Elsie out of the way to grab Ernie for herself and receive an even more awkward kiss from the young man for her efforts.

Noel was, it had to be said, a little ashamed of his cousin, and he scowled and pushed his hands in his pockets, trying not to say anything that would spoil the party before it had even begun.

'Yes. I'm quite sure Ernie and Pearl have been busy being married,' said Elsie a little coldly. 'And, as I say, I saw them arrive but, as for the rest of you, I didn't know *you* beautiful people were here.' She smiled and nodded briefly at Emma, then scanned the room until her eyes alighted on Noel. 'There you are, hiding away from us!' Noel quickly rearranged the scowl into a half-smile and nodded, retreating further into the shadows. He didn't really like the attention. 'Ernie. Noel. Pearl. Emma …' Elsie began. Noel bit his lip and ducked his head, trying not to laugh. That was Emma neatly put in her place. 'This is my great friend from college, Holly

Sawyer. Please excuse us turning up like this, but it's just simply exhilarating out there. Isn't it, Holly? Holly – this is everyone. We're just waiting for Louis and my cousins now.' She repeated all their names and the girl, Holly, looked wretched as she nodded at everyone in turn.

Noel noticed she was twitching at her skirts, and he wouldn't have been surprised if she dipped into a curtsey, but he took pity on her and watched as she tried to melt into the shadows on the opposite side of the hall.

Ah well. He couldn't just let her stand there all alone, could he? He pulled his jacket together, straightened his shoulders, stepped out of his corner, and headed to hers.

Chapter Nine

Christmas Present

They chatted easily over the lattes and the mince pies. Sorcha sat down at the table with her gingham apron on, a flashing Christmas badge on the shoulder strap, and joined in the conversation.

'Thanks so much for indulging me,' Locryn Dyer said as Sorcha pushed another mince pie towards him. He'd already had two and shook his head with a grin. 'I don't think I'll be able to move if I have another one. You're right, Merryn – they are amazing.'

Sorcha nodded. 'Merryn would know. I have to hide them from her normally. Well, like I said, you can take some home with you, Locryn. I don't think anything can beat a homemade mince pie. I'll give you a pot of brandy butter to take with you as well, if you like. I doubt it'll be something you whip up yourself, what with sorting out the exhibition and everything. You'll be pretty busy, I imagine. And maybe your kitchen isn't a decent enough size to work in comfortably. Or maybe it is. I wouldn't know. Ignore me. Sorry.' She laughed.

'You can certainly tell where your priorities lie, Sorcha.' Merryn drained her coffee. 'And they are very good priorities, I have to say.'

Locryn smiled at her again. He had a really nice smile, all open and friendly, and it lit his whole face up. Sorcha couldn't help smiling back.

'It's not a bad size, considering, but I'd say it was functional rather than impressive.'

Sorcha nodded. 'I've worked in some places that were neither functional nor impressive. My kitchen here is small, but it does what I need it to do. And what I need at the minute is space for Christmas food. We've got some Festive Afternoon Teas scheduled and I've got lots of bookings in already. Merryn might be getting some weird and wonderful experiments to try, but I'm sure she'll be fine as a taste tester. I think I'm doing something interesting with pistachios, although I haven't quite decided what yet.'

'I'm more than fine to try anything you bake. Those spiced flapjacks you made the other week were gorgeous – happy to sample your stuff any time—oh!' Merryn's phone rang and she looked at the number. 'Hello, Coren. What's up? We're just in the tea room. Discussing spiced flapjacks – you'll be pleased to know we'll be getting some soon.' She winked at Sorcha.

Sorcha laughed and stood up to clear away the empty mugs, now that everyone seemed to have finished. 'I'll get you a bag for those, Locryn – if you really want them.' She indicated the pies.

Locryn widened his eyes and deliberately pulled the plate towards him. '*If* I want them? I suspect I absolutely *do* want them!'

Sorcha laughed again. 'Okay. Let me have the plate and I'll sort it out.'

Reluctantly, teasingly, Locryn released the plate and pushed it back towards her. She put it carefully on the tray.

'Okay – I'll pop back over.' Merryn was still chatting to Coren, nodding every so often. Then she said her farewells to him and hung up. 'Sorry, guys. I'm going to have to go back to the house. There's some mix up about

74

a wreath-making workshop. I've been trying to sort it out, but there's still some problems.' She frowned. 'I'd better go and have a look at the information we've got as the facilitator sounds a bit stressed, apparently. Coren's not great at the people skills, bless him, and Kit's trying to fix some installation up in Rose's Garden or he would have helped. Just as well we're both here today, isn't it? Sorcha, will you be okay to show Locryn the exhibition space?'

'Oh! Of course. If he doesn't mind being lumbered with me? I'm not very professional about it. My domain is down here.'

'I don't mind at all,' said Locryn. He smiled at her again, his voice soft, and her heart did a weird little pounding thing and her stomach went squishy. It had been a long time since a smile had had that effect on her.

Sorcha was involuntarily transported back to a school Christmas party where the boy she had fancied all year – well, since September anyway – had asked her to slow dance with him. Yes – those little butterflies had woken up after a ten-year sabbatical, and a fair trampling from Martin, and decided to flap around, despite it being very unseasonal for them. It was a weird, yet not unpleasant, sensation.

'Lovely.' Merryn stood up, interrupting the moment, which probably wasn't a bad thing to be honest, as Sorcha felt she must have a rather vacant, staring sort of expression on her face. 'Will you come over to the house when you're finished, just so we can say goodbye to you properly and you can meet Coren?'

'Yes, of course we'll pop over.' Sorcha was glad of Merryn's cheerful voice – she had found it hard to take her eyes off Locryn, truth be told. 'I'll bring a couple of the leftover mince pies as well – Kit and Coren might as well have one each too.'

'Excellent. See you soon then. Locryn, if the space is no good for you, don't be afraid to tell us. I know it won't suit everyone.'

'I'm sure it'll be fine. See you soon.' Locryn raised his hand and Merryn nodded, hurrying out of the tea room towards Pencradoc.

'If you're ready, I'll take you upstairs. It *is* a nice space – but maybe I'm biased.' Sorcha pointed to the staircase Locryn had noticed when he came in. There were some cheerful Christmas prints in frames ranged up the walls alongside it.

'Did you do the decorating? Nice touch. I love the theme.' He followed her to the staircase and they began to climb up.

'The sign and the pictures? And the tinsel everywhere? Yes. I love Christmas. Normally I've got some other pictures on there – sort of like film posters, but for fairy tales. With it being like Rapunzel's tower, they seemed fitting. I think it's because I've got relatives from Ireland and Germany, and the folk tales are so important, aren't they? Oh – and scary! Don't get me started on Little Red Riding Hood.'

'I know. It's terrifying – talk about warning young girls off relationships!'

'Ah! You know about it. Excellent.'

'Yes, I've got a bit of an interest in that sort of thing. Again, it's a family connection.' Locryn laughed. 'Amazing how these tales change in translation, isn't it? I'll see if I can find some things in the shop for you, for when the tinsel's down – pretty sure I've got some old books of Grimms' Fairy Tales and Hans Christian Andersen stories; an old toy theatre, even, with little cut-out figures that might bring it a bit to life. Maybe it's something Coren could consider exhibiting in the future?'

'I'm sure he'd love something like that. They really want to make Pencradoc more family friendly. We've got some children's Christmas crafts sessions arranged. And card-making too, as well as those wreath-making workshops Merryn mentioned. I love anything like that. Anything Christmassy. In fact, give me a few more days and I'll have this place even more like Santa's Grotto.'

'Santa's Grotto! Hey that's a good idea – has Pencradoc got one of those? That would encourage the families in.'

'Actually, no – but if you're offering, I'm happy to tell Merryn?' She paused and grinned at him over her shoulder.

'Maybe next year. It might be a little too much doing this exhibition and sitting in a grotto while it happens.'

'Very true. Look – here's the room. It's all nice and bright. I love how it's whitewashed. It makes all the pictures jump out from the walls.

'Oh! Yes. Yes, I can see how that works.' Locryn stood in the middle of the room and looked around him. Sorcha had even put some decorations up in the exhibition space and some tasteful bowls of festive potpourri, the scent of which mingled beautifully with the spices from her recent baking session downstairs. 'What's that over there?' He pointed at a piece of Perspex on the wall.

'It's some old graffiti by Rose, one of the previous Duchesses. They think she wrote it when she was a child. It's quite special. Makes her come to life a little more, I think. You should go and have a look at it properly some time – it's lovely. But anyway, as you can see, we've got nothing official on display up here at the minute. All of these pictures are Kit's. He's Merryn's partner. He just puts his work up when we're empty, so to speak. Nothing worse than a bare wall, which is why I've tried to mitigate any possibility of that with my decor. We've also got a couple of cabinets, see? So the things you can't hang on the wall, or want protected a little more, can go in those.' She indicated some glass-topped units, currently displaying some painted pebbles and stones. 'Again, this is Kit's work. Like I say, he's not precious and will take it all away if you want to use everything.'

'Thanks. I think it's exactly what I envisaged. I've got some framed photographs and pictures that I don't mind hanging up, and some more delicate things as well – old postcards, Christmas cards, invitations to parties and some antique glass baubles. That sort of thing. I can put those in the cabinets, if that's okay?'

'It's not my call, but it sounds nice to me. I love the idea of an old-fashioned Christmas.'

'There are certainly some interesting things which survived. I've got items from the Victorian era, but also from the Edwardian times, so I couldn't really think of an all-encompassing title for it. I really just wanted to put my stamp on the area, you know? Let people know I'm here, and hopefully get to know a few more people as well, if we can tempt them across with nibbles. My Aunt Susie is doing a good job of promoting me, but I think I need to take a bit of responsibility for it myself.'

'Well, nibbles are always good. In my experience, they *always* help. Hey, have you thought about doing some Christmas ghost stories as well? Dickens and M.R. James? That kind of thing? Cordelia Beaumont would be a good one to ask. I can put you in touch with her. She's training to be a drama teacher, but she has a background in the theatre and she's really good. She could read them out.'

'I love it! Get people in the mood for it – hey! "The Spirit of Christmas". That's kind of catchy, isn't it? That would be a good title.'

'Sounds like you'd want to get people tipsy on sherry – not that I mind that!' Sorcha held her hand up, looking comically shocked. 'How about "The Spirit of Christmas Past" instead?'

'It has a certain ring to it. I like it.'

'Good. I can go really traditional with the nibbles then. Excellent.' She clapped her hands. 'Sorted.'

'Great.' Locryn found he was genuinely enjoying himself, chatting with Sorcha. The conversation was so easy, he felt as if he'd known her for years. 'Do you think Coren would go for all of that? It's kind of exploded into more of an event than it was, even just within the last few minutes.'

'He'll love it. Anything that will bring in the visitors is good. We'll mention it to him when we go over to the house. Have you been inside Pencradoc yet?'

Locryn shook his head. 'Not yet. It's an incredible building and from what I've heard, the things they've done with it for the Arts Centre are great. I was telling Merryn earlier that some of my family, decades ago, came to the house. Apparently, they knew some of the Pencradocs, And I think the village is great too – I was lucky that the shop came up at the right time.'

'Some things are just meant to be – it's good you're managing to settle in so quickly. Sometimes taking that first step to do something new is the scariest, but I don't think I could *ever* be scared by Pencradoc. It's a little sad it couldn't be used as a family home any more, but it's just not practical. What Merryn's team have done has made it accessible to everyone though. And Coren lives here in an apartment, so it is still technically home for at least some of the family. Merryn and Kit have a couple of rooms as well, for when they come and stay, so it works well, really. Plus it means people like me can get into it officially.' She laughed, and he couldn't help but smile again. 'And it's even more beautiful right now with the decorations up.'

'I bet it is. But hold on – "officially"?'

'It means I used to visit unofficially … but we're not going to talk about that right now. I need to take some mince pies to the boss and tell him we're going to rope in Cordy. It's all about channelling that Christmas cheer we need to focus on.'

'We?' Locryn teased.

'Oh! Sorry. Sometimes I just don't know when to keep quiet and, knowing me, I'll end up taking over. Just tell me to stop. Seriously. I'll have what I think is a brilliant plan, and it's just based on impulse.' She flushed a little. 'I know how annoying it can be when someone starts telling you what to do with your business. But at least some of my crazy plans seem to work out okay, thankfully.' She pointed down the stairs. 'Like my little empire here.'

'It seems as if it's a good little empire. I'm happy with what I've seen up here as well. I think I'm ready to head over to Pencradoc and chat to Coren and Merryn about it all. Is that okay?'

'Sure. I'll just close it all up as we go and get those mince pies sorted, and we'll head over.' She smiled up at him and nodded decisively.

Locryn indicated that she should lead the way back

downstairs, and he followed her down, waiting while she efficiently shut up shop and got ready to go across to the estate with him.

And, as he watched her wind a scarf around her neck and pull a red woollen cloche hat over her shiny, dark hair, he couldn't help but think that he was very happy indeed with what he had seen that day – on rather more than one level.

He was looking forward to seeing more of Sorcha and realised that he was very willing to listen to more of her impulsive and very brilliant Christmassy plans. He thought they might get on quite well.

Chapter Ten

Christmas, 1906

'Wonderful entrance. You couldn't have planned it better if you'd tried.'

Holly looked up, startled. A tall, rangy man was looking down at her. Clean-shaven, with his dark blond hair styled in a fashionable side parting, his features were regular and his smile polite, but his green eyes were kind and twinkled with mischief. This, then, must be Noel. The faces and introductions had passed her by in a haze of horror, but he wasn't the man in the car and he wasn't Louis so, by process of elimination, he had to be Emma's cousin.

Holly's cheeks were burning even more warmly than the cheerful fire in the grate. The charm of a fireplace surround decorated with holly and ivy and little sparkling decorations faded into the background of the worst mortification she considered she had ever felt. 'They must think I'm barmy on the crumpet,' she replied, then flushed even more hotly. 'Sorry. That won't even make sense to you. I sometimes don't think about what I say.' She clamped her lips together, wishing the floor would just open up and swallow her. Honestly, even if she was dragged down to Hell, it had to be better than the way she was feeling right now. *Barmy on the crumpet?* Like he would know what that meant!

To her surprise, Noel laughed. He leant down towards her and his breath was warm on her cheek as he whispered into her ear: 'You're not crazy. Even I can tell that. If you're anything like me, you're probably thinking of a million other things you could be doing right now.'

Holly nodded, her eyes on Elsie as she chatted with Emma. 'I don't even know why I'm here.'

'Because you're as unfortunate as I am?'

Holly laughed reluctantly. 'Perhaps.'

'So how do you know Lady Elsie?'

'We go to the Liberal College of the Arts together. She's incredibly talented.' Holly frowned. 'Incredibly … liberal … as well. It's hard to believe she's quite the rebel when you see her here at home.'

'I think much of it depends on the circle you're born into – and of the society you're brought up in. You don't have to be taught how to behave or act around people; you just know it automatically.'

'Elsie's one of a kind.' Holly suddenly realised her mistake. 'I'm sorry, I'm terribly rude.' She held her hand out. 'I'm Holly.'

'Oh.' A smile twitched at the edges of his lips. 'I'm Noel. Obviously.' He took her outstretched hand in his and, to her surprise, kissed it. She scolded herself inwardly. Not everyone was as common as she was. A firm handshake, in her opinion, was the accepted greeting. And here was this sophisticated friend of Elsie's kissing her hand. 'I'm Emma's cousin, in case you didn't realise.'

'I realised. You're not Ernie, and Louis isn't here yet, so …'

'Louis. Hmm.' He raised his eyebrow. 'I've heard rumours about Elsie and Louis.'

Despite herself, Holly laughed. 'That's terribly inappropriate! There's nothing to "rumour" about.'

'I'd like to see for myself. I—'

There was another commotion, and both Holly and

Noel turned as one to see the door being flung open and two blonde girls come striding in, just as confidently as Lady Elsie. Clara and Mabel: Elsie's cousins. They both had long, curling golden hair, and dark, intense eyes which roved around the entrance hallway, seeing who was there. And who, apparently, was not.

'I told you.' Mabel, the smaller one with the slightly younger, rounder face, addressed her older sister. 'We're late. As usual.'

'Not everyone is here though, are they?' Clara answered, quite snippily.

'No – Louis isn't here for a start. Is he?'

Clara nudged her younger sister sharply with her elbow. 'Mabel!'

'Clara! Mabel!' Elsie drifted seamlessly over to them. 'You know everyone, don't you?'

The girls nodded in unison as greetings flew forth between the other guests. Holly pressed herself further into the wall. She felt quite outnumbered now. Clara and Mabel seemed like different beings completely, all dressed up and ready to mingle with Society.

'Mama and Papa told us to tell you that Aunt Zennor and Uncle Teague and the little ones are quite safely installed at Wheal Mount. And so is Biscuit, of course. Medora is spoiling him quite terribly already,' said Clara. She nodded towards the door. 'We brought the carriage back with us. Obviously.' Clara and Mabel lived with their parents, the Duke and Duchess of Trecarrow, at Wheal Mount – a family property a little further south in Cornwall. Zennor and Teague had announced they were staying there overnight with their other children – *quite simply to avoid Elsie's exuberance*, her step-father had told Holly wryly.

Holly knew that Elsie's parents were putting a huge amount of trust in their eldest daughter by letting her host the party, but Elsie would carry it off with aplomb as usual. Nothing ever fazed her.

'I think we're just waiting for Louis now,' said Elsie.

There was a discreet cough from the side of a hallway, and one of the servants stood there with a letter in his hands. 'Excuse me, Lady Elsie,' he said, 'but we've just received this. I believe it's addressed to you.'

'Oh!' Elsie hurried over to the gentleman and took it from him, ripping it open. 'Oh no! *Damn* it!' Holly felt her own eyebrows raise at the vehemence of the comment and she heard Noel disguise a quiet laugh. 'It's Louis.' Elsie looked at Holly, the only one who possibly had an inkling of the disaster which had befallen her party. 'He can't come. He has a fever of some sort and he's dosing himself on lemon and honey and whisky, of all things. He's terribly sorry. Well. Damn it all to hell.' She crumpled the letter up and stuffed it in her pocket angrily. 'Splendid.' Elsie's cheeks flushed and her eyes shone with what might have been frustrated tears.

'But we're all still here,' said Emma in some surprise. Emma, Holly suspected, was a person who rarely recognised much beyond her own little self-centred bubble.

'We are. Yes. Yes, we are.' Elsie's smile was forced, her voice shaky, but Holly wasn't sure anyone else noticed.

Holly pushed herself away from the wall, trying not to pay attention to the curious glances at her rather dishevelled figure as she went over to hug her friend. 'Let's not spoil the party, darling.' She leaned closer and whispered in her ear, 'It means Cousin Clara can't pay him any attention anyway, doesn't it?'

Elsie laughed sardonically and hugged her back. 'It

does,' she whispered back. 'Thank you, darling Holly-Dolly. I knew you were the perfect person to have here. Righty-o. Pull myself together.' She took a deep breath and pasted on a brighter smile. 'That means we are now *all* here. So I suggest we get everyone shown to their rooms and get back together in the drawing room for some drinks and some games just as soon as we can. Dinner will be at seven, but, well, we can start the party whenever we all convene. Mabes, would you be a brick and ring that bell for us?' Elsie was standing with her hands out now, encompassing all her audience, as Mabel scurried over to press the button on the wall. Again, Holly wasn't surprised her friend's artwork was focused on the stage. Elsie was a born extrovert, a born leader, as well as a born artist. She was hiding her feelings well now. Holly knew that only she could detect the little spark of sadness in Elsie's eyes.

Opposites attracted, she guessed, which was why she and Elsie got on so well. She just wished she didn't feel quite so like a fish out of water at Pencradoc today.

Noel watched Holly walk over to Elsie and put her arm around her when she read the letter about Louis not coming. He had sensed in that moment a genuinely warm person who clearly put her own discomfort aside to make sure her friend was all right. He'd also seen the way Emma seemed vacant and unconcerned, and the way the two blonde girls had looked at one another – one in teasing delight and one in horror and disappointment – and the way Ernie had been pinned to Pearl's side, trapped there by a gloved hand on his arm.

Fair do's, it wasn't an earth-shattering disaster, but it was obviously important to Elsie, God love her.

There were murmurs of assent from the people in the hallway, and gradually they all peeled away, led by various maids to the rooms they were staying in that evening.

Noel had brought an overnight bag, which he had carried in and stashed in the hall beneath the branches of the Christmas tree – early, he'd noted, as the tradition was not to put the thing up until Christmas Eve, but obviously Elsie and her family didn't hold much with tradition – and he headed back over to where he'd left it.

'Let me do that, sir,' said a young lad who'd materialised out of nowhere to show him upstairs.

'No, it's my luggage. I'll carry it, thanks.' Noel smiled down at the boy. He was probably no older than thirteen – only ten years younger than himself. 'You just tell me where I'm to lay my head tonight, and that's fine and dandy. No need to add to your graft, young man.'

The lad let out a gurgle of laughter. He had freckles across his cheeks and his hair was untamed. In fact, it looked damp and Noel had the feeling that he – or the Cook or someone – had slicked it down in the kitchens before he'd come to see the guests.

'It's up here, sir. You can follow me. I'll show you.' His accent was glorious; thick as clotted cream and just as cheerful.

Noel grinned at him. 'Lead the way, old chap.'

The lad laughed again and headed up the stairs. Noel glanced across at Holly as he made his way after him. She was standing with Elsie deep in conversation, and he hoped, bizarrely, that their rooms wouldn't be too far from one another. And also that she was pretty close to him for the duration of the party. She was refreshing, and he liked that.

When he was almost at the top of the stairs, something made him look back down into the hall. Holly was standing, looking right up at him, clutching a big book in her arms while Elsie fussed with something on a table. The girl blushed and quickly looked away.

But Noel smiled and took the last few stairs two at a time. Maybe this wouldn't be as awful as he'd anticipated.

Chapter Eleven

Christmas Present

Sorcha liked Locryn. He was easy to talk to and was open to her ideas, which was novel. She thought back to this time last year when she'd been with Martin.

She was glad she'd washed her hands of him and thrown herself into her business instead. That had been a *very* good decision. It was lovely to be able to chat with a potential customer like Locryn and have her head spin with all sorts of exciting things to hopefully make the event better. The Penhaligons just let her get on with what she was doing and, even though she jokingly referred to Coren as the "boss", he wasn't really. The Tower Tea Room was all hers, and all the business that came through it her responsibility. It was nice, though, to combine it with something like this forthcoming Christmas exhibition. She'd already provided some traditional afternoon teas for the local WI when they'd had their mini art exhibition earlier in the year. Luckily, the day had been glorious, so they'd all sat outside on fancy little tables, bedecked with gingham tablecloths and cheerful pastel crockery with bunting fluttering around the folly.

This time, it would be quite different, but just as nice. She was already thinking of table decorations – both for her Festive Afternoon Teas and for Locryn's exhibition. *Candles*, she thought, *with tiny twists of holly around them; tea served in little fancy cups* – if she could get some nice vintage ones, that would be even better—

Hang on.

'Locryn – am I right in thinking that you own an antiques shop?'

'You are.'

They were heading up the steps outside Pencradoc now, and she paused by one of the grey stone pillars.

'Would there be any chance of some vintage tea sets? I'm willing to pay for them. I just think if we can aim for some authenticity in the set-up, then it'll all work quite well together. It would be great to use them for the Festive Teas too.'

'Yeah, I've got a few tea sets like that.' Locryn nodded. 'You don't have to buy them though. I'll loan them out to you.'

'Oh! Thanks, that's great. I'll pay for any breakages though; it's only fair.'

Locryn laughed. 'If you insist.'

'Oh, I do. Come on – welcome to Pencradoc. Not that I have any ownership of it at all. It's just such a wonderful place. I often daydream about the people who lived here and wonder what they were like. I was always sure princesses lived here, sweeping down the stairs like Cinderella at her ball. It's quite refreshing to think that we've got people like Merryn sweeping down them now. Normal people.' She pushed the heavy old door open and stood back against it so Locryn could get the perfect first impression of the house – the entrance hall, all bedecked for the festive season ahead.

'Wow.' Locryn stopped dead still and stared around him – exactly the reaction Sorcha had hoped for, and she hid a smile. The hallway looked particularly spectacular today, with a huge Christmas tree up and the banisters decorated with holly and ivy. A cheerful Christmas-themed vase stood on the hall table, host to a big twiggy arrangement that hid tiny twinkling lights within the branches amidst twists of silver wire. It was extremely pretty and a nod to the more contemporary art that Pencradoc boasted throughout the year.

'Who's that?' Locryn walked over to the marble bust of a little girl at the bottom of the stairs. Someone had wreathed white Christmas roses around her hair and, if possible, she looked even more proud of herself than usual because someone had given her a bit more attention. 'She's very sweet.'

'That's Lady Elsie. Coren and Kit are descended from her. Her stepfather was Ruan Teague, the artist, and he taught her well. She became quite famous in her own right after she'd finished her studies at the Liberal College of the Arts in London and went on to do some work with the Slade School after that. I'd love to know what she got up to in London. She had a reputation for being the life and soul of the party; a bit of a wild child, I suppose. Photography, art, drama – you name it, she shone at it.' Sorcha smiled at the figure. 'I think you can tell even by looking at this what she turned out like.'

'I'd like to have known her, I think. I wonder if she's the one my relatives knew? That would be amazing. In fact, this *place* is amazing.' Locryn stared around him at the mixture of artwork on the walls.

'Isn't it? The workshop rooms are upstairs, and there are some retreat rooms for people who want to stay for a short period of time. You already know they're doing wreath-making workshops. Those are in addition to the usual painting workshops. They're doing candle making ones too in a couple of weeks. Kit's got a studio and a business in Marazion, but he teaches some of the art courses, and his friend Matt comes up as well to do some. Matt's with Cordelia – he's also an art teacher, so we can only really rely on him for the odd weekend and school holidays.'

'And you think Cordelia will be up for doing the readings?' Locryn turned to her, his eyes hopeful. 'I honestly couldn't have hoped for a better location for this exhibition. I mean it.' She could see that Pencradoc was already having an effect on him; it was, she had discovered, that sort of place. Locryn looked as if he was about to turn into quite a champion of Pencradoc, and she liked that idea.

'We can only ask, but she is really good. Look – let's go along here to the offices and we'll find out what Coren thinks.'

She led the way along the corridor to the rooms at the back: the newly refurbished offices – Coren's domain, naturally. She knocked at a door on the right and a gruff voice called for them to enter, followed by a lighter voice scolding the gruff one and then a rumble of male laughter.

'Hey everyone – we come in peace and bring mince pies.' Sorcha offered the mince pies up on a plate and bowed her head theatrically.

'Coren, I think that deserves more than a grunt, don't you?' Merryn was in there and also Kit, who was half-sitting on the windowsill, his hands in his pockets. He had been the one laughing at his brother's scolding.

'Sorry – yes – thanks, Sorcha.' Coren forced a smile onto his face, but he still looked a little grumpy. 'Hi, Locryn. Hope we're living up to your expectations? It's good to meet you properly, anyway.' He stood up and shook hands over the desk. 'The wreath workshop thing threw me, but, really, you are very welcome here.'

'Yep, we all know how my brother likes to be in control,' said Kit. He pushed himself away from the windowsill and held his hand out to Locryn. 'I'm Kit. Very pleased to meet you. And welcome to Pencradoc.'

Locryn felt another smile breaking out onto his face. He held his hand out in response and shook the dark-haired man's enthusiastically. Coren, he noticed, was fair-haired and the men looked completely different from one another, despite apparently being brothers.

'Thanks. I feel pretty welcome now – everyone's said that to me today. It's great to meet you all.'

'We've had a brainwave.' Sorcha looked at Merryn. 'Cordy. Christmas ghost stories.'

Merryn's eyes widened and she tilted her head to one side. 'Excellent idea. Including ragged urchins?'

'Nope. No ragged urchins.'

'Shame. But yes, that's fab. Shall I text her?'

'If you don't mind – if Locryn is sure he wants to do it?' Sorcha looked at him, her forehead furrowed a little in the middle, as if she'd maybe had second thoughts. 'And Coren's good with it?'

'I'm good with it,' said Coren. 'Anything to widen the appeal, and we know Cordy's usually up for that kind of thing.'

'And I'm sure about it too. Why wouldn't I be?' added Locryn.

'Because sometimes I speak without thinking – and you really need to rein me in and not be polite about it.' Sorcha pulled a face. 'I'm under no illusions, and I know I can be quite annoying at times.'

'No, it's great. Not annoying at all. Please, Merryn, would you be able to ask her?'

'Sure.' Merryn smiled and pulled her phone out of her pocket, slapping Kit's hand away from the mince pies as he reached for his second one. He'd sloped off to the table Sorcha had put the plate on.

'Hey,' he said mildly. 'I was getting one for my brother.'

'No, you weren't.' Merryn didn't even look at him as she texted. 'Right, that's gone. Thanks, Coren. Okay. Now let's see if she replies. So, Locryn, was everything okay? I'm assuming it was, seeing as Sorcha has effectively expanded your exhibition.'

'It's all great. The room is perfect. And we've sorted out some vintage tea services for the party.' He shot a look at Sorcha whose cheeks were turning scarlet. She knew what was coming. 'And Sorcha has also come up with a title. "The Spirit of Christmas Past". She thought it was better than my vague interpretation of it.'

'Sorry.' Sorcha was fully scarlet now. 'I *have* taken over a bit, haven't I? And that was only in the time since Merryn left us alone. I did warn you.'

'No, it's all good.' Locryn winked at her, and she laughed.

Just then, Merryn's phone bleeped and she picked it up to read the message. She punched the air and gave a quiet cheer. 'Yes. Cordy says of course. Just to tell her the details. She also asks about ragged urchins.' Merryn texted back and read the words out as she texted them: 'Not unless Matt wants to dress up.' Then she pressed send. 'There. That should do it. Excellent.' She looked up. 'We've got an event organised. Yay! Let's finalise the dates, and we can get started on clearing the exhibition space out for you.'

'Sounds good,' said Locryn. Coren indicated a chair,

and he sat on it while Sorcha perched on the table by the mince pies.

Together, they went through all the details and, when everyone was happy with it, they shook hands again and Locryn stood up. 'Thanks again. I'll be in touch when I've got the things ready to bring across.'

'Looking forward to it,' said Merryn.

'I'll take you back to the gatehouse,' said Sorcha, 'if you're all done?'

'Sure.' Locryn nodded and waited until Sorcha had said her farewells and led him back out into the corridors.

They paused in the hallway, both of them stopping almost involuntarily. A weird sort of silence descended and cocooned them, and he felt a little disorientated. There was a very strange feeling in that place as the hairs on the back of his neck began to prickle.

'Locryn …' Sorcha's voice was nervous and seemed to come from a long way away. 'Do you feel …?'

He nodded, unable to answer as they looked at one another. Locryn was sure his expression must mirror hers; one of fear and uncertainty. *What on earth was going on?* Nothing had changed since they had last been here. The tree was still there, the wreath still around the little girl's marble head, the garlands on the staircase, yet—

Then he saw it – a movement on the staircase caught his eye and he spun around abruptly. The figure of a fair-haired girl was descending it, swathed in a bluey-green dress, her shoulders set, her head up, looking straight ahead of her. The skirt of the dress was clutched in her fingers and she glided silently down the stairs, the bottom of her gown lost in a swirling white mist. Without a sound, she headed straight towards one of the rooms and drifted through the closed door.

Locryn's heart was pounding. He'd heard rumours this old place was haunted – his customers and new friends in the village gleefully regaling him with tales of Pencradoc's ghosts and hinting at its dark secrets when he'd mentioned his exhibition idea – but he had just smiled and laughed along with it all, never ever thinking he'd come into contact with anything – and now he'd, apparently, seen something in the middle of the afternoon, of all times. *Good God*. It was Sorcha's princess, but whether she was real or imagined, he wasn't quite sure.

'Sorcha – did you see that? Did you see *that*?' He pointed to the door, his hand shaking and thoughts crashing around his head. A ghost? Had he really seen a *ghost*? And not only that, but there was a vague sense of knowing her that floated away with the girl – her face, her hair, her eyes; they were all familiar to him.

'I saw something – I did. I definitely did. Did *you*?' He turned to see her pointing in the complete opposite direction; behind the Christmas tree, of all places. 'Did you see him? A man – standing just under there. He didn't move; he was just standing there. Bloody hell!'

Her eyes were wide and her gaze moved to his outstretched arm. She slowly dropped her own arm. 'What are you pointing over there for, Locryn? He was here. *Here*.' She jabbed her forefinger at the tree. 'I thought it was just a jumble of shadows in the branches at first, then I saw him, I saw his face really clearly, and he was looking at the door. But he didn't move. Good God! I just saw a Pencradoc ghost!'

'So did I.' He was surprised his voice was as steady as it was. 'But mine was a woman. And she was coming down the stairs. And she just walked through that bloody door.'

Chapter Twelve

Christmas, 1906

'Do you like him?' The question was asked in an amused sort of fashion, and Holly quickly looked towards her friend.

'What? No! No. I mean, he seems nice. He seems friendly. But I don't even know him. No. No, I don't *like* him. Not in the way you *like* Louis.'

'Ouch. That was below the belt, darling.'

Holly immediately felt guilty. 'I'm sorry. I didn't mean it like that …'

'Yes, you did. You absolutely meant it like that. It's all right. I'm being a josser, aren't I?'

'No! You're not being a fool. Louis would have come if he could have done.'

'It's a bloody cold he's got. He's not dying!' Elsie scowled. 'He *could* have come. *I* would have come.'

'You're being a bit harsh. It's maybe more like influenza. A cold wouldn't keep him away.' Holly hitched the book closer to her. It was a heavy old thing. 'And do you really need a Visitors' Book this big?' Those words were embossed in gold block on the cover – it wasn't hard to work out what it was. Elsie had pulled it out of a drawer in the side table as soon as her guests were being escorted upstairs. She'd shoved it at Holly to hold while she hunted down a pen.

'Pencradoc had a lot of visitors back in the day,' Elsie said. 'Papa-Ellory stopped that. Horrid man.'

'Elsie! That's your father you're talking about.'

'Mmmm. Maybe. But yes. We do need a Visitors' Book this big. I intend to resurrect the tradition. Ah – there's a nib that doesn't blotch. Excellent.' She scratched some squiggles onto a piece of blotting paper. Holly saw the squiggles were actually a quick sketch of a robin sitting on a snowy branch similar to the one she'd drawn on the window in their college bedroom – a few simple, careless strokes and there was a mini-masterpiece. *Typical Elsie.* 'They stopped filling that one in somewhere around the last century.' Elsie nodded at the book. 'I think it would be nice if my friends could fill it in and then I, at least, can have something nice to look back on when I'm in my dotage.'

'When you're in your dotage and have a hundred children and a handsome husband at your beck and call,' teased Holly.

'If he's not been laid out by a damn cold by then.' Elsie muttered the words under her breath, but Holly heard her and hid a smile.

'Maybe,' she echoed. 'Seriously though, this is a lovely idea.'

'Would you like to be first?' Elsie held the pen out to her.

Holly put the book on the table and opened it. 'Why not?' She took the pen and turned to a fresh page. The names and dates, she noticed, looked exciting – so many different people had visited that it quite made her head spin. As she flicked through, she saw politicians and poets – even royalty.

'Oh my goodness.' She peered down at the book, at one of the last entries. 'You've even got Lily Valentine in here!'

'Yes.' Elsie smiled. 'Remember, I told you she came to

surprise me one day when I was small? When I took that photograph? I made her sign the book to prove she'd been here and then, like I say, I took those photographs as well, just to make sure. Poor Edwin, her husband. He barely got a look in – but he knows I love them both, so he can't ever be cross with me.' She laughed. 'Go on. Start a new page after Lily. I know you want to.'

'I do indeed.' Holly turned the final inscribed page and smoothed the thick paper out before she wrote on a fresh sheet. 'Christmas Party, hosted by Lady Elsie Pencradoc, 22nd December 1906,' she said as she scratched the words out. 'And here I am as the first guest: Holly Sawyer.'

'Perfect.' Elsie clapped her hands. 'Now, let me just add some suitable adornments to the page, then we can leave the pen there and head upstairs.' She pulled Holly's plait affectionately. 'I shall send my maid in to see you, and we'll see if we can do something with that.'

'My hair is perfectly acceptable, thank you.' Holly batted her friend's hand away. 'I just need to brush it out and re-plait it, that's all.'

'No, it's not.' Elsie shook her head. 'This is a Christmas party. An excuse to get dressed up and have fun. Come on – let's not be so serious. I promise, you'll not recognise yourself after I've finished with you.'

And that, thought Holly with a frisson of fear, *is exactly what I'm so scared about …*

Noel, after tossing the young lad a shilling, unpacked his luggage in the room he had been allocated. He had, admittedly, kept his door ajar until he heard voices coming along the corridor. He peeked out and saw, with disappointment, that it was Ernie and Pearl.

He knew, from his eavesdropping, that Elsie's cousins

were in the other wing, sharing the room they always used, and that Emma was a couple of doors down from him. And Ernie and Pearl were obviously in his wing too.

When it all went quiet outside with no more scuffling footsteps or sounds of people, he realised with a sense of strange regret that Holly was more than likely in the family wing with Elsie. He supposed it made sense for them to be together, as Holly didn't know anyone else. *Oh well.* He would have to hope that he managed to sit near her for at least part of the evening. And the way to do that, he determined, was to struggle into his formal dinner suit just as fast as he could and be waiting for her when she walked in.

He laid out his clothing, noting with distaste the starched collar, white bow-tie and waistcoat Emma had insisted he bring with him, and began to get ready.

Really, he was so much happier in his more casual suit. He didn't need to pretend he was someone he wasn't. He was quite happy to be himself, truth be told.

He was definitely more interested in finding out everything he could about Holly.

Chapter Thirteen

Christmas Present

'I really don't know what I just saw.' Sorcha was staring at the Christmas tree again. 'But I know I saw a man, not a woman.'

'I definitely saw a woman. I'd like to think it was our imaginations, but for us both to see different things at the same time … it's just a bit weird.' Locryn raised his hands to his head and ruffled his hair in evident astonishment. 'God. So this place really *is* haunted? The stories are true?'

Sorcha forced a laugh. It was high-pitched and nervous sounding. 'Can we just go with a weird trick of the light thing? Maybe too much sherry in the mince pies? Duchess Rose was the only one who was supposed to be here, and even she was only meant to be in the gardens. Merryn told me.' She nodded at the beautiful de Amato portrait that hung on the staircase wall. 'That's Rose there. Was she the one you saw?'

Locryn shook his head. 'No. She had blonde hair – almost silvery blonde. It wasn't the lady in the portrait.'

Rose's dark beauty filled the frame and Sorcha nodded, although she wasn't quite sure why as nothing made sense at that moment in time. 'I've never heard of any ghosts being … *here*.' She indicated the hallway around her.

Locryn was shaking his head now and looking around him. 'Have you ever wondered what goes on in these houses when there are no people around? What if that happens all the time, and nobody ever sees it?' Sorcha saw him shiver. 'Things could be happening all over Pencradoc right now, and nobody would know unless they were in that exact place at that exact time …'

It was Sorcha's turn to shiver. 'But this is the middle of the afternoon. There are often people around. Granted, it's not always got the tree up or the decorations. I wonder if that's stirred it all up? Something in the atmosphere bringing back ghosts of Christmas Past? Ugh. Makes our "Spirit of Christmas" thing a little too close to home. Come on. I think I need to leave.' She hurried out of the hallway and didn't look back, although she was conscious of Locryn following her pretty closely.

They managed to get out and shut the door behind them, and even then Sorcha didn't linger. She tramped down the icy path purposefully, her hands stuck in her pockets. 'I just need to leave here, I think. Get away for the day. Ask Merryn if there's anyone else hanging around when they're meant to be dead.'

Locryn, however, slowed down and stopped halfway down the driveway. Sorcha, aware that there was now a cold draught behind her rather than an actual person, turned to chivvy him along, wanting to put as much distance as she could between herself and Pencradoc until she sorted out her scrambled thoughts and emotions. It wasn't simply fear and shock she felt – it was more. She had felt herself connect with the figure by the tree in some way. That was the only way to describe it.

For as much as she told Locryn that the man had just been staring at the door, motionless, she knew there was more to it than that. Yes, he had stood still, his hands behind his back as if he was waiting to greet someone formally, but his eyes had fixed on her … and he'd smiled.

And he'd had the most incredible smile; a smile just like Locryn's. And she didn't quite know how that made her feel.

Locryn's knee-jerk reaction was to get the hell out of that house. Pencradoc was beautiful and amazing and he already loved it, not just as a house or an arts centre, but for what it could *do* for him – what it promised him, deep down.

It was an even stranger, more powerful feeling than he'd had before when the woman had walked down that staircase. For, although he was frozen to the spot in terror as he saw her, he'd had the most overwhelming desire to follow her into that room and engage her in conversation.

'Locryn?' Sorcha's tentative voice brought him back to reality and he turned to face her. 'Are you all right?'

He shook his head. 'Not really. Just seen a ghost.' It was a bad attempt at humour and she didn't even laugh, just stared at him out of those brown eyes. Bizarrely, he wanted to say something funny, make her smile, see that dimple appear in her cheek again. But instead, here they were just staring at each other on a rather cold and wintry day like two strangers.

He gave himself a mental shake. They *were* two strangers. He hadn't even met her up until a couple of hours ago – but seeing that woman in the hall, and now seeing Sorcha looking at him … it was as if a connection was made somewhere deep in his psyche and he knew, he just *knew*, they'd met before. Where or when it had been, he had no idea, but Pencradoc was involved somehow. And it was as if the earth and the sky and the old house itself all knew; it just had to make the pair of them realise that too.

Wow. That was deep. Deep and very weird. But still he stared at her, couldn't take his eyes off her, and it seemed as if the world stopped turning for a second then stuttered back into life.

'This is going to sound strange,' he said, 'but when I was in there, it felt as if that was where I was meant to be. And then I saw ... her ... and I wanted to run away. But now I'm outside, I'm ... well, I'm ...' his voice trailed away. It sounded pretty stupid, spoken aloud like that.

'You're wanting to be back inside? To see what she's trying to tell you? Because you're drawn to the house, and you know there's something about it that's connected to you?' Sorcha flushed and bit her lip, seemingly afraid of having said too much.

Locryn nodded, a sense of relief flooding over him. 'Yes. Exactly that. Am I crazy?'

'No. No, I don't think so – but it's probably a good idea to give yourself some space from Pencradoc just now.' There was a pause. 'I'm feeling exactly the same. That man ... he was ... so ...' This time her voice was the one that trailed away, and she shrugged helplessly, her hands still in her pockets. 'Perhaps we both need to leave and come back another day. I've always felt drawn to it. You see that gap in the trees over there?' She nodded to the boundary of the estate.

'Yes.'

'Well, this is a huge secret, and nobody else knows what I used to do. But there's an old padlocked gate built into the wall. It's probably a delivery entrance or somewhere they used to use if they just wanted to walk and didn't need to get a horse or a carriage out – I'm not certain. But it's made of wrought iron and it's in a wall about ten-feet high. When you're quite an agile young kid who doesn't always think about her actions before she does them, and who's desperate to get a look at the big house whatever it takes, you'll climb that rusty old gate and you won't give a thought to the fact it's so rotten it could break under your weight. No, you just climb up the gate, hoist yourself over the wall and scramble down the other side. Then you can wander around the gardens at leisure and imagine the people who lived here and the people who visited, and you can pretend you're someone else for a few hours. You know?'

Locryn looked at her and nodded slowly. 'Yes. Yes, I do know. And I think I would have done the same.'

Then she surprised him again by saying softly, 'Yes. I think you would have done too.'

Chapter Fourteen

Christmas, 1906

Holly sat on the bed, dreading the knock on the door that meant Elsie was approaching. A maid had popped her head in, just as Holly was slipping into her simple tea-dress.

'Miss Sawyer, Lady Elsie asked me to tell you to wait for her before you get ready for the party.'

'But I'm ready.' Holly indicated the dress. It was grey and elegant and not too fussy.

'She was quite insistent, Miss.'

'She would have been,' muttered Holly. 'All right. Thank you. I'll just wait here then.' It was pointless arguing.

'Very good, Miss.' The maid bobbed a curtsey and hurried away, closing the door behind her. Holly felt truly entrapped now. She eyed her art materials and her half-finished portfolio. How she longed to open the portfolio case up and start painting instead! Things could actually get quite hideous after all. It wasn't every day you bounded into a hallway of Society people inappropriately. How lovely it would be to just get on with her college work instead of having to face them all again – yes, she'd be *happy* to work on it here at Pencradoc, all curled up on that window seat overlooking the parkland. She sighed lustily. *Bloody Elsie and her bloody plans!*

'Well now. How *do* you do, my darling Holly?' The door burst open immediately after a peremptory knock, and Elsie barged in, her arms full of blueish-green fabric.

'How do *you* do, Lady Elsie?' Holly's voice was flat, And yes, rather sarcastic.

'Very well, thank you. Very well. Now. I found this for you. So you can abandon that rather dull little dress and put this on instead.'

'I *like* this dress.'

'I *know* you like the dress. *I* like that dress. But really, you need something special for tonight.'

'Why? Why do I need something special?'

'One word: Noel.' Elsie grinned and Holly felt herself blush to the roots of her hair.

'Elsie. That's *enough*. I don't even know the man, and he won't even want to know me. What's the point of me dressing up like ... like ... Emma? Or Pearl? Or *you*?'

Elsie was dressed in an elegant black lace gown with silvery threads woven into it. It had simple, short sleeves and a square neck, back and front. It suited her dark beauty perfectly.

'No reason for me to dress up. That's why I'm wearing such a gloomy frock. Nobody for me to impress. Now, here we go ...' Elsie, whose dress was definitely *not* gloomy, was like a magician. In one graceful movement, she had shaken the fabric she was carrying out, and the dress floated into the air, like a silvery-blue blizzard of crystals and lace, overlaying a greenish underskirt, before gliding back to settle like a sparkling snowdrift on the bed.

Despite herself, Holly was impressed and reached out a finger to stroke the fabric. 'It's beautiful! One of yours?'

Elsie shrugged her shoulders. 'It's one I wore for a ball last winter. Don't worry. Nobody who is here was there, so they won't know. I've decided that we're going to create a secret identity for you as well. It'll be great fun.

And will hopefully put Miss Emma in her place, awful creature.'

Holly didn't think Clara or Mabel would comment, even if they did recognise it – they were nice girls and Holly had always got on well with them. Emma, she wasn't sure about. But she was glad the gown was unknown to the group, regardless. And yes, she may be being a little shallow, but it really *was* pretty. Also, a little devil on her shoulder was encouraging her to play along with Elsie's game. The Christmas angel sitting valiantly on her other shoulder was not going to get an audience today.

'You're a fairy godmother in disguise, aren't you? Or are you an evil fairy, and you'll make *me* turn into a pumpkin at midnight instead of my glass coach, secret identity notwithstanding?'

'I'm not *that* evil,' scoffed Elsie good-naturedly as she unfastened the hooks and eyes and tiny buttons on the bodice. 'Give me some credit at *least*, darling! Now. Look. See? The gown is from House of Worth.' She indicated the neatly embroidered label. 'Nothing but the best. I thought you could set it off with your hair up, because it's got these tiny little lace sleeves, see, and it looks almost off the shoulder.' The dress had diagonal draping across the bodice and a white lace *fichu* which melted into the sleeves. The skirt had looped trims around it and a small train.

Holly smiled. 'All right. Come on. Help me into it.'

'Splendid. And we have shoes here too – they're even older than the dress, and well danced in, but they'll set it off beautifully if you're not too dancey in them. Then I'll do your hair.'

Holly was already taking the tea-dress off. She

apologised to it silently as she replaced it with the gorgeous blue-green creation and stood while Elsie bent and fussed around her, pulling the fabric straight and picking off imaginary pieces of fluff.

'Sit down. We'll sort that hair out now,' she commanded, and Holly obediently did so. The dress rustled and the train dragged beautifully behind her. She loved the feel of it. She caught sight of the firelight flickering off the crystals in the mirror as she sat down and her heart began to pound excitedly. Maybe Noel wouldn't even take a second glance, but as far as she was concerned it wasn't for him. It was for her.

At least that was what she told herself as Elsie brushed her hair out and created something magical in the style, chattering all the while. The thing was, Holly wasn't even convinced she had convinced *herself* by reasoning that she didn't care what Noel thought, even as the thought of those mischievous eyes and that engaging smile floated into her head. She did want to look beautiful for herself – who wouldn't? – but the icing on the Christmas cake would be if Noel noticed that too …

Eventually, Elsie deemed Holly ready to make her grand entrance. 'We'll go in together,' she said, leaning in to the mirror to tweak a stray piece of wild, curly hair back into place. 'Just take your lead from me. You're going to be the mysterious Lady Holly Victoria Sawyer, and Emma will simply be furious. That girl has been chasing a title since she was in her infancy. I'll have to remember to amend the Visitors' Book as well, later on. That'll be fun, won't it? We'll record you for posterity as "Lady Holly".' Holly smiled, rather liking the idea of a title for the evening, and dipped sideways to let her friend primp and preen over her head. Elsie's curl immediately sprang back to where it shouldn't be, and, shrugging, Elsie stood up again. 'I tried.'

Holly sat upright and then, pushing a diamond pin into her hair more securely, she stood up. 'You did. But you don't have to try. You look beautiful. And thank you. For this.' She swept her hand down her body, indicating the outfit. 'And my title, of course.'

'Don't mention it. Just don't turn into a pumpkin.'

Holly laughed and nudged her friend. 'You said you weren't that evil.'

'But I have no prior experience of being a fairy godmother!' Elsie made her eyes go wide. 'I could be terribly mistaken! Or I could be *genuinely* evil, and just *pretending* to be nice to you.'

'I hope not!' Holly linked arms with her friend and they headed over to the doorway.

'Once more unto the breach, dear friend, once more,' Elsie intoned as they walked out into the corridor and made a deliberately stately procession along the hallway towards the top of the stairs. 'Actually, you should do this bit yourself,' she told Holly. 'Just hold onto the handrail, keep your head up and your eyes straight ahead. You're the one who's commanding attention. Only don't lose your glass slipper on the way. At least not yet.'

'You go first!' said Holly with a giggle, lifting her skirt so the delicate dance shoes with their neat little heels were exposed briefly. 'I'll copy you.'

'Very well.' Elsie inclined her head, and her face became a mask of serious imperiousness. Holly was terribly impressed. 'Follow me.'

Elsie glided down the grand staircase, which was decorated with holly, ivy and pine garlands, ignoring the cold gaze from the portrait of Ellory, Duke of Trecarrow, and reached the bottom as elegantly as if she was melting snow running down a waterfall. Someone had even wound a festive wreath around the marble hair on the sculpture of a very young Elsie that graced the bottom of the staircase, and it suited the mischievous little face perfectly.

The evening was just starting to get dark and the lights were on – Pencradoc had the luxury of electricity, which was wonderful – and Holly's dress caught the lamplight in all sorts of beautiful ways. She pressed her hands together, sticky as they were with perspiration. She'd fall, she knew she would, but descending the staircase elegantly was all part of the game and she had to try it.

Elsie looked up at Holly and grinned. 'There. Simple. Your turn. Oh – I've changed my mind. Curses upon my mercurial temperament, ho hum, but I've decided that you should leave loose of the handrail because it's more impressive if you hold your gown up.'

Holly nodded and arranged her face appropriately, desperately wanting to giggle but holding it back the best she could.

She'd made it down to the first landing when Elsie suddenly shouted out, 'Oh! Wait. Wait again, just one moment.' Elsie hurried over to the drawing room door and took hold of the handle. '*This* is how one makes an entrance. I'll pretend to be a footman and open the door for you. Now – continue.'

'Very well, Lady Elsie.' Holly nodded mock-haughtily and continued drifting down the staircase.

Even as she clutched her gown, trying desperately not to crush the fabric, and put one foot carefully in front of the other, part of her mind was on the image of a fairy tale princess doing exactly the same thing. It was something she could use in her portfolio, and she felt a little quiver of excitement. She had a good imagination, but this had just given her a little push in the right direction – a little spark of inspiration …

'May I present Lady Holly Victoria Sawyer,' droned Elsie as she flung the door open and bowed theatrically, indicating that Holly walk past her. Elsie kept her head bowed, her eyes to the ground as Holly drifted through, fully in character now, her nose in the air, her skirts held primly between her thumb and forefingers.

'Good evening, Lady Holly. It's very pleasant to meet you.' The male voice was warm and amused and Holly started, her eyes widening in horror as she saw Noel Andrews standing with his back to the fireplace, his hands clasped behind him. He looked absolutely divine in his dinner suit and she could tell he was fighting back a smile.

To her horror, he took a few steps towards her, even as she was frozen to the spot, her skirts suspended over her ankles. She felt like a child who had been caught stealing biscuits from the kitchen.

'Oh no,' she muttered. 'No. *No.*'

'It's a pleasure to meet you, Lady Holly.' Noel stopped in front of Holly and bowed, almost as low as Elsie had done. He had seen the door open, seen the little bit of play-acting going on behind it and found it desperately amusing. Maybe it was the wrong thing to do, but he joined in anyway. He hoped that Holly would take it in the spirit it was intended.

'I'm not really a L—'

'*Shhhh.*' He stood up and held his forefinger in front of her mouth, then mirrored the movement on his own face. 'It's Christmas. You can be anything you want to be.'

'But—' The girl looked panicked, as if something which had seemed a good idea at the time suddenly wasn't any more.

'Again, *shhhhh*.' He smiled. 'You look magical. I mean, you looked lovely before, but now … now you look incredible. You look …' He bit his lip. It wouldn't do to fumble his words. He knew what he was trying to say but felt the need to tread a fine line between letting Holly know what a bobby-dazzler she was, and how pretty and natural she had been before. He shook his head. 'I know what I'm trying to say. And don't look like that, Holly. It was a compliment, no matter how much I made a hash of the words.'

But Holly had found her voice. She dropped her skirts and pressed her palms together. 'I'm so sorry. Elsie and I were just having some fun, and I didn't mean to embarrass us both by waltzing in here like that. Gosh, I'm so silly. Making up a secret identity, goodness me. They'll all know it's a lie anyway.' She looked around helplessly, searching, perhaps, for Elsie to come and give her some back-up. But she was out of luck. Elsie had slunk off to the drinks table, waved away the footman who was standing beside it, and was studiously pouring some glasses of wine for the three of them.

'Why are you always apologising?' Noel was simply curious. On the two occasions he had met her, she had made, admittedly, grand entrances, but he thought it was endearing and natural. It made her stand out in a good way. He had been dragged to too many of Emma's friends' homes recently, and he found them all to be rather bland and Emma-like. Holly and Elsie – especially Holly – were invigorating.

'Am I? Sorry – ah!' There was a twitch of her lips

which threatened a smile as he raised his forefinger again and wagged it in front of her. 'All right.' She took a deep breath and nodded. 'It's just I'm in a highly unusual situation here.' She twitched her frock again and made the crystals catch the firelight. 'Elsie and I go to a very liberal college, as you know. There are, naturally, many people of many different backgrounds there. I don't feel as if I fit in very well with the sort Elsie *should* mingle with.'

'But she mingles with you, so that's good, isn't it?'

'It is.' Holly nodded.

'And I guess that if you put all the artwork together – it is arts that you study, isn't it? I thought so – I couldn't imagine Elsie studying anything else from what I know of her – that nobody would know if it was an average person who had painted it, or the Queen of Sheba. Or Lady Holly Victoria, come to mention it.'

'Very true.' Holly had recovered herself a little and nodded mock-seriously, as if she was remembering that she was actually "Lady Holly" at the moment. She stuck her chin in the air, apparently as an afterthought.

'Good. Now, would you do me the honour of sitting down over here?' He took her elbow gently, indicating a couch at the other side of the room. 'I think I'd like to know a little more about Lady Holly Victoria and her secret life beyond Society balls.'

Then she smiled and a dimple appeared in her cheek, and he had to blink as he momentarily lost the ability to breathe, think or even exist. She was truly breathtaking: a fairy tale princess come to life at a Pencradoc Christmas party. At that moment, he also felt the unmistakeable stirrings of his imagination coming to life as well.

She was exactly what he needed.

Strangely, seeing Holly here tonight had made him reconsider his fairy tale book. He genuinely wanted to pull the crumpled notebook out of his luggage and start writing again. Yes, he had even brought it here – part of him hoping that he might get some inspiration from Elsie's exploits at least, which he felt a little guilty about.

But as Holly walked over to the couch with him, he had in his mind a heroine, a princess who looked and sounded exactly like Holly. Fragmented pieces of folk tales, mythology and fairy tales that had captured his imagination aeons ago came back to him, and he knew, he just knew, that as soon as he left Pencradoc and returned to his real life his princess would become a reality on the page as well.

Chapter Fifteen

Christmas Present

The next day, Sorcha woke up far too early, her head full of strange images – largely of the fair-haired man standing beneath the Christmas tree at Pencradoc. She just couldn't get him out of her mind. Every time she closed her eyes, he was there with that smile and with those eyes looking right at her.

She turned over in bed and pulled the pillow over her head, but instead of taking her mind off him, she only thought about what it would be like to wake up in his arms and have those eyes looking straight at her in real life, and see that smile for real—

And Locryn could provide all those things but ... *urk*. She flipped over in bed again and laid on her back. Maybe she could accept the smile and the eyes right now – but it was just a bit early to be thinking about sharing a bed with the man. She'd known him less than twenty-four hours, and the thoughts she was having made her sit up, her cheeks burning. 'Bloody hell. Sorcha, you are a hussy. Plain and simple.'

She gave herself a good talking to all the way to the bathroom and all through breakfast and then decided, when she couldn't stand it any longer, that she should probably get out of the house. She had cards to post and Christmas presents to buy, and a morning spent in the town wouldn't be a bad thing. The tea room was closed today, so she needed to take that opportunity.

There was a strange, milky light in the sky and the

gardens were white with overnight frost. She raised her face to look up. *Snow*. There might even be snow, which would be quite exciting. Not that it ever lay for long in Cornwall, but it would make her feel even more festive at least. *Plus it's a good way to take my mind off him.*

Off Locryn.

Because she was still obsessing over him.

In fact, her imagination had merged the two stories from yesterday together, and she did her errands mechanically, whilst in her head she was the woman walking down the staircase at Pencradoc and he was the one waiting for her ...

The one waiting for her in the drawing room, beside the fireplace, his hands behind his back, his smart dinner suit and his starched white collar suiting him extremely well, but she knew he'd rather be in his less formal clothes – the clothes she'd seen him in when they were all in the hallway and the scent of the Christmas tree had been tickling her nose and Elsie was holding court ...

'Stop it!' she hissed to herself – as if that would make her stop anything. She clutched the handles of her bags until her knuckles were white. That was one thing she could acknowledge about herself; she had a hugely creative imagination. It was probably one of the reasons she was so good at her job. But even when she had been a child, creeping through the shadowy gardens of Pencradoc, she had imagined being one of the little girls who played there. The ones who were enjoying that party she'd yearned to join in with—

'What the hell?' She stood stock-still in the middle of the street. There'd never been any children there, had there? She'd just accepted that memory for all these years, but Pencradoc had been owned by Coren and

Kit's elderly aunt, and they said they'd been the only kids who'd ever gone there. She knew they didn't have any sisters.

The memory of those children had stayed with her – and only now, now when she was in her mid-twenties, had she begun to question who they were or why they were there.

She started shaking. She had a good idea who they were and, more than likely, they had been there about a century ago.

Wildly, she looked around her – she needed a coffee and she needed to sit down. Her knees were trembling and she thought she might throw up. Ghosts, spirits of the past, memories, shadows, shades, whatever you wanted to call them – yesterday wasn't the first time she'd seen one, was it?

Was that why she was so drawn to the place – even as an outsider? Was it letting her in, bit by bit?

Her gaze caught a shop just over the road, and heedless of any traffic driving through the brightly decorated streets, she raced across to it.

Locryn Dyer Antiques.

It was the best place she could be right at that minute. It was the only place she thought might bring her back to earth a little and ground her. Seeing Locryn would definitely take her mind off what may or may not have been a ghostly birthday party.

Locryn was busying himself getting out photos and old Christmas cards and dusting off china tea sets. He'd not slept well, if he was honest, and he'd been down in the shop since about eight o'clock.

He'd sold a few things throughout the morning, which

was nice, and had some browsers in as well who'd queried the exhibition. He'd also printed out some posters and stuck them around the shop.

And at least he had a title for the exhibition now: "The Spirit of Christmas Past". A bit too close to the truth, given the events of yesterday – he still shivered every time he thought of that girl. He wanted to know her, wanted to understand more about her – and that was a bit freaky, because then wouldn't he have to be, at the very least, dead too? No. Christmas had its traditional ghost stories, but he didn't want to be a ghost himself, thank you very much.

'Ugh.' He shuddered. He'd much rather be kind of alive and spending some more time with Sorcha, but once again the ghostly girl's face floated into his head, and he could almost imagine her voice—

'Locryn? Hello.'

Well, okay, there it was. He had imagined it a little softer – but he would take the owner of this voice over a ghost any day – *God, he so would.*

'Sorcha! How are you?' He hurried across the room to her, his hands out. He was hardly aware he was doing that, and he forced himself to drop his arms and to slow down as he went to meet her. She looked a little discomfited and he frowned. 'Are you okay? Still thinking about yesterday?'

'Yeah – yeah. I'm okay – and I'm trying *not* to think of yesterday, so let's just … not, eh? I'm just keeping busy. You know. Rushing around. So I don't end up doing everything last minute. My mum always calls me Tail-End Charlie …' Her voice petered out, then she seemed to recover herself and smiled. It looked a little strained, but that dimple was there and that made him smile back.

'Anyway. I've never been in your shop, obviously. So I just thought I'd pop in and have a look. See you. See the shop, I mean.'

'Well, here it is.' He swept his arm around, taking in the books and paintings and oddments within the place. It was, someone had told him, like a treasure trove. 'I've got the things for the exhibition separate, but I've tried to make the shop floor festive.' He folded his arms and looked around him. 'I'm not quite at the stage you're at with decorations, but you know, I'll get there.'

Sorcha suddenly seemed to relax and put her shopping bags down. 'I might have a look around, if you don't mind. See if I can buy anything for the tea room.'

'Is this any good? It's a serving bowl with a Christmas scene painted on it. See the children throwing snowballs and the little dog running around? You could put something in it – potpourri, or maybe even cakes?'

'Oh! And there's a snowman on it. And the church, all lit up. Yes. Perfect. Christmas scones. That's what I can put in there. Wonderful. How much?'

'What? Oh no – take it. It's fine.'

'No! Honestly, how are you ever going to make a profit if you keep giving stuff away? I've already got the promise of the tea sets, remember? I'll ask again. How much?'

Locryn laughed and shook his head. 'You're impossible. Okay.'

He named a price which was a good twenty per cent less than he had been planning on selling it for. Sorcha clearly realised that as she narrowed her eyes suspiciously. 'Sure?'

'Yes! Yes. I'm sure. Tell you what – pay that and give me two scones and we'll call it quits.'

'Deal.' They shook hands. 'So how soon do you want to collect the scones?' Then she flushed. 'Oh – sorry, I don't mean to drag you away from work like that, just to get a scone. I know you must be really busy. Just come when you can. It's fine. I'm open Wednesdays through to Sundays at the minute, ten until three. Just call in any time.'

'Any time.' He nodded and folded his arms again, smiling. 'I like "any time". I'll come on Thursday then. I can start bringing things through for the exhibition and I'm giving myself a half day on Thursday anyway. I'll see you after lunch. Is that okay?'

It was Sorcha's turn to grin. 'Yes. More than okay. I'll keep two back for you, and I'll even throw in a latte. How does that sound?'

'Perfect.' And they shook hands again.

It was possibly the best deal Locryn had made in quite some time.

Chapter Sixteen

Christmas, 1906

Holly allowed herself to be led to the couch and willed herself to move as elegantly as a real Lady. She was conscious that, as she and Noel sat together in the shade of the huge Christmas tree, Elsie had drifted off again and had taken up Noel's post at the fireplace, sipping her wine and looking studiously out of the open drawing room door, to all intents and purposes waiting for her guests.

Holly knew that her friend was deliberately staying away from them and was clearly hoping they would make some sort of connection. Elsie fancied herself as a matchmaker; she had hinted that Holly should get involved with young men at college before, but Holly found many of them very odd and quite earnest, and often reluctant to leave their own groups of acolytes and talk to a wider range of people. Ah well, it took all sorts.

She found Noel easy to talk to and was just regaling him with the sort of art she was most interested in – 'Arthur Rackham is my absolute hero! And I can't *wait* to see what Edmund Dulac produces for the Brontë illustrations!' – when there was a shift in the atmosphere. She looked up, a smile still on her face, as Noel stood politely to acknowledge the next guest.

Or rather guests, as everybody had decided to arrive at once, it seemed. Clara and Mabel drifted in, beautiful little replicas of one another, followed by Ernie and Pearl, and finally Emma.

Emma's smile was wide and, Holly noticed, directed

straight at Noel. The smile faltered as the girl took in Holly sitting primly on the couch near him.

'Oh. Noel. You're here. I thought you might have waited for me. We were supposed to be attending the party together, weren't we?' Her voice was light and playful, but the meaning of her words was anything but.

'Well, we travelled together, but I don't think that is classed as attending together, Ems.' His voice was just as light, but the meaning in his words was just as unmistakeable.

There was a snigger from Mabel which turned into a polite cough, as Clara glared at her – but not before a glint of amusement had sparked in the girl's dark eyes.

Holly felt a little better then. Clara and Mabel seemed to share her opinion of Emma, and it was quite amusing that the girl was so obviously ... *obvious* about everything, wasn't it?

Really, Emma was incredible. And not in a good way. She was a member of his family, and he would always acknowledge her as such, but that was as far as his feelings went. That look she had shot him when she had noticed him with Holly was quite worrying.

He really wished that his grandfather had never mentioned that damn "Honourable" rubbish – he could pinpoint that conversation as the moment Emma had decided to make him a target for her attentions and it didn't sit well with him.

Indeed, he remembered with a chill that he had found it darkly amusing when Ernie – who seemed like an awfully decent fellow, to be honest – had inherited his title and his estate, and had begun to be the sole topic of conversation from Emma in her letters to Marion.

That poor chap! If this is how she went on with him, no wonder the man had shied away from her eager attentions and married Pearl instead. And soon after that, there had lurked the inkling that Noel might be granted an "Honourable" title …

'Good God,' Noel muttered, not wishing to think about it. He took a gulp of wine and shook his head. He sat down again next to Holly and turned to face her. 'What sort of games do you think Elsie will be inclined to force upon us?'

Holly pulled a face. 'Charades. Most definitely. And there's a hideous one she loves called Dogs and Cats, which involves finding playing cards and making animal noises when one does so.'

She looked so indignant that Noel spluttered with laughter. 'Oh no. I'm not prepared for that.'

'It's one of her specialities. She made us do it for her birthday, but as she's got so many small people in her family, it made it better somehow.' She laughed. 'Less embarrassing, anyway. Her youngest brother scolded me terribly for not barking loudly enough when I'd found my card.'

'Delightful! Anything else I should worry about?'

'Mittens.' Holly nodded sagely. 'If there's a pair of mittens beside your place setting, worry. I mean it. She'll be making us eat dinner whilst wearing them.'

'Oh dear me. Is it too late to run away?' Noel made a big show of looking furtively around, as if planning his escape route. His gaze locked on something beyond the door and he hesitated. He half-smiled, stared at what he thought was someone in the doorway there, then blinked and shook his head 'Sorry – I thought we had extra guests. Latecomers. Not to worry. Trick of the light. You were saying? Games? Hideous games? What next?'

Holly laughed. 'Sardines. Sardines is a good one if you need to run away. I've got a wonderful hidey-hole for that. Another one of my little secrets. I seem to store them up in Pencradoc, don't I? Secrets, I mean.' She tweaked at her dress, as if reminding herself that she was still in the guise of Lady Holly.

'And where, pray tell, may that be?' He realised their heads were very close together, but she didn't seem to be complaining. Her eyes, when he was this close to them, were flecked with silver and pale blue as well as grey. They were the most delightful eyes he'd ever encountered.

'If I told you that, then it would no longer be a secret, and you might come and find me.'

'And would you object to that?' His voice was low, and she searched his face with her eyes.

'Actually. No. No, I don't think I would object *too* much ...'

'Excellent.'

Holly looked as if she was about to say something else when there was a resounding clap from the fireplace. *Elsie. Of course.*

'Good evening! And now we are all here, let's start with Charades, shall we? I'll go first.'

Of course Elsie would go first. Of *course* she would. Noel couldn't help but laugh, and he raised his glass to her.

'Do you mind if I just stay here, just sitting next to you, Lady Holly?' he asked.

'Not at all, Sir Noel.' Holly smiled and nodded her head regally, and he raised his glass to her this time and settled down.

Chapter Seventeen

Christmas Present

Despite all the weirdness and all the strange realisations that Sorcha was having, the days flew by and Christmas was coming closer and closer. But the image of the man beneath that Christmas tree wouldn't leave her. There was just something about him that constantly brought his face and his smile back to her – usually in those strange moments between sleeping and waking, when she'd imagine herself the heroine of her own fairy tale, and the man smiling down at her, bowing mock-seriously, a twinkle in his eyes as he asked her to dance at an enchanted ball …

But real life beckoned and she needed to focus. She'd almost finalised her menu, and Merryn was eagerly popping down to the tea room far too often, on some pretext or other, to see what experimental bakes Sorcha was producing. Merryn's favourite so far was a peppermint slice, as crunchy and sweet as a candy cane, but with an added layer of dark chocolate to set it off, and pink and white mint-flavoured icing twirled on the top to echo the traditional tree decoration.

Locryn's exhibition had been scheduled to run for the week before Christmas. It would close on Christmas Eve, along with the tea room, and then after the festivities Locryn would dismantle everything and they'd get back to some semblance of normality, ready for Sorcha re-opening after New Year. She was hoping that, with it still being pantomime season, she could persuade the

Penhaligons to allow her fairy tale exhibition to happen shortly afterwards. Locryn had shown her some of his collection in the shop, and she thought the items would go well with her usual prints once they were back in place on the staircase. Coren had cautiously agreed, but unlike Sorcha and her sometimes reckless ideas, he wanted to plan it out more thoroughly and run it more towards Easter. Sorcha was happy to accept that and was already thinking of the decorations she could use.

Cordy had also produced a list of potential ghost stories, and Locryn and Sorcha had subsequently spent a fun couple of hours choosing which ones the actress should read. They settled on extracts from *The Turn of the Screw*, *The Signal Man* and *Martin's Close* and tried to read them to each other, but it just made them laugh – and then stop laughing a little bit as they remembered the eerie figures they had encountered in Pencradoc.

'Maybe continue this later,' Sorcha had said, pushing the papers away.

'Maybe, yes,' Locryn had responded, pulling a face. Then they'd looked at each other, laughed again, and talked about something else entirely more festive.

Sorcha was also looking forward to spending Christmas Day with her family and was even more delighted to be having someone else cook the Christmas lunch – but she'd be bringing along the pudding as was tradition.

It was now a fortnight or so before the exhibition was due to open, and she was taking the opportunity to make the pudding in her little kitchen at the folly.

It was a huge excuse, of course – the main reason she was happy to hang around the folly for all that time was because Locryn was busy putting the exhibition together.

She'd had to come over several times to open up for him especially early and had begun to look forward to it.

He was bringing awfully small amounts of stuff over each time, and he had just arrived with the next delivery. 'It's just easier this way,' he said, unpacking a beautiful tea set with blue and white snowflakes painted on it. 'I don't want it all banging around in the van.'

'And if anything's worth doing, it's worth doing properly,' Sorcha commented, leaving the pudding to finish off, placing Locryn's latte next to him, and sitting down to join him. 'That's a very pretty tea set, by the way.' They had fallen into a nice little routine and she was enjoying spending time with him.

By tacit agreement, they hadn't mentioned the ghosts in the house again, beyond the stories they'd tried to read, but she knew he thought about the girl just as much as she thought about the man. They'd both found reasons to be in Pencradoc after that, but she knew for definite that she hadn't seen her person and, even though there was a crushing disappointment associated with that, it was helping her deal with her feelings about Locryn a little better. She had a feeling that his ethereal woman hadn't made an appearance again either; if she had, he certainly hadn't told her, and she thought that he might have done.

However, it was still nice to sit like this and just chat – because, sometimes, if she was on her own in the tea room, she had taken to standing at the window upstairs and staring out towards the house and replaying all sorts of images in her head that all seemed to involve the man she had seen in those odd waking-dreams. She was aware of snippets of conversation and the hum of voices and the crackling of logs in the fireplace as she smoothed down the skirts of her beautiful blue-green dress ...

'It's Christmas. You can be anything you want to be.'

'You look magical ...'

'I'm in a highly unusual situation here ...'

And she'd end up shaking herself back to reality and stomping back downstairs, making a great deal of noise, afraid of losing herself to her daydreams again.

'The snowflake set is one of my favourites, but I like the robin one best.' Locryn was still discussing the tea set, and she forced herself back into the room, away from the fairy tale qualities of her daydreams. Unaware, he held up a saucer and squinted at it. 'Thought that was a crack, but I think it's just in the glaze. That's okay.' He put it down carefully and pulled his mug over to him. 'Something smells good.' He sniffed appreciatively, looking towards the kitchen.

'Oh yes.' She pushed ideas of floaty gowns out of her head. 'Christmas pudding. With a whole lot of alcohol in it.' She grinned. 'I'm making one for the Management as well. They're all heading to Coren and Kit's parents for Christmas Day, so I said they could take one with them. What are you doing for Christmas?'

'Same.' He smiled at her. 'Going home. My parents live in deepest Cornwall, so it's a bit of a drive, but I don't see them that often, and it'll be good to see my brother and sister and their spouses and their kids as well...' He shrugged his shoulders. 'And I'm taking Aunt Susie down too. She usually comes to us, so the company for the drive will be nice.'

'Do you always go home for Christmas?'

'Hmm. Last year I had it at my place. Well, our place – my ex-girlfriend and I lived together at that point. It was a miserable, miserable day. I couldn't wait to get back to work.' He laughed. 'That relationship was doomed to failure. We did nothing but argue. I think we'd thought – well, I'd thought – we should try to embrace the Christmas spirit and have a nice time and all that.' He shook his head. 'We both just felt trapped. Realised we didn't get on all that well, and she moved out between Christmas and New Year. When I eventually sold up, I came here. The house we were in was mine originally; then after all that went on, it just wasn't a very happy place any more. But I was kind of glad we broke up when we did – it meant we could both start the New Year with a fresh start. It had been going downhill for a while and that just finished us off. This year has *got* to be better!'

Sorcha nodded. 'Yep. My ex did nothing but moan on the whole time. He was a chef and didn't like working over Christmas. He was very lazy, really. You don't go into that career thinking you get weekends and holidays off. He also wanted me to take him on as a partner. I think he thought I'd give him an easier ride. But it was never going to happen.' She balled her hands up into fists and knocked one set of knuckles against the other. 'We got to being like that, the whole time. Just butted heads, and he couldn't understand why I wouldn't let him meddle with the tea room.' She looked around at the decorations. She'd snuck even more in since the last time they'd been in here. It was going to be dreadful taking them down. The place would look so bare, and the cards she'd strung up across the walls were so very pretty. 'But this was my dream, not his, and I put my heart and soul into it. It's not big enough to share.'

'I'm the same. Part of the reason I left my old premises was because I didn't get on with the guy who owned the building. He wanted a cut of the profits, which was fair enough, I suppose, but then he kept putting the percentage up as well as the rent, and it was getting to the point where it just wasn't going to be cost-effective. Thank God I salvaged it all and the place in Pencradoc came up. It's just about perfect.' He smiled at her, that incredible smile again, and she felt her defences begin to crumble.

'If I told you where my hiding place was, then it would no longer be a secret and you might come and find me.'

'And would you object to that?'

'No. No, I don't think I would object too much ...'

She stood up abruptly, forcing herself not to listen to the whispered voices. 'We're better off here, I think. That's the time almost up on the puddings. Look, I did an extra one as well – I wasn't sure what your plans were and didn't want to think of you eating a supermarket one, so you can have it.'

'Ah. And now Pencradoc *is* perfect.' He sat back and his smile grew even wider.

Sorcha couldn't help but respond with one too. 'I'm going to package them up and take one over to the house. Do you want to come too?'

The unspoken words between them were, *if we're both together, they might come and see us again.*

Locryn studied her for a second, then nodded slowly. 'Yes. Yes, I think I'll come with you.'

'Great. I'll give you a shout when I'm ready.' And she scurried into the kitchen.

And, oddly, she knew that this might just be what they needed to do.

Locryn couldn't help but wonder if the ghostly girl would be there today. The draw of the house was increasing the closer he was getting to it, and he guessed that Sorcha was feeling it too. The atmosphere had shifted slightly, and it was as if the house was hiding behind a sheet of glass. He could see it, and it looked familiar enough, but it somehow appeared different – it looked as if it was apart from everything, and just sort of … off. Skewed, almost.

He cast a glance down at Sorcha and her brow was furrowed, her eyes searching the place as if she was looking for something behind the façade. 'Is it just me or …?' She didn't finish the sentence.

'No. It's not just you.'

The world had gone silent and insubstantial. The trees were still there, stark in their wintry beauty, the grass still crispy underfoot with a hoar-frost and the sky a gathering grey where clouds were building up. But there was nothing there that made him think they were in the twenty-first century. No traffic noise. No airplanes overhead. *Nothing.* Not even the constant rushing of the waterfall he had grown to love.

'Locryn!' Sorcha's voice was sharp and cut through the silence. 'Look! Over there! Do you see her? Do you see *them*?'

She stood stock-still, her hand reaching out to stop him from moving forwards. The Christmas pudding in its jauntily wrapped muslin bag swung forgotten from her fingers. Instead, she pointed to a pathway coming around from the Wilderness area, leading through Rose's Garden.

Two girls were pelting through the landscape, skirts grazing their ankles, berets on their heads, coats flying free. Below their skirts were black boots. One girl had wild, dark, curly hair blowing freely behind her; the other a silvery-blonde plait bouncing as she outpaced the dark girl.

There was the impression of them laughing and teasing one another. Then they hurtled up to the closed front door, pushed it open and disappeared straight through it.

Chapter Eighteen

Christmas, 1906

Holly had learned it was best just to let Elsie get on with it. She allowed her friend to wallow in the Charades game as much as she wanted to. A couple of times she guessed the correct answers way before anyone else did. But if she was quiet and didn't shout out, then it would never be her turn to act it out and it would give Elsie longer in the spotlight.

Her strategy was working. Noel was complicit in it, even without being told, and they used the time to whisper to one another about many, many things not related to Charades, and nobody paid them any heed. She may have caught one or two glances their way from Emma after the girl had made quite a carry on during her turn – probably, Holly thought, to get Noel's attention – but she wasn't concerned. It was nice just being able to talk to him. He seemed just like her – the same ideals, the same sort of lifestyle; in fact, it felt as if she had known him for an absolute eternity. It was most strange, and she didn't want the evening to end. Not this part of it. Not the part where she was with Noel.

All too soon, however, it was dinner time. At least, thank goodness, there were no mittens by the plates, although Elsie did make one decree: 'Before dinner, you need to do something. And that something is to find a peanut.'

'Elsie!' Clara was horrified. 'Not your silly peanut game!'

'Yes, my silly peanut game.' Elsie laughed. 'There are several peanuts hidden around the ground floor rooms – it's up to you all to find a peanut and, if you're really lucky, you might find a fig. And if you get the fig, you get first choice of dessert!'

'What about a peanut and a fig?' asked Mabel. 'If I find both, do I get *two* desserts?'

Holly bit her lip to stop herself laughing. Mabel obviously had her priorities straight.

'I suppose I could have allowed that – it *is* almost Christmas.' Elsie blew a kiss at her younger cousin, who clapped delightedly until a sharp nudge from her sister reminded her of her station in life. 'But it would be delightful if you could just bring one thing each – either a fig or a peanut. It means the game is over more quickly and we can eat! Good luck everyone.'

'Peanuts. This is an experience.' Noel was trying not to laugh as well.

'This is Elsie. Come on. We'd better do it. I know the places she usually hides them so we won't have to take too long over it. If you know Elsie well enough, you know she always puts them in places that mean something to her.'

Noel stood up and offered her his hand. She took it and he bowed as he helped her up. Holly felt her eyes widen as a little fizz ran up her arm and she stared at him in surprise. That was one thing she wasn't going to mention to him. It was her imagination, it had to be. But now that they were holding hands, she didn't really feel like letting go.

'I'll escort you to your chosen destination. If you don't mind?' Noel frowned a little, as if he might have overstepped the mark. His voice was a little too controlled and, going by the way he was now squeezing her hand as if his life depended on it, Holly could only assume he'd felt that funny little tingle as well.

'The library,' she managed to respond. 'Top shelf, beside a volume of Shakespeare that she's particularly fond of – something to do with her Lily Valentine obsession – and there'll be one behind the photograph of her mother and Teague at their wedding. It's in the reading nook. There'll also be one in the study – next to a pen portrait she did of her cousins one summer.'

'We have a chance for at least one peanut each then.' They began to walk out of the room, Noel still escorting her as he spoke in a low voice. 'Will it look too obvious if I simply don't let go of your hand and we walk into the library together?'

'A little.' She dipped her head and smiled. 'I'd better take the library, and you can take the study. Oh. And if it comes to it—' she looked up at him as they stood in the hallway, and she knew she couldn't hold his hand forever '—if you're not familiar with the house, and you ever feel the need to escape the riotous peanut hunt or the wild guests, the linen press room on the first floor is my particularly excellent hidey-hole. I feel obliged to tell you. It's one of my more secretive destinations because it looks as if it's part of the panelling halfway along. Excellent for Sardines. I've used it on more than one occasion. I will be forever grateful to Master Arthur Teague for showing me it.' Reluctantly, she eased her hand out of his. 'However, for now we are on a peanut hunt, and I will see you at dinner. Thank you for a lovely evening so far.'

'The evening has certainly been better than I had expected anyway.' Noel let her go and bowed again. 'Lady Holly, I take my leave. And thank you for sharing the linen press room's whereabouts with me. Most generous.'

Holly curtsied and fought back a giggle, then ducked into the library. She couldn't help it though – she opened the door a crack and watched his tall figure stop and look around, getting his bearings in the hallway, before he strode off to the study.

Then she closed the door gently behind her and walked over to the reading nook. She didn't fancy clambering up the ladder to the top shelf tonight – not in this gown, at least.

Noel was searching for the study when Emma appeared, seemingly out of nowhere.

'Noel! I was wondering where you had vanished to.' She took his arm and pulled him closer. 'It seems an absolute age since we had each other all to ourselves.'

Noel extricated himself very gently. 'We have only been here for this afternoon, Emma. And you know we will have all of Christmas together.' The thought depressed him, it really did.

'I suppose.' Despite no longer being attached to him, she walked very closely to him, and he found himself forced to stop and face her. 'Where are you going to search for your peanut?' She pulled a face. 'It's rather a silly game.'

'But it's your friend's party and it would be nice to play along, Ems.'

'It would be an altogether nicer party if that girl wasn't here.'

'Pearl?' Noel knew, of course, that Emma meant Holly. 'But she seems quite quiet – can't see she's done you any harm, old girl.'

'Not Pearl! Although I could do without her as well, to be perfectly frank. That Holly person.'

'Lady Holly?' Noel deliberately made his eyes wide and his voice sound as if he really was in awe of the titled lady who had appeared at the party.

'*Lady*? She wasn't introduced as such!' Emma was miffed, he could tell. He knew Emma always felt annoyed when she met girls with titles.

'I don't think Elsie introduced anyone with their titles, did she? Lady Clara, Lady Mabel or even Lady Pearl?'

Emma pressed her lips together and glowered. 'She still seems quite common to me. It must be that place they study at.' She folded her arms.

'That's entirely your opinion. Now, if you would excuse me, I think I need to head into the study and find a peanut.' He indicated the room to his right.

Emma's eyebrows shot up. 'In here? There's one in here? Wonderful.' And she barged past him to stampede around the study.

'Quite,' he murmured. So he turned on his heel and walked back the way he'd come.

Chapter Nineteen

Christmas Present

'That's her. That's the girl from the staircase.' Locryn looked at Sorcha. 'The blonde one. The one that ran ahead.'

'You saw them? You definitely saw them? It wasn't just me?'

'I definitely saw them.' Locryn shook his head. 'Are we supposed to go in? Follow them?' He stared at the door, and Sorcha realised she was now clutching his hand. There seemed no urgency on either side to release their grip, so she kept her hand in place and felt grateful for the touchstone to reality.

'I don't know. Do you think they went in there? In there *properly*?'

'I don't know. They just disappeared inside.' He looked at her and she was aware again of his eyes and his smile, and the image of the man she had seen under the tree flashed into her mind once more. She wanted to go in – she so wanted to go in to Pencradoc and see if he was there.

She took a deep breath. 'Yes. Let's follow them.'

Clutching each other's hands, they ran after the girls. Sorcha knew they weren't real living people – there was no reason for anyone to be on the premises dressed like that. Pencradoc was closed today and Merryn would have told her if they were expecting anyone.

And, anyway, the atmosphere was so absolutely charged with something she couldn't describe that deep in her heart she knew they were ghosts of times gone by. But, like Locryn, she needed to see what lay beyond the door.

The door was closed and Sorcha halted, almost reluctant to open it. Then she took a deep breath and stepped inside.

The hallway was eerie – there was a fire burning in the grate and a tree, but it was unlike the tree that had been there before. The decorations were different, the paintings were different. And, horror of horrors, a chilling portrait of a man she didn't recognise was on the wall where Duchess Rose usually resided. The only thing that was familiar was Elsie's marble bust – still with her wreath of Christmas roses around her hair. Sorcha focused on Little Elsie and tried to steady her breathing. Her heart was pounding and she thought Locryn was bound to hear it, but he seemed as disorientated as she did. Then he spoke.

'It's different. It's ... not ... Pencradoc. Not the one I know, anyway.' His voice was quiet. 'What the hell's going on?'

'I don't know.' Her voice was equally quiet, and she looked around her, trying to spot anything else remotely familiar. To her great disappointment, the man she had originally seen was nowhere in sight – but she could almost sense him all around her. Perhaps that was just because she and Locryn were now standing so close to one another that she was completely aware of his warmth and his breathing right beside her. Then she slowly became aware of murmured conversation and the clink of glasses, the odd laugh coming from one of the rooms to her right. 'The drawing room,' she whispered. 'Someone's in there.'

They walked to the door, Sorcha hardly able to

comprehend how she was even managing to put one foot in front of another to make herself move across the hallway.

Then she suddenly halted and forced herself to take hold of the door handle. However, before she could do that, the door quietly swung open and revealed a room full of people.

And he was there – *he was there*, talking to a woman with silvery-blonde hair, completely absorbed in their conversation. It was the girl they had seen outside, leading the way into the house. Somehow, by running through the magic mirror that was Pencradoc, the wayward, laughing girl had transformed into a calm, beautiful, ethereal ice princess. But it was him she focused on.

He was dressed formally this time, and his eyes and his smile said that he was already in love with this woman. Amongst the tumult of emotions that suddenly swamped her – fear, panic, confusion – Sorcha felt crazily bereft, as if she'd just found him, then lost him to this gorgeous creature.

She also felt, for a split second, that the scene seemed entirely familiar to her – perhaps it was the girl's dress; perhaps it was the way they looked at each other as if the rest of the world didn't exist. But something in that scenario spoke to her; spoke to her of long-ago dreams, visions of princesses in stories she'd read, fairy tales and happy ever afters. It was the most peculiar feeling – almost as if she had stepped into the coloured plates in one of her treasured childhood books.

Then the man looked up, his eye seeming to catch hers, and she was frozen in terror. Then he half-smiled and turned back to the girl in the fairy tale dress.

Sorcha watched, unable to move, as the scene gradually

faded from view and there was a slight shift again. Then, as if the scene had never happened, she was staring at the room she knew. The room that had exhibition catalogues on the tables for visitors to read; the room that workshop attendees assembled in whilst they enjoyed a coffee or a tea as they waited for someone to take them through to their event. 'Locryn,' she said, when she had found her voice. 'What if ... what if *we* were *their* ghosts?'

Locryn tore his eyes from the room and looked down at Sorcha. He was utterly speechless which, for him, was quite something.

'Bloody hell,' he managed eventually. 'What did we see? What *was* that?'

'That, I think, was a Christmas party. And we weren't invited.' Sorcha attempted a laugh, but it came out all wrong. 'Oh God, I'm sorry.'

'No, no, don't apologise. I'm kind of glad you saw it too.' He moved towards her, his arms outstretched, intending to pull her into them, to give her some sort of support and reassurance, but she held up her hands and shook her head.

'No, Locryn. Please. I can't ... I just can't.'

He felt as if he had been slapped and dropped his hands by his side. Then he raked his hand through his hair, utterly confused, before shoving them into his pockets. *What the hell was going on?* One minute, they'd been close as anything. And now – now she was effectively pushing him away. How had that scene had that effect on her? Her connections to it must have been even stronger than he thought. She'd been here longer than him, been part of Pencradoc since she was a child. And if his mixed-up feelings for the silvery-haired girl were scrambling his brain, then what must be happening to her? He somehow knew she felt something for that man – and the mere fact that he and Sorcha had only ever seen these things when they were together pointed to the pair of them being the catalyst for whatever was going on here.

Her voice broke into his muddled thoughts. 'That girl you described – the one running across the garden just before – she was the one chatting to the chap I saw. They were together.'

'Yes. Yes, I saw. I'm kind of a bit sad I didn't take much notice of the rest of it. Might have been a decent party.' It was his turn to attempt a laugh.

Sorcha shook her head. 'I didn't take any notice either.' She closed the door of the room firmly and stepped back into the hallway. 'I don't know if the rest of it was ours to see.'

'Maybe not.' However, despite everything that was competing in his heart and his head for attention, in the back of his mind the faces of the woman and man he had focused on were now even more familiar than they should have been. How did he know them? Where had he seen them before? Apart from here, at Pencradoc, of course. It was the way they were posed as well – she was sitting and he was standing, and he couldn't get the image out of his head. It was unnerving.

Then Sorcha suddenly stepped away from the doorway and away from him, walking a few steps across the hallway. She turned to face him and folded her arms. *Dammit.* The body language was definitely not encouraging and neither was the expression on her face.

'There's more, and I need to tell you this, because if I don't share it, I think I'll finally crack. And it's just as crazy as ... as *that* ... as that scene we just saw.'

'Really?' He was thrown. That wasn't what he had expected to hear. 'What's up?'

'You know how I said I used to sneak into the grounds of Pencradoc when I was little?' Her body language was even more defensive.

'Yes?'

'Well ... once I did it, and there were some kids playing in the garden.'

'And? Have you just realised that you might have got into trouble if the adults found you? Been grounded for a month?' He tried to make a joke about it, but the way she looked at him, her mouth set and turned down slightly at the edges, was similar to the look she'd given him when he'd tried to make a joke a little while ago. He felt himself grow hot and cold in embarrassment. He'd totally misjudged the situation yet again, and it reminded him how little he knew this girl after all – but every time he thought that he wanted to shake his head and deny it, because it really did also feel like they'd known each other for years.

And there must be *something* there between them, because why the hell were they only seeing these things when they were together? He didn't have time to ponder that too deeply as she was speaking again.

'Under other circumstances, yes. And I *was* grounded for weeks at a time. But this time, the time I'm talking about, there weren't actually any kids in the garden playing.' She looked up at him and, despite the distance between them, he was looking down into her eyes, and they were so familiar they made his heart stutter and he had to blink.

He brought himself back to the conversation with some difficulty. 'What do you mean? They weren't ... real? You imagined it?'

'I didn't imagine it.' Her voice was quiet but firm. 'They were there – but I think *they* were ghosts as well; or memories, at least. Or hey, maybe I was really there for a brief moment in time. It certainly felt real, even though the whole atmosphere was different. It was quiet and still, and there weren't even any birds singing. It's like imprinted on my mind – I thought it was because I'd seen those children playing, and I daydreamed about them for ages afterwards. I kept going back to find them and I never did. Now though, I think it's because I knew subconsciously how weird the whole place felt. Even though I was only seven. Because it felt just like it did today, and I think that's why I didn't run away screaming when we walked into Pencradoc just now. I knew whoever was there couldn't hurt us. I knew they wanted us to see something. That's why we both felt it. And yes. Yes, I *did* want to see what it all meant.' She bit her bottom lip as she seemed to struggle to get what she wanted to say straight in her head. 'And I think the children were Elsie and the little girls from Wheal Mount. There now. I've said it. Pencradoc and its ghosts must have been in my life forever. Part of why I loved playing "Let's Pretend" – then again, although it felt homely, in a way, I never felt I belonged at the house itself. I still don't. I feel as if I'm passing through for a purpose. Just visiting. Not meant to be at Pencradoc forever.'

'I'm not sure what to say. I understand. I do. I just keep wanting to go back there because I feel there's something waiting for me. Something someone needs to say, or something I need to know.'

Sorcha nodded. 'Yes.' She must have realised she still had the pudding in her hand, because she raised it and stared at it. 'Okay. I'm not delivering this today. I'll do it tomorrow.' Then she fixed him with a direct gaze and his stomach lurched. *This was it*. He knew what was coming. 'I'm so sorry, Locryn. I think I probably just need to go home and be on my own. It's really shaken me. I know I shouldn't be so cut up about the ghost of a man I've never met being in love with a girl I've no clue about, at a party I wasn't invited to over a hundred years ago. It's just … messy. But I *am*, and I don't know why, and you really don't need this.'

There was a beat. 'Again. I understand.' He felt crushed. They'd just shared something so desperately weird and, yes, personal – and this was her effectively telling him to leave her alone. 'But I really don't mind. Honestly.'

'But I do,' she said quietly. 'I just need to … think.'

Well, he could respect that.

But that didn't mean he had to like it.

It was a battle he knew he couldn't win and, after a moment, he nodded. 'I'll head off then. Goodbye, Sorcha.' He pushed his hands deeper in his pockets and took a last lingering look at her. Perhaps things would be different tomorrow.

Perhaps they'd be different by Christmas.

Or please God, by the time his damn exhibition opened at least, because that was why he'd been taking dribs and drabs of stuff over, wasn't it? So he could see her. So he could spend time with her. So he could be with her. So he had an excuse.

And, after miserably acknowledging that to himself, he turned and walked out of Pencradoc and didn't stop walking until he had jumped in his van and roared away from the estate.

Chapter Twenty

Christmas, 1906

Holly had retrieved her peanut. It had been, as she suspected, hidden behind a raft of family photographs. More pictures had appeared since the last time she had been to Pencradoc, and someone had decorated the little display with messy paper chains – possibly one of Elsie's younger brothers or sisters. Holly took a moment to look at the family – there was Elsie, the tallest of all the siblings, standing at the back of the group, the younger children ranged around her.

Holly smiled. Elsie always talked about her brothers and sisters as if they were still small, but in reality some of them were not much younger than she was. Laurie, for instance, was already studying at Charterhouse, and it wouldn't be long before he was at university. Isolde and Medora were at Roedean; Medora longing, by all accounts, to join the same college Elsie and Holly went to, Isolde desperate to go to Newnham, the women's college at Cambridge. They were all fairly ambitious and, despite how liberal their parents were, the children were all going to get the best education they could.

Then there was a noise behind her, like the door handle turning and a draught as the door itself began to open. Then someone spoke: 'Oh! I'm terribly sorry.'

Holly jumped and turned around. 'Pearl! No need to apologise. There are plenty of peanuts for everyone. There's at least one more in here.' She frowned as she realised how silly that might sound to someone of Pearl's sophistication.

To her surprise though, Pearl laughed. 'Peanuts. Sure. Terribly charming. I guess I'm holding out for the fig though.'

'Is dessert so important to you?'

'Yes. Yes, it is.' Then a shadow fell across Pearl's face and the sophisticated Dollar Princess came back. 'All right, I guess I'll leave you to it. I'll go find another room ...' She waved a gloved hand towards the door.

Holly suddenly understood that Pearl absolutely felt just as out of place as she did and just as nervous about being in the company of Elsie's guests.

'Oh! No – really. No need to. Not on my account, anyway. I'm just as baffled as you are by all of this. Look – I can show you where Elsie will have hidden one, if you want to know?'

'You'd do that?' Pearl looked surprised.

'Of course.' Holly was confused. 'Why wouldn't I?'

'I don't know. Some people are just a little ... standoffish with me.' Pearl flushed. 'It's kind of nice to find someone who isn't.'

'Goodness me, I'm anything but standoffish. Believe me, I'm simply here as Elsie's college friend. I'm nothing else beyond that – despite what she dressed me in this evening.'

Pearl seemed to relax a little and smiled. 'I'm glad to hear that. So – where can I find one of these darn peanuts?'

'Up there.' Elsie pointed to the top shelf. 'There's a hefty volume of Shakespeare up there. It'll be behind that.'

'Oh.' Pearl stood and stared up towards the ceiling. 'So how do we ... get up there?'

'The stepladder.' Holly went over to a fixture against

the bookshelves and dragged it over to where Pearl stood. It was on some sort of track and could whizz around the library at great speed if one was so inclined – or so Elsie had said with a wink once.

'Ah. Thank you. I … ummm … I don't like heights.'

'It's really not that high.' Holly took hold of the ladder and climbed onto the first rung. 'It's easy.'

'No. No, I don't think so.' Pearl flushed, and again Holly looked at her in astonishment. Then she saw it – the fact that Pearl's hand hovered protectively somewhere around her midriff, then dropped as if she had suddenly realised what she had done.

'Ah. Not a problem. I'll get it for you.' Holly smiled at her. 'I might need you to hold the ladder for me though. Are you happy to do that?'

'Why yes! Yes, of course.' Pearl smiled again, and Holly noticed her shoulders slump and relax a little. The American girl moved forwards and held the rail, and Holly stepped up further and felt around for the peanut she was certain was there.

'Oh! Ha! You got the fig after all!' Her fingers closed around the sticky fruit, and she began to make her way down the ladder, careful not to get tangled in her long skirts.

'Thank you! Even better!'

'Perfect, I'd say, but—' Then disaster struck. Holly took her final step down to put her foot on the floor and turned her ankle. There was a tiny *crack* and the heel snapped off one of the delicate dancing shoes. 'Damn! Oh no! Oh, how *hideous*!' She bent down and picked up the heel as she stood at a strange angle, one leg bent at the knee.

'Are you all right?' Pearl looked horrified and reached

out to touch her on the arm. 'That's my fault. I'm so sorry—'

'No, no, it isn't your fault. Don't be silly.' Holly tested her foot and thankfully realised it was all right – *no damage done, except to my pride. And the poor shoe, of course!*

'It *is* my fault, I should never have come in here and asked you to do that. I've spoiled it all, haven't I? Your poor shoe! And Emma – Emma hates me. I suspect you will too, after this.' Pearl's mouth turned upside down and tears glistened in her perfect blue eyes.

'What? No! No, don't be silly. These things happen. They're only shoes, and old shoes at that – Elsie told me when I borrowed them. Look. I'll just take them off and get the heel repaired after Christmas.' She lifted her feet, one after the other, and took the shoes off.

'Are you sure?' Pearl stared at her for a moment, different expressions flitting across her face, until she took a deep breath and smoothed her skirt down. 'Confession time. I suspect you guessed why I was kind of reluctant to do that? I know I'm crazy, but I'm, well, I'm worried. If I'd fallen … I know, I know, chances are I wouldn't have done. And I'm sorry you did when you were only trying to help me.'

Holly looked at Pearl. 'That's not crazy. And I didn't really fall, did I? I just sort of stumbled at the final fence. But I'd be worried too, I think.' She smiled and nodded at Pearl's stomach, trying to reassure her. 'Does anyone know yet?'

Pearl shook her head. 'Only Ernie. And it's such a huge thing for us, and for the families, that I'm so worried I'll mess it all up.'

Holly felt sorry for her and instinctively put her arms

around her and hugged her quickly. 'You won't mess it up.'

'I hope not. My family are back in New York and I feel quite alone, if I'm truthful. It's my first Christmas away from everyone, because last year they were here, and ...' The sentence remained unfinished, and this time a tear did roll down her cheek.

'It is – it's hard, but Ernie loves you, and now you know me, so we can write to one another if you want to. And I think Emma hates *me* as well, so you're in very good company.'

Pearl laughed and, very quickly, almost as if she was scared of prolonged contact and wasn't quite sure it was the correct thing to do, returned the hug. 'Thank you, that all makes me feel a whole lot better. You're right, of course. And yes – if we can write to one another, that would be so special. Say – can I suggest why Emma hates you as well?'

'Suggest away! I've never met her before today, so I really don't know what I've ever done to her.'

'Noel likes you – it's so obvious. And she, I suspect, likes Noel. I doubt the feeling is reciprocal. They are some sort of cousin, I think, so Ernie tells me. He says she's been chasing the poor man ever since she realised Ernie wasn't going to fall for her – and Noel isn't interested at all.' Pearl pressed her lips together, possibly afraid that she'd said too much.

Holly suspected that if her jaw was as slack as it seemed to be, she must look rather stupid.

'No!' She felt her face flush. 'Really?' She wanted to deny that she had an inkling Noel found her attractive – but really, deep in her heart, she knew it. Even if they had only known each other for a few hours, she was strongly attracted to the man, and it seemed he was to her too.

'Really.' Pearl smiled. 'I think after Christmas, I might have to persuade Ernie to have a party of some sort. And I'll have to invite you and Noel.'

'And Elsie.' Holly's voice was faint, even as she heard herself speak.

'And Elsie. I do like Elsie. She's kind of crazy as well. But in a good way.'

Holly nodded, still reeling a little from Pearl's comment. 'My goodness.' She smoothed her skirt down, realising too late that her hand was still sticky and covered in sugar from the fig. She frowned as she tried to rub the mess off her skirt and only succeeded in making even more of a mark. Elsie would probably never lend her anything else ever again!

Noel had just about given up. He had mooched around several rooms and was rapidly losing patience with the evasive peanuts. Much as he wanted to go back to the library and, despite walking past it several times, he made a great effort not to push the door open and see her again. *No*, he thought, smiling to himself, *I have to wait*.

'All right.' Eventually he came to a stop in the hallway and looked around him. 'So what's so special to you in here, Lady Elsie? Any peanuts hidden in here, perhaps?' His eyes settled on the book that Holly had been holding earlier. *Earlier?* He had to stop and think. It had only been a few hours ago, but it seemed as if they had known each other forever. He shook his head, moved over to the table and opened the book.

He smiled – there she was: Holly Sawyer.

Then he had to laugh. Next to the date and title of the

event – *Christmas Party, hosted by Lady Elsie Pencradoc, 22nd December 1906* – was a perfect depiction of a peanut, surrounded by a wreath of detailed holly and ivy leaves. 'Well, I think this one will have to do,' he said and picked up the Visitors' Book.

Just as he was heading back to the drawing room, he heard whispered giggles and turned around. There was Holly and, surprisingly, Pearl, coming out of the library. Holly was holding her shoes in one hand, and it looked as if she had something clutched in her other hand, which he assumed was the peanut she had successfully located. Pearl was examining something she was carrying, and Noel smiled. He guessed she had found the other one from the library.

Holly looked up and caught his eye. She flushed again, but a shy smile was threatening to break through. He stopped, intending to wait for the girls, when Emma again appeared out of nowhere and tapped him on the shoulder.

'I found it. In fact, I found two.' She held her palm out to him, and indeed there were two peanuts in it. 'One was by some drawings in the study, and then I found one on an easel someone had left in the orangery.

'An easel. That "someone" was most likely Elsie. Why didn't you leave that one for someone else to find? We just needed one thing each.'

Emma shrugged. 'Why *not* take it? Nobody else was even in that area. And besides.' He saw her eyes slip towards Pearl and Holly who had come to a standstill, clearly not wanting to come any closer to him whilst Emma was in the vicinity. 'There are some people in attendance who probably shouldn't be here anyway, so what does it matter?'

'It matters.' Noel was finding his cousin most irritating today. Had she always been so selfish? Or had it just been that he had blithely ignored that selfishness of character until he realised that her vitriol was directed at his very own recently discovered fairy princess?

'Oh, don't be such a spoilsport.' Emma stuck her chin in the air and grabbed his arm possessively. He really wished she would stop doing that. 'Nobody is going to be denied dinner anyway. Why are you carrying that book?'

'Why not?' His answer was as brief and cool as he dared, echoing hers.

Elsie, in the meantime, had come to the door of the drawing room and was clapping as her guests appeared from various corners of the ground floor. 'Come on then. Come in. Who has what?' She was peering eagerly at everyone's spoils as they showed her what they had found. To Mabel's delight, she had found a second fig, hidden in plain sight on the mantelpiece in the morning room. It had been beneath a portrait of Zennor, Elsie's mother, as she told everyone excitedly, 'It was the first place I looked. Elsie *always* hides something there!'

'Hush, Mabel! You're giving all my secrets away,' said Elsie with a laugh. 'Now, who got the other one?'

'Pearl did,' offered Holly from just behind the door.

'No – *you* did.' Pearl smiled at her, then back at Elsie. 'Holly had an inkling where it was and she helped me retrieve it.'

'I already had my peanut.' Holly held it aloft. 'I didn't need two tickets for dinner.'

'I suspect you didn't.' Noel heard himself speak before he'd really formulated the words in his head. He also felt Emma stiffen next to him and didn't dare look at her face. He knew she wouldn't own up to taking two peanuts now. Honestly, it was comical – a Peanut War, for God's sake!

'But Noel – what about you?' Elsie came over to him. 'And what, may I ask, are you doing with my Visitors' Book?'

'I couldn't find a peanut,' he admitted, pulling a sorrowful face which made Mabel giggle. 'But I did find an excellent picture of one. Here.' He extricated himself from Emma's clutches, glad of an obvious reason to be able to do so. 'I was going to sign it, but got side-tracked by the artwork. Will that suffice, or must I starve?'

'Oh!' Elsie laughed. 'You won't starve, don't worry. But you'll have to forgive me. I get a little carried away with ideas. I drew that so I'd remember, in years to come, what sort of games we played tonight. But, now we have it here – Clara, you're closest to the door, darling – please would you bring that pen and the ink from the hall table in here? Then we can all sign it.'

And, because Elsie had decreed it, and decreed it so charmingly, everybody – including a silently furious Emma – wrote their names in her Visitors' Book; the final task they were allocated before they were allowed to move into the dining room for dinner.

Chapter Twenty-One

Christmas Present

Locryn didn't come to the Tower Tea Room the next day. Or the day after that. And by the third day, Sorcha felt even more bereft than she had done when she had seen the shadows of that long-ago Christmas party. She missed the real Locryn-type person more than she even missed the ghostly man's smile. Locryn was the one who was stealing into her daydreams and quiet moments: *Locryn.* Locryn, who wasn't coming anywhere near her, thanks to her stupid performance in the hallway.

Merry bloody Christmas to yourself, Sorcha! See what you've done by thinking this whole thing is like a magical bloody fairy tale?

She opened up at ten every day and smiled and made sure people thought she was happy, and she served her customers, many of whom were just taking advantage of the beautiful 'Winter Wonderland Walk' at Pencradoc. Kit had done an incredible job of his installations, and she had a collection of postcards by the till for people to buy, along with packs of Christmas cards they'd had made up. Everyone was cheerful.

Everyone except her, of course. She knew that Locryn had only done what she wanted him to do and left her alone that day, but now she wondered if she'd been a bit too direct. She hadn't exactly said, 'I'll be fine tomorrow, I just need today to think about things.' And he was, to be fair, respecting her wishes. But she missed him. She *actually* missed him.

Several times she picked up her phone, wondering if she should call him, then put it down again. They were just friends after all. Maybe they were even just colleagues? There was no reason why they should be in daily contact. She'd see him at the exhibition opening night, anyway. He'd been in touch with Merryn, apparently, saying he felt pretty much sorted and didn't think he needed any more access to the premises just now. It made her cringe when she thought about how she'd pushed him away that day, when he was probably just as shaken up as she was.

But at least, on the positive side, Sorcha knew exactly what treats she was making for opening night. She reasoned if she could just get through the next few days, she'd see him and they'd be all, 'Oh hello, lovely to see you, let's not ever talk about the fact we saw a ghostly Christmas party ever again, ha ha, or the fact I sent you packing and I don't think I really meant to *do* that, tee hee.'

But it felt very crap, not seeing him. As she thought about it again, she felt her mouth turn down at the corners; even more so when she saw the Christmas pudding she'd made him still sitting on the shelf.

Locryn wasn't faring much better, despite business increasing in his shop as curious villagers popped in to see what treasures he had, looking for special Christmas presents or simply buying little treats for themselves.

Between customers, just like he was right now, he kept replaying the conversation he and Sorcha had had after they'd seen that ghostly Christmas party. They were some *real* spirits of Christmas Past, he thought wryly – and several times he stared at his phone, wondering if he should call Sorcha, just to make sure she was all right. Then he pushed his phone away, figuring that he couldn't rush things. Who knew what emotions he might stir up? Goodness knew that he felt a bit odd about the whole thing as well. It was a blessing that he had the shop there to take his mind off it all. He was pleased she had the tea room; that they each had something else that was tangible, rather than this odd four-way sort-of relationship between a guy and a girl, and a dead guy and a dead girl.

Part of him wondered whether the complicated feelings he had were anything to do with the family connection he'd been told he had to this place. His Aunt Susie had always been the one who had championed Pencradoc. He was close to his aunt and had loved hearing the stories she told about this area. Susie had also made him swear to visit her for Sunday lunch at least once a month as soon as he was settled, and it was a promise he wasn't finding difficult to keep.

Although, he had to admit that part of him had hoped that the next time he visited Susie, Sorcha would be with him. He sighed and popped Susie's invitation to the event in an envelope, along with one of the little Edwardian Christmas *cartes de visites*. He didn't want to do this exhibition without Susie being involved in some way and so he was taking advantage of a little downtime in the shop – quite unusual at the minute, but in a good way, he acknowledged – to tie up some loose ends before opening night. He eyed the pile of flyers behind the counter. They had been Sorcha's contribution to the cause. She'd printed them out after her initial meeting with him and he'd subsequently seen them stuck all over the village. It made him smile every time he saw one. It made him think of Sorcha every time he saw one too.

That had felt a little more uncomfortable these last couple of days.

'The greatest enemy to action is inaction,' she'd told him as she piled them onto him during one of his visits to Pencradoc, suggesting that he put some up in places she may have missed. 'Or something like that, anyway.'

'Something like that,' he muttered today, thinking of her again. He sealed Susie's envelope, wrote her name on the front of it with a vintage fountain pen he was particularly fond of, and smoothed it out. He laid it on the counter and looked at it. He'd give it to her next time he saw her. Then his gaze drifted again to the flyers. They were sitting alongside a small pile of Christmas cards he'd been writing out as well.

It was as good a time as any to post those cards, he reasoned. Then, with his heart pounding, he stood up and knew exactly where he was going and what he was going to do, right after he had visited the post box.

Sorcha's Christmas had seemed so full of promise a few weeks ago – and now it just felt grim. She knew she had no right to complain, really. But it didn't stop her feeling miserable.

Eventually, on the "Day of Ultimate Gloom", as she had christened that miserable December day, three o'clock came and she locked the door, turning her little sign to say "Closed". She sighed and tidied up the last few tables, cleared up and washed the crockery, and felt even more miserable when she opened the cupboard to put it away and saw all the vintage stuff Locryn had loaned her.

When she felt like this, there was only one thing to do – and that was to stomp around the grounds of Pencradoc and let her mind drift so it could clear itself. She'd do her own circuit of the Winter Wonderland Walk and hope that the place would work its magic on her. It had been snowing lightly and the landscape was white and clean around her. *Timeless*. The sort of landscape Elsie and her friends would have known and loved.

The landscape that she, too, knew and loved with something deeper than her conscious mind.

And today there was also an inexplicable urge associated with it. She knew she just had to be there, to be out in it, and to find whatever it was that was drawing her towards it; just like the heroines in her beloved books of fairy tales as they wandered into the enchanted forests.

Sorcha was about halfway around the trail when she came to the clearing in the foliage that hid her secret gateway. She stared across at it, remembering those long-ago days when she had snuck in. Memories of the bright birthday party and, following on from that, the images from the shadowy Christmas party she'd encountered played around her mind.

Not knowing why she did it really, except that she felt she absolutely had to go there at that very minute, she ploughed across the ice-covered grass towards the rusty old gate. Her heart was pounding and her breath was catching and, once again, she felt that pull towards it. The frost was dusting it and she knew, if she got close enough, there would be tiny icicles hanging off the wrought iron pattern.

And she did get close to it, and she stood in front of it, and a shadow moved on the other side of it …

And her breath caught again as the shadow resolved itself and spoke. 'Sorcha? How the *hell* did you ever manage to get in this way?'

Locryn was facing *her*, facing Sorcha, right through the

bars of the gate. He stepped forwards and took hold of the old metal. It was cold and wet through his gloves and his breath came out in a little cloud as he exhaled, trying to control his emotions.

She was there, and bizarrely she was the first and last person he had ever expected to encounter.

'Did you really climb over this? I'm surprised it didn't crumble into dust.' The words were trite but he didn't know what to say. 'Bloody secret bloody gates!' He rattled it for good measure.

'It was twenty years ago. It wasn't quite so rusty.' She was looking at him, some strange emotion flickering across her face. 'I had smaller feet. I could squeeze them into the loopy bits.' She waved vaguely at the pattern on the metal. 'See. Loopy bits.'

'Ah.'

There was a pause, then they both spoke together.

'Locryn—'

'Sorcha—'

'You first.' He needed to know that she was happy to see him. *God, this was a stupid idea, it really was.* He'd been posting his cards, walking his bad mood off around the village, second-guessing himself the whole way around, when he'd suddenly diverted and acted on his earlier decision to head to the old gate. He knew he'd been out of sorts since his last visit; didn't know if she would want to see him, didn't know if it would ever be quite the same between them. It wasn't exactly every day that two people saw a sight like that and could move on from it without it messing up their minds and their – well – relationship to some extent.

If they even *had* a relationship. If it wasn't just one big mixed up Santa sack of emotions because they'd been spending so much time together, and when they did, weird things happened. This could work out well. Or it could work out very, very badly indeed. Their own story, he acknowledged to himself, was as yet unwritten and he wasn't quite sure which way it would go.

'Where have you been? Why haven't you been over to Pencradoc? Sorry.' Sorcha shook her head. 'I don't mean it like that. It's just, I've kind of missed you.' She blushed. 'And I know it was my fault you stayed away … because I had that sort of meltdown. But the truth is, I didn't like not seeing you. And I've still got your damn pudding in the tea room! There. I've said it now, and you'll think I'm an idiot, so I completely understand if you stay away a bit longer.'

'Sorcha.' He gripped the bars tighter and leaned closer. God, he wanted to be closer to her still, he really did. 'I don't want to stay away. I *didn't* want to stay away. But you made it pretty clear you wanted to be on your own, so it was the only thing I could do. You've no idea how much I wanted to come back. I was trying to think of some stupid excuse to come over, but nothing seemed right. And yeah.' He shrugged helplessly. 'The excuses were *all* stupid. You know as well as I do that everything for the exhibition is over there now, everything's in place. I know I've only been away what, two days—?'

'Three. This the third day.' There was a twitch at the side of her mouth as it began to turn upwards, and his heart leapt. *That's a good sign, right?*

'Three days. I'm not counting today. Because I'm here.' He rattled the gate a bit more to make his point. 'I'm here.'

Sorcha stepped close and she took hold of the bars as well. 'Locryn. You don't need an excuse to come and see me. You *didn't* need an excuse. You could have just come and told me I was stupid and needed to get over myself.' Her voice was soft. 'I'd have been so happy to see you. You're the only one I've told about the children in the garden. You're the only one I've told about this gate and my dodgy past record of breaking and entering. It's not something I really want to share with Merryn or anyone else. And me and you … we've got our ghosts in common, Locryn. We … we *should* be together. Shouldn't we?' She looked fearful, scared perhaps of what he would say.

But he nodded slowly, unable to tear his gaze from her. He had to agree. If one thing was clear this Christmas, that was it. They had those damned ghosts in common – and, he dared to hope, a lot more besides.

Then she surprised him once again. 'Locryn. Kiss me. Please.' And she leaned in towards the gate, and he leaned closer, and somehow, with the chilly metal not impeding them in the slightest, they kissed.

Sorcha pulled away first, and he wished he could tear the bloody gate down and take her in his arms properly.

'Go on,' she said, smiling suddenly. She indicated the gate. 'Get yourself over that thing and we'll go to the folly. It's warmer in there.'

'It's rusty!' He couldn't help but laugh.

'If you do it quickly, you'll be over the top faster though. I can tell you where to put your feet.'

'Oh really?' He stood back and folded his arms.

'Yep.' She nodded and pointed to part of the metalwork, then traced her way upwards. 'Got it? Then it's just scrambling over the top. You can probably jump down from this side. I'll wait for you.' And she took a few steps backwards and folded her own arms, putting her head expectantly on the side.

'So long as you *do* wait for me,' he said with a laugh and gripped the metal.

And he could have sworn that somewhere, just behind him, a man's voice whispered, '*She's waited this long to see you again. Don't let her down, old chap!*'

It was all the incentive he needed, and he began to climb.

Chapter Twenty-Two

Christmas 1906

Dinner was actually a lovely affair. Holly could still taste the cherry tart as she finished her coffee in the drawing room.

As always, Elsie had dispensed with tradition, and all the guests were assembled in the drawing room instead of separating the men from women – but as there was only Noel and Ernie who would have had to stay in the dining room, it made a lot of sense.

At least it did to Holly, who had managed to sit down for dinner perfectly positioned between Pearl and Noel, with Elsie just around the corner at the head of table. Clara sat importantly at the other end, being the daughter of a Duke and a Lady with an equal rank to her cousin. Clara's father, Jago, and Ellory had been brothers, and Jago had inherited the title after Ellory died. Mabel sat next to Elsie, laughing with Ernie, who looked more relaxed every second in the young lady's company, and Emma sat scowling between Ernie and Clara. Clara was far too polite to engage in any of Emma's gossip, and Holly was quite pleased that she was at the other end of the table.

However, once they were back in the drawing room, Emma perched primly on the sofa next to Holly – clearly so Noel couldn't sit there, she imagined. She sighed inwardly. There always had to be someone to spoil things—

'What's that stain?' Emma's voice was loud and seemed to ring through the room. 'That there – on your gown.'

'This?' It was too late before Holly realised she'd lifted the skirt a little too high and her bare feet peeped out of the bottom.

'You have no shoes on!' Emma was aghast. Loudly aghast, and everyone turned to stare.

Holly felt herself grow hot under the scrutiny. 'Well, the stain is sticky stuff from the fig Pearl and I found.' Her voice was more calm and steady than she thought it would be. 'And I have no shoes on because the heel broke on one of them.'

'Where did you leave your shoes? Because that's a bad show, leaving discarded footwear around someone else's home. Where's your room? Surely you could have changed them before coming down to dinner?'

'My room is right next to Elsie's, and I didn't have time before dinner or that would have been quite discourteous to Elsie. But the shoes are quite safe. Nothing for you to worry about.' In fact, Holly had tucked the broken shoes behind the Christmas tree in the hallway, fully intending to take them up to her room when she got a chance. But when she thought about it, then yes, that had been a poor show. She should have taken them straight up – but that would have meant less time with Noel ...

Her treacherous, unconscious glance across at him as he talked to Ernie caught Emma's attention. 'He's spoken for, you know.' Emma's voice was triumphant. 'You might as well give up now, Lady Holly.'

Holly opened her mouth to protest that she had no such title, but then closed it again. *Dammit, why shouldn't I pretend to be someone a little more glamorous just for one day?* Especially to this horrid, spoiled girl next to her, who she was beginning to find less and less appealing as the evening wore on. That little devil on her shoulder smirked though and did a little jig of delight that the ruse had worked and Holly's secret identity was continuing to protect her like a layer of silvery ice.

'I see.' Holly nodded in her best imperious fashion, channelling all Elsie had taught her. 'And to whom is he betrothed, pray tell?'

'Oh. Well. To *me*, of course.'

Holly's stomach churned, but she kept her demeanour rock solid. 'Well, I was unaware of that. He hasn't exactly spent a lot of time with you this evening. It isn't very obvious. Allow me to offer him my congratulations—'

Inside she was screaming, but she held onto Pearl's words: *she's been chasing the poor man … Noel isn't interested at all.* And hadn't Elsie said he was just visiting family over Christmas? If anyone knew the truth, then Elsie would have known it and told her.

'I'd rather you didn't. It's not common knowledge yet,' Emma said. 'I wouldn't want him to think I'd been gossiping. We're going to announce it at New Year.'

'I see.'

'And may I suggest you cover your feet up? It's rather vulgar having them on show.'

And before Holly could say another word, just as she realised she still had her skirt hitched up, Emma stood up and swept over to Noel. She took hold of his hand and stood on tiptoe, whispering something in his ear. She cast a sly glance towards Holly and smirked, before wandering over to Elsie and shrieking in horror, 'My word, Elsie! What are you doing?'

'Drawing pictures of my guests.' Elsie was working away with a pen on the open pages of the Visitors' Book. She had her feet up on an occasional table, legs crossed at the ankles with her black slippers on show and her frock pooling onto the floor in a midnight sky of twinkling black and silver. Only now she had added a huge white Christmas rose from one of the household arrangements to her hair – there was, in fact, a big gap in the bowl on the table she was using for her feet. No comments *there* about *Elsie* being vulgar and showing her ankles, were there?

'And what are *they*?' Emma continued, jabbing her forefinger at a couple of small watercolours next to the depleted arrangement. 'Darling, do you really have unframed Rackhams lying around the place? My word! That's so *bourgeois*.'

'Rackhams?' Elsie glanced up vaguely. 'Oh. Those? No, Lady Holly painted those. *Too* accomplished. Brought them with her portfolio. *Jolly* good.' Holly glowered in their direction, even though part of her wanted to yelp with laughter at Elsie's laconic voice and the use of her made-up title. She'd forgotten to take the watercolours upstairs before the party. Elsie had been giving her some constructive criticism on them.

'Oh! Ah – yes. Now I study them, I can see they're rather amateur attempts at copies.' Emma was, it had to said, truly hideous.

Holly was gratified to see that Elsie ignored her and didn't deign to dignify the snipe with a response. Instead, her friend sat with the tip of her tongue sticking out of her mouth, putting the final touches to her own masterpieces. 'There. All done. Now—' she snapped her head up and stared around the room, blanking Emma quite beautifully. 'Who's for Sardines? Don't answer – I'll tell you who's for it: all of you! Every single one of you!'

There was a collective, good-natured groan and the rustling of fabrics as people shifted and got to their feet.

Wonderful. Sardines. Holly looked at Emma and was sure her face betrayed her thoughts. *Please God, do not let me end up in a hiding place with that awful woman!*

Elsie looked around the group and smiled. 'Clara. You know the house as well as anyone. You can be the one to hide. Everyone – we have to find Clara, and then stay quiet as mice until someone else finds us. Last person to find us all is the odd man out.'

'Would you like to tell us where we can hide and where we can't?' Clara asked, quite politely.

'Of course. This floor, the basement and the next floor up. The rooms we can't access are locked, so don't even try.' Elsie smiled around at the group. 'And obviously everyone's bedrooms are quite off-limits. Now – Clara, we're going to count to one hundred and then start searching. One. Two ...'

Clara turned on her heel and ran out of the room, slamming the door behind her so nobody could hear her speeding through Pencradoc. Holly counted along with everyone but had no intention of even trying to find Clara. She knew where she was heading, and if she was the odd man out, so be it.

Chapter Twenty-Three

Christmas Present

Locryn had landed perfectly well on Sorcha's side of the gate, and they'd kissed again and held each other properly and said all sorts of lovely things to one another. And then, giggling, she'd grabbed his hand and they'd run back to the folly, where she fumbled with the lock before they barged right inside, and they kissed far more ardently and passionately than she'd ever thought it possible to do in a place of work.

But then there was a noise outside and the door handle wiggled and, guiltily, they sprang apart, just as the door opened and Merryn came in, her pretty face flushed with the cold. Under her arm was tucked a big brown book

'Am I too late to add this to your exhibition?' Merryn asked. 'I knew we had it somewhere – I made Coren dig it out. He wasn't impressed I dragged him away from his Easter planning.' She rolled her eyes. 'Honestly, I know we need to plan ahead, but he can never just live in the moment.' She shook her head despairingly. 'He should be looking forward to Christmas, but *noooooo*, not Coren. Anyway.' She laid the book down on the table in front of her, apparently oblivious to Sorcha's flushed face and Locryn's half-unbuttoned shirt, and brushed her hand over the cover. 'I thought you might find it interesting – and it's something you can use that truly links to Pencradoc. It's the old Visitors' Book and, if you flick through it, you can see that it wasn't used for years. But look – in 1906, Lady Elsie seemingly resurrected it, and we've got some details of some guests she had for a Christmas party. She's made some little sketches in it too, which confirms the fact it was for Christmas – a tree, a robin and whatnot. But she's also done a few doodles of people's faces. I think that's one of the most interesting things about it – plus, some of the names in it are quite exciting.'

'Anybody famous?' Sorcha felt flustered and desperately hoped her face wouldn't give away their activities of a moment ago. Meanwhile, Locryn turned away and discreetly re-buttoned himself, and Merryn, bless her, still seemed oblivious.

Instead, Merryn nodded. 'Yes.' She pointed to some names in the book. 'Try these two. Holly Sawyer and Noel Andrews. We'd like to think that this is the place they first met.'

'Who?' Noel's name was vaguely familiar, but it took Sorcha a moment to work out why. 'Oh! Noel Andrews! Didn't he write that book, *The Enchanted Princess*? It was as popular as *Alice*, wasn't it? I had a copy when I was a little girl. I saw the ballet as well when I was about twelve. It was wonderful. She's a fairy princess, but her wings are frozen as she's under some awful enchantment, and she has to live amongst humans in a magical castle surrounded by winter until her true love releases her.' Sorcha smiled as she drifted back into her childhood. 'Then a handsome prince comes along and they dance at an enchanted ball, and she knows she has to leave the ball to go with him, but she has no way of walking on the snow because she'll die if her skin touches it.' She wagged her finger at Locryn thoughtfully. 'But the wicked princess has taken all her shoes away. The princess refuses to be carried everywhere, so the prince comes back and fits her with a pair woven from moonlight, and she leaves with him, and her wings come back and she takes him off to Fairyland, and they rule both there and in his kingdom, and she keeps the moonlight shoes forever ...' She finally took a breath. 'God, I *loved* that story. It was like Cinderella and the Snow Queen all mixed up.'

But Locryn was frowning. It seemed he hadn't just picked up on the author's name. 'Holly Sawyer? And Noel Andrews?'

'Yep.' Merryn pointed to the names. 'Right here. Although—' she laughed '—it's actually got "Lady" Holly Sawyer. Looks like the word "Lady" is in a different handwriting though – Elsie's, I think, judging by other things we've seen. Who knows why – everything I know about Holly Sawyer points to the fact that she certainly didn't have a title, but it's too much of a coincidence to have her name there next to Noel Andrews and for it not to be the illustrator Holly Sawyer.'

'Holly illustrated Noel's book,' said Locryn. 'They had just got married when the first edition was published. The early copies go for a fortune. In fact ...' He tapped his lips with his forefinger and it did funny things to Sorcha – she knew now exactly what those lips were capable of. 'I'll be right back. I promise.'

Then, right in front of Merryn, he grabbed Sorcha and kissed her again. He leaned his forehead against hers and their eyes locked. 'I'll be right back. Don't go anywhere.'

'I ... I won't.' She stared after him as he ran out of the tea room and she saw him disappear across the wintry ground, leaving a neat row of footprints in the crisp, white snow.

Locryn now understood – he understood how the girl on the staircase had been so familiar to him. There was something in particular he had been seriously tempted to bring to the exhibition, and he hadn't done it. He didn't know why he had been so reluctant. Instead, every time he looked at it, he had found an excuse to leave it where it was on the wall of his flat. His favourite watercolour painting – that incredible fairy tale forest scene he loved so much …

It had never seemed quite the right time to remove it from where it was and to display it elsewhere. Now, though, he thought he might have found it a holiday home. Now was its time to shine – and a very special girl would be there to help it get the recognition it deserved.

Chapter Twenty-Four

Christmas Present

'What is it? What is it with my friends and the fact they all fall for people who we bring to Pencradoc to do a job?' Merryn's eyes were sparkling with mischief. 'What with Cordy and Matt, and now you two. Honestly!'

'*You* came here to do a job.' Sorcha couldn't help grinning. 'You never left, did you? You found Kit.'

'Fair comment.' Merryn laughed. 'Wow. Well, now Locryn's vanished into thin air, do you want to have a look at these drawings? Elsie has worked her magic beautifully.'

Sorcha moved towards the book, even though her heart was hammering, still reeling from that last kiss. Sure enough, Elsie had done some doodles on the page; some more recognisable than others.

'What on earth is that?' Sorcha pointed to a strangely shaped thing surrounded by a wreath.

'A peanut, I think? Apparently it was a popular game in those days. "Find the Peanut".'

'Oh my.' Sorcha couldn't help laughing. 'Hey – I recognise those two. Clara and Mabel, of course.' The faces were perfectly in proportion, the family resemblance between the two girls evident. Sorcha had seen pictures of them before and was delighted to see them recreated in miniature.

'Indeed. Look at this signature – Emma Carew. She later became Lady Fleming and married an MP. They were quite the Society entertainers, and she swore she'd

174

run the best *salon* in London. A very ambitious lady, I think. And that's Sir Ernest Elton and his wife Lady Pearl Arthur Elton.' Merryn put on a grand voice as she indicated a surprisingly young man and a pretty, if brittle-looking, young woman. 'Sir Ernest inherited a house a few miles north of here when he was only twenty-one – it's bigger even than Pencradoc. Pearl was American and so the story goes she was brought over to England and paraded around Society, along with her fortune, to find a husband and a title. She found Ernest.'

'Poor woman.' Sorcha was horrified. 'She's just like a chattel.'

'They seemed happy enough though. They had twins a little while after they were married, and several more children at regular intervals after that. She was great friends with Elsie – Elsie's little brother apparently adored her because they shared the same name – and she was also very close to Holly. In fact, I think Holly and Noel were godparents to one of the children, but don't quote me on that. It's just bits and bobs I've picked up over the years. We saw some of Holly's work in London. She really had an extraordinary talent herself, and I think she went to art college with Elsie, which is probably why she was here that Christmas. She came into her own with the illustrating. I think she and Noel were good for one another. Although that was the only book they ever did together.'

'*It was the only one we needed to do together.*'

Sorcha jumped. A voice had whispered in her ear, and her heart began to pound. It was the voice she had been hearing around the estate over the last couple of weeks and now she got the distinct impression someone was standing beside her, reading the book over her shoulder.

Merryn was still talking, but Sorcha couldn't concentrate.

Because, even as she studied the next sketch, the sketch of Holly, she knew without a doubt that the faint figure she had seen running through the gardens and sitting in the drawing room before quickly fading was Holly's. And the man who had been waiting for her beneath the Christmas tree was Noel.

She cleared her throat. However, the images of Holly and Noel somehow seemed even more familiar now – as if she'd seen them more clearly at some point. Not just from the shadowy figures she'd encountered, because all she'd ever really focused on were Noel's eyes and his mouth – and that had been enough. But that wasn't something to share with Merryn.

Instead, she said, 'I think Holly liked it here. I think you're right – Holly and Noel met here that night and the rest, as they say, is history.'

'Yes. And doesn't Noel seem a handsome chap?' Merryn smiled at the final miniature. 'He's got a bit of a look of Locryn about him, wouldn't you say? I would have loved to have been here that Christmas to see how they got along with each other. I wonder if anyone might have predicted they'd get married and live happily ever after? It's just like a fairy tale.'

Chapter Twenty-Five

Christmas, 1906

Noel counted along with everyone else and clapped as they reached one hundred. The group swarmed out of the door and scattered upstairs, downstairs and throughout the ground floor. He popped his head out of the door and caught sight of Emma heading upstairs. For some reason Holly was squeezing behind the Christmas tree, as he himself put on a good show of looking confused yet calculating.

He waited a few moments, then shut the door and ran back to the occasional table Elsie had abandoned her artwork on.

He caught his breath. The pictures that Holly had created were stunning – absolutely stunning. The girl was, quite simply, one of the most talented artists he had ever encountered, despite her work being right next to Elsie Pencradoc's on that table.

He already knew in his heart he had no intention of searching for Clara that evening; seeing those paintings had strengthened his resolve even further. He hurried out of the drawing room into the hallway, then ducked into the study and peered out as Holly, looking as furtive as he must have looked himself, came rustling out of the enormous branches, setting the decorations wobbling quite alarmingly. To his surprise, dusting off pine needles even as she walked, she had those shoes in her hand again. *Was that what she was doing?*

He watched her hurry into the drawing room and

emerge with her paintings in her hand. She ran upstairs and disappeared towards the wing her room was in. After a few moments, she came back into sight, without her paintings, but was now heading the other way – towards the wing he was staying in. In a few moments, Emma appeared from a corridor, ran along from the family wing, then rushed downstairs. Noel ducked back in the study, waited until her feet had pounded past the door, then ran up the stairs, heading in the direction Holly had disappeared. *Where was that door again?* The one she'd mentioned earlier … the door to the linen press room.

He strode along the corridor until he came to it and paused outside. Then he took a deep breath and opened it – just a crack, but it was enough. She was sitting there, bathed in the glow of an electric lightbulb, her knees drawn up to her chin, slightly breathless.

'Holly! May I?' Now he was here, practically in the linen press with her, he felt nervous. Would she even want him with her? He would respect her if she chased him out, and he'd go back to joining in the game, but—

'I don't mind,' she said. 'But your fiancée might.'

'What? What the hell?' He stepped inside and closed the door, well-hidden in the panelling as she had said, behind him. 'My fiancée? I don't have a fiancée!'

'Are you sure? Emma seemed rather clear that you were going to announce it in the New Year.'

'Emma?' He was horrified – and, yes, angry at his cousin. 'No. No, I'm not engaged to Emma. Who on earth said that?'

'As I said. Emma did.' Holly shuffled over so she was pressed against a shelf of fresh sheets and blankets. She laid her head against them and stared at him, cocooned in the midst of the smell of soft soap and clean linen.

'You don't have to stand on ceremony. You can sit down, you know?'

Noel did as he was bid and they sat, very close together, in a very small space. He could feel the heat of her body, sense every time she breathed, hear, it seemed, every heartbeat. 'Emma is my cousin. Nothing more. I think she'd like to feel we had an understanding, and she's doing her damndest to make me think it's a good idea. But it's not. I'd never marry Emma. We are completely incompatible.'

'Why? I'd say she was a safe prospect. The families might approve.'

'Emma is desperate for a title – they'd approve more of that. I might be an Honourable one day, but there's no guarantee. I'm certainly not born into – well – title-ism.' He was pleased to see a smile twitch at the sides of Holly's lips at that phrase, even if it quickly disappeared again. 'And there is no expectation from any of our parents that we should make a match.'

'So it's just Emma that thinks that? Or is she just warning me off?' The question was so direct that for a moment he couldn't speak.

Then he said something that quite possibly wasn't the most tactful thing he'd ever said – but it had to be said, nevertheless. 'I don't want you warned off. Quite the opposite.'

'So you want me to be encouraged?'

'You could say that. Yes.'

'I've had a little too much wine with my dinner.'

Her tone was conversational and he was thrown once more. 'And?'

'And I think I could quite easily be encouraged. I go to a liberal college. I'm not exactly the traditional young lady you're probably used to meeting.'

'I see.' He risked moving his hand to cover hers and she didn't move it away.

'I'm not an easy person to be with. I argue and I challenge and I sometimes don't know when to say nothing. And I rarely admit when I'm wrong.'

'I'm not easy either. I'm flippant and grumpy and argue back.'

'But I am loyal. I'm loyal to the core.'

'Me too. Life is never dull.'

'Never.' She paused for a moment and looked at his hand covering hers. 'What did she say to you? In the drawing room – before Sardines?'

'Emma? She told me that my find of the peanut drawing was ingenious, and she wished she had thought to look there.'

'Is that all?' Holly suddenly laughed. 'Oh, she's such a card, that one.'

'Why do you ask?'

'You didn't see the look she gave me afterwards. I suppose I should feel sorry for her.' Her voice was amused and she raised her eyes to him.

His heart gave a little jolt as the electric light made her skin glow and her hair shine like moonlight on snow. She was the very image of the Enchanted Ice Princess he wanted to write about. He wished he could save this moment and preserve it, but he feared he'd never have the words to do it justice.

'Holly, I want to write about you.' The words tumbled out before he could stop them. 'Is that all right? Would you mind? If I wrote about a heroine just like you?'

'Me? A heroine?' There was still a faint trace of wine on her warm breath; still a sense of amusement in her tone.

'Yes. You see, I'm a writer. I write stories, silly stories, popular tosh that sells and the newspapers and periodicals devour. I can barely keep up with the demand. But you see, I want to write a proper story. Like a cross between *Alice's Adventures in Wonderland* and Grimms' Fairy Tales. I know I could do it. And I've had an idea that's been buzzing around my head for an eternity, but I've never known exactly what it was I needed to put down on paper. But now – now I know.' He felt himself grow even warmer. 'It's you. You're my Enchanted Ice Princess, and I would like your permission to write your story.'

To his surprise, she laughed and turned her hand over in his, curling her fingers around it. 'I don't think I've ever been called an Enchanted Ice Princess before. I rather like it.'

'You're Lady Holly tonight though.'

'I am. I am.' She nodded. 'But I'm only pretending. Elsie has been my Fairy Godmother, and I fear it'll all come crashing down when this is all over. When we're back in real life, and Emma is scowling at me over breakfast and I'm comparing myself to Elsie, who is the wildest, funniest, most talented girl I know. But, ah well, fairy tales aren't meant to last, and there's always an element of warning in them for the poor characters. I'll simply abandon my beautiful ballgown and my fancy slippers. It was nice while it lasted, but it won't be difficult to go back to being me.'

'You don't sound as if you're too concerned at that prospect?'

'I'm not. I quite like "me", really. I'm more Holly than I am Lady Holly, and anyway, I can be a princess instead. I've done all right, I think, at being Cinderella. I even broke my glass slipper.' She poked her toes out from her dress and wiggled them, then motioned across to her shoes. 'I was going to put those back in my bedroom too, but then by the time I rescued my paintings, I saw Emma along there, and, well, I just shoved the pictures in my portfolio and ran back out. I wasn't thinking – I have *no* idea why I didn't leave the shoes. I'm blaming the wine.' She stared at the shoes in rather a confused and puzzled fashion, and it was all Noel could do to bite his lip and not laugh. 'Anyway. I brought them with me. I *do* hope she didn't realise which bedroom was mine – I was in such a rush, I left my door unlocked and my portfolio lying around. But I'm sure my artwork isn't really to her taste anyway. It would be one more thing for her to rag me about.'

'Your artwork? Your illustrations?'

'Yes. Those ones.'

'I saw the ones in the drawing room – the ones you rescued. You have an incredible talent. Your pictures would go quite well with my book, wouldn't they? May I possibly commission you to illustrate it? When it's written, of course.'

'Ha! Thank you. They weren't meant to be on public display, but I'm quite proud of them, to be honest. When your book is written, I will certainly offer my services.' She nodded elegantly.

'Wonderful. Now, Cinderella, may I perhaps do something?'

'It depends on what that is.'

'I think we need a little more fairy tale magic.' Noel leaned across and took the unbroken shoe. 'Whomsoever this shoe fits will be my Enchanted Princess!' And he lifted her foot and slipped the shoe on.

Holly giggled. 'Why, my Prince, it fits.'

'It most certainly does. Now, may I steal a kiss, Princess Holly?'

'Absolutely.' And she moved towards him, then stopped an inch or so away from his lips. 'Oh. I have to say something as well. Before I find myself hell-bound and give myself so freely to a man I've only met once, which I understand is the way of fairy tales. I think we may both be receiving an invitation to another party – at Pearl and Ernie's home. It's not until after Christmas, and I have to go home tomorrow – my train is at eleven. So it means I won't see you for a week or so after that. Will you be attending?'

'I would say that if you're attending, then I shall most definitely be attending too.'

'Good. Noel – I'm sorry to say this, but I think this is the part where we *do* sort of have a kiss. We've done all the rest of the fairy tale. You know my true identity. You've even made sure my shoe fits.'

'I do love a good fairy tale. I think you're right – we need to do the story justice.'

He leaned towards her again, hardly daring to believe this was happening. In a linen press of all things!

And this time, they did kiss.

And it was magical.

Chapter Twenty-Six

Christmas Present

'Fairy tale?' Locryn just heard the last word as he barged back into the folly. He had a folder with him and his heart was thumping in excitement. He had an idea how well this would be received, but one could never be sure. 'Hold that thought. May I?' He indicated the table and the women nodded in unison. Merryn moved the Visitors' Book a little, and he put the folder down. 'This is what I went back for. I've had it for ages – since I moved into my first house. It was given to me by my Aunt Susie and it's been hidden away in my home ever since. One of *my* biggest secrets. I think it was waiting for the right time to come out and shine.'

He opened the folder and smiled as he heard Sorcha and Merryn gasp in delight.

'It is, it's beautiful!' Sorcha leaned in towards it, and Merryn sucked in her breath.

'Wow,' said Merryn. 'Is that what I think it is?'

'What do you think it is?' Locryn knew, of course, that Merryn would have the best idea of all of them what it was.

'A Holly Sawyer print. Am I right? From the book? Or Holly Andrews, as she would have been then, I guess.'

'Close – try again. Look at it in the light.'

Merryn moved around the table and whistled. 'That's not a print. That's an original. I can see the brush strokes. Incredible. Look, Sorcha.'

Sorcha wriggled in between Locryn and Merryn, and Locryn was pleased she was close to him again.

'I remember this page! It's the Ice Princess – just as she's becoming a fairy again! Look! Look at her shoes! The Prince is putting them on her feet. I love it.'

'It's got the look of a Rackham or a Claude Shepperson,' admitted Locryn, 'but there's her signature at the bottom – H. Andrews.'

'Hold on.' Sorcha peered at it again. 'It's different. It's different from the one I remember.' She tucked her hair behind her ears as it fell down and obscured her view. Locryn desperately wanted to do that for her but decided to restrain himself with Merryn being around. 'Can I see the Visitors' Book again, Merryn. Please?'

'Sure.' Merryn pushed it over to her and Sorcha placed it next to the watercolour.

'Oh, how lovely – I *knew* it. Their faces are the same as the ones in the book – it's Holly and Noel. I *knew* I recognised Elsie's doodles from somewhere. But there's more. Look – just beside the Princess. There's a little crib, just hidden away in the icy foliage next to her. There's a tiny baby in it, all tucked up, with a garland of holly around the crib. How sweet! That wasn't in the book.' She looked up and smiled at Locryn. 'I wonder if she did an original for themselves – maybe when they had a baby, and she hung it in the nursery? This is wonderful. Thank you so much for bringing it here.'

'What a find. You're so lucky, Locryn, to have been given that. We might never know why she did an original like that, but I like Sorcha's theory.'

'She's probably right.' Locryn smiled. 'I'm related to Holly and Noel – not too sure how or where I fit in, but I definitely fit in somewhere along the line, Aunt Susie discovered the connection through my great-grandfather. That's how she had the picture – she got it from him. And I don't think your theory is too far from the truth, Sorcha. That picture's hung in our family nurseries since the year dot. I'm certain they must be the relatives that had the connection to Pencradoc. It seems to fit perfectly. Susie said the family nickname for Holly was "Milady", so I don't know how that came about.'

Merryn grinned and clapped her hands. 'Brilliant! The answer's in the Visitors' Book, I reckon! But why on earth they did it, who knows? It's another one of Pencradoc's secrets – but a nice one, I think. How marvellous. And the Prince in the picture does have a bit of a look of you in him. I said Elsie's doodle did too. How exciting.'

'Well, I'm going to display this painting at the exhibition, now we know there's definitely that connection to Pencradoc. It'll look great in the cabinet next to the Visitors' Book, won't it?'

'It'll be awesome. Kit and Coren will be delighted. I'm sure Coren will want to add it to the press release, and we'll get something written up about the Noel and Holly connection to use in the exhibition. I'll run it by you first though. Have you got the keys for the cabinets? You can put it all straight in if you're happy to do that. I'll leave the Visitors' Book with you.'

'I've got the keys.' Locryn patted his pocket. 'All sorted.'

'Great! Okay, I'll go and see the boss and catch you both later then.' Merryn smiled and pulled her gloves back on. 'See you soon!' And she clapped once more, then headed out of the folly.

Locryn and Sorcha said their farewells and watched her leave. Then, once they were sure she had gone, they turned towards one another. Locryn smiled and said, 'Where were we?'

'Just wait one second. I know exactly where we were, hence why I'm locking that door.' Sorcha tore herself away from Locryn and hurried after Merryn. With a peek outside, she closed the door and firmly locked it. Then she turned, leaned against the door, and smiled. 'As I said, I know exactly where we were. But before I do anything about it, let's go and put the book and the painting upstairs. I don't know – it just feels wrong with Noel and Holly watching us. And in the presence of that tiny baby too!'

'I knew I recognised them – this is how. From this painting. It all makes sense. Why we both felt it, why we both needed to be here to see them.' Locryn walked over to her and took her hands in his. 'Why I felt such a connection to the place. My family actually started here. It's incredible.'

'You're right. And that'll be why I fancied Noel something rotten. I could see you in him, and it all just merged together – my feelings for you, and seeing him there, looking at her like that. I wanted you to look at *me* like that. And then I acted like an idiot and almost pushed you away. Have I told you I'm sorry about that?'

Drawing her closer to him, which made her feel ridiculously weak-kneed, he smiled that slow, thoughtful smile of his. 'You did. And you don't need to keep apologising.'

'You think the same as me then? It's been them hanging around Pencradoc in the run-up to Christmas?'

'I think so. I think it's not really them though. I think it's more their memories – it's their happy place, if you like, and I think they felt it so much that it's tinged the atmosphere with their love – a bit like Holly's watercolour there. Good grief, I might come back and haunt here myself once I'm dead and gone. Only I'll be in the Tower Tea Room, and I'll be chasing a dark-haired woman with a teapot in her hand.'

'I won't run away from you, I promise.' As if to prove her point, Sorcha stepped even closer to him and raised her face to his. 'I'm pretty sure they won't mind us having perhaps one tiny kiss while they're watching us from the table. And look – mistletoe.' She nodded upwards. 'Don't know why I put that there. It seemed like a good idea at the time.'

'We can't waste it then, can we?' Locryn smiled into her eyes and Sorcha realised she had no intention of wasting that mistletoe at all.

Chapter Twenty-Seven

Christmas 1906

'Holly! Hols! Lady Holly Victoria Sawyer!' Elsie was obviously wandering along the corridor looking for them. The pitch of her voice changed. 'Holly-Dolly. Come out now. Please. The game's over. I need your sensible personage to stop a very silly squabble.'

Holly shifted position and turned to look at Noel, pulling a face. 'Must we?' she murmured. She had been quite cosy in the linen press, leaning against Noel, whose chin was resting on her head, and she was feeling pleasantly drowsy to boot.

'I suppose we must. The thing has probably descended into carnage without us. I believe we are the best party guests in the history of party guests.'

'I'd be inclined to agree. Hush! Listen, though. I think we're rumbled.' She pressed her forefinger to her lips and Noel pulled her closer as the door to the little room opened.

'Ah-ha!' Elsie's flushed face appeared in the gap. 'Found you. I see you're having your own game of Sardines. How absolutely delightful.' She didn't seem perturbed in the slightest. Rather, she simply pulled the door further open and indicated with a jerk of her head that they should come out of the tiny room. 'Emma and Mabel are almost coming to blows and I think I'll have to slap some sense into one or both of them if your calming presence doesn't work.'

'What's going on?' Holly began to crawl out of the linen press, conscious that Noel was close behind her.

Elsie stood back until they were both out of the room and standing slightly awkwardly next to one another. Elsie reached out and smoothed Holly's hair down, tucking a pin back in, and continued her conversation as if nothing was amiss.

'Mabes said she saw Ems wandering around the upstairs corridors. The issue was that she was in the family wing and not the guest wing, and Mabes said she looked guilty as hell and she wanted to know what she was doing along there. Emma said she was lost and it wasn't her fault that Pencradoc was, and I quote, "so ridiculously Byzantine" and Mabel said that was a load of tosh because she'd been before on a number of occasions. Then Emma countered with "well, you were up there too", and Mabel said "of course I damn well was because I'm part of the damn family". And then Clara interrupted and became all superior and told Mabes to watch her language. And I said "calm down girls, it's a damn party." Then *Emma* turned to me looking all sour and angry, and said, "I think *you* should be more concerned about where Lady Holly is and where my cousin is, because they haven't participated at *all*".' Elsie shrugged, unconcerned. 'So, before I told her that it was none of her damn business where the hell you were, and I hadn't held you hostage to playing the silly old game, I just made a comment about people being overly excited and becoming crotchety, and came up here to drag *you* two out of *there*.'

'I see,' said Holly slowly, not really seeing at all how she could help. 'I don't actually know how I can help with that one. And anyway, how on earth did you know where I was?'

'It's your go-to spot, darling. I was there when little

Arthur showed you it, remember? At dear Biscuit's birthday party – and I saw how delighted you were with the place. It didn't take me a great deal of time to work it out. Now.' She looked at the pair of them appraisingly. 'Noel, straighten your jacket and tame your hair. Hols, your dress is awfully wrinkled and your face is awfully red, but I think we can get away with that if we tell the truth about where you were. Don't look at me like that. You were perfectly entitled to be hidden away in the linen press during a game of Sardines. You did awfully well, by the way. Noel, I think we can say you were in the night nursery, perhaps in the large cupboard in Nanny's room. We didn't say that was out of use, and it's logical you might have found your way in there. Come along then. All agreed. Excellent.' She dipped a curtsey and ushered them past. 'Noel – give us five minutes, darling. Can't look suspicious.'

Holly looked up at Noel, and the look in his eyes told her he was definitely trying not to laugh. 'Capital plan,' he murmured. Then, to Holly's surprise and delight, he locked gazes with her and dipped down to kiss her.

'I'll see you soon, my Enchanted Princess.'

She felt herself flush from her toes right up to the roots of her hair, but Elsie remained stoical. 'Come along, Holly. Mustn't look suspicious.'

Elsie took her arm and pulled her along the corridor, her black gown sparkling in the electric lights as it swished along the floor. Elsie seemed slightly shorter, Holly thought, so she must have decided to take her shoes off as well. Emma would be doubly appalled at that one!

As they scurried along towards the grand staircase, Holly couldn't help but throw a glance behind her, just to check she hadn't imagined the time that had just passed.

But no. Noel was there, and he lifted one hand and waved at her, still with that smile on his face.

She couldn't help but smile back, even as Elsie was ushering her away.

'We shall discuss this later,' said Elsie, almost pulling her down the stairs and into the drawing room. No grand entrance for them this time – it was more of a flustered hurry, and Holly could hear the raised voices even as they approached the doorway.

'I don't trust her at *all*. She says she's a Lady but she certainly doesn't seem to have the breeding required. And if you ask me, she's set her sights on Noel and that's simply unacceptable. Where do you think she's been all this time? I suspect she's been with *him*. Singling him out somewhere private. And *you* complain that *I* was in the corridor!' That was Emma, and Holly pulled back at Elsie so they came to a sudden halt.

'Me?' she asked.

'Apparently.' Elsie blinked. 'Want to?' She nodded to the door.

'Oh, most definitely.' Holly pulled her shoulders back and drew herself to her full height, then flung open the door in her best "Lady Holly" manner.

'Good evening, Emma. May I ask what all the commotion is about?' she enquired politely. 'I heard my name mentioned. I'm terribly sorry, but I was still engaged with the wonderful game of Sardines, so I have missed all the excitement. Mabel! Pray tell – who won in the end? You look delightful, by the way. I don't think I told you before. So utterly grown up.' She smiled at the younger girl. 'Very ladylike. Now. Emma. Please share with us your comments again. I'm afraid I didn't hear it all. I was, you see, hiding in the linen press. My word, what a teeny, tiny room that is! Yet such a delightful place to hide. And I do believe Elsie has tried to find Noel and lure him out of wherever he was hiding.' It wasn't a lie.

Emma stared at Holly, and her face grew bright red as she apparently tried and failed to come up with an excuse.

Eventually, she must have decided that attack was the best form of defence. 'Everyone knows your game, *Lady* Holly. We all know you're desperate to attract Noel. He'll have a title one day, and you already know where I stand with him. You won't manage to do it, you know? You just *won't*.'

Holly had had enough. She was just about to respond and tell the girl exactly what she thought of her in a very unladylike manner, when a light breeze lifted the damp curls on the back of the neck and a shiver ran down her spine – a shiver that had nothing to do with the breeze and everything to do with the person who had caused it by walking into the room.

'I say, I think my hiding place was perhaps the best one of the evening.' Noel smiled around at the assembled company. He held up a stuffed rabbit. 'The things you find in the night nursery. Elsie – is this yours? Never mind. It's a splendid rabbit anyway.' He looked at it, then handed it to Mabel with another smile, which had the desired effect of distracting the girl. He continued conversationally. 'I heard Elsie shouting in the corridors, and I thought it was either a particularly ingenious way of flushing us all out, or I'd really spent far too long in that room and Sardines was over. Do you know, I sat in the cupboard for a bit, then I became terribly bored, so I climbed beneath the covers of the bed and I swear I fell asleep for a little while? My thinking was that if anyone came in, then all they'd see would be a jumble of covers and perhaps think it was just a rather messy unmade bed.'

'You're quite right, Noel. You did hear me. It was the end of the game and I needed to herd you all back here so we could settle ourselves down for some music and some chatter, and then drift off to bed.' Elsie smiled at him. 'I'm glad I found you both. Stragglers! Now – if we're all accounted for, shall we continue from where we left off? Oh – and because we make our own rules up here and why not, I ask? – the winner of our game is … Ernie! Because he found Clara first. We don't really care about odd-men-out, do we? A round of applause for Ernie, everyone!' And, incredibly – or maybe not incredibly, because it was Elsie after all – the guests obliged. Well, all the guests, Noel noticed, apart from Emma, who was standing on the outside of the group, her fists clenched and looking as if she was about to cry.

Noel wasn't a cruel man, and after a quick glance at Holly and some marvellous unspoken communication between them to make sure she was all right about it, he walked over to Emma. She was his cousin, after all – and family, despite her faults.

'Do you want to tell me what's going on?' he asked her quietly. 'There seems to be a little bit of a fuss happening.'

Emma looked up at him and her bottom lip began to tremble. 'I want to go home, Noel. I have quite a headache. I want to leave this awful party. Take me home.' She added, he noticed, a little stamp of her foot, which, under other circumstances, might have been amusing.

He didn't want to leave Holly though – not when he'd just found her.

But, as he wrestled with his conscience and tried to think of a feasible excuse, he realised that he didn't have much of a choice at all. Emma was, to all intents, verging on hysterical and most definitely miserable, and to encourage her to stay would make everyone else miserable. Mabel, distracted briefly by the rabbit, wouldn't stay distracted for long, and then Clara would defend her and the three of them would probably start arguing – and he didn't want Holly to be in the middle of it all.

'Emma. Are you sure?' Well, he had to try – he had to try at least!

'Yes.'

'Positive?'

'Positive. Yes!' She glared over at Holly, and Noel decided he didn't want to push the issue.

He tried not to sigh too loudly. He would have to take her back. 'All right. Come on – let's go to your room and get your things.' He reached out for her hand, but she shook him off in a temper.

Emma cast an angry glance at Holly and said in a small, tight voice, 'I can manage. Just tell them we'll be ready soon and get them to collect our luggage and take it to the front door.

'"Them",' murmured Noel. '"Them" have names, I'm sure.' He turned away from Emma, looked at Elsie apologetically, and took in the slightly stunned faces of Pearl and Ernie, the steady dark gaze of Clara and the furious little face of Mabel. 'Terribly sorry, chaps. Looks like we're skipping out early. Good to meet you all. Jolly good.' He bowed to Elsie and took her hand, then kissed it politely. He did the same to Clara, Mabel and Pearl, then shook Ernie's hand. Then he turned to Holly and smiled afresh. He locked eyes with her and held his hand out. 'I've enjoyed this evening though. I really have. More than I thought possible.'

Holly held his gaze and took his hand. How he wanted to kiss her again properly! And not just on the hand! But he couldn't, not here. 'I enjoyed it too. It was nice to meet you, Noel Andrews.'

'A pleasure, Lady Holly.' He bowed and drew her closer, hands still together. Then he dipped his head and allowed himself to kiss her hand, and he hoped that Holly knew he meant it a thousand times more than he had when he'd kissed the others.

Chapter Twenty-Eight

Christmas Present

Sorcha couldn't wait for the exhibition to happen. It was only a couple of days away now, and when they hadn't been working, she and Locryn had been practically inseparable since the revelations of the painting.

Holly and Noel Andrews! Fancy that!

'I actually can't wait for Christmas, and for your exhibition,' Sorcha had told Locryn over a tasty pizza at the little Italian restaurant in the village the day after they'd found everything out. 'And I equally can't wait for the New Year when we can start planning the fairy tale exhibition.'

'I'm happy to loan Merryn whatever you need. You know that I've got loads of resources, and I've got my eye on a couple of other things as well. There's an auction coming up in Exeter, so I'll be heading down there. I think there are some of those old jigsaws going – the wooden block ones?'

'Oh! I've seen them in museums! The one's with six pictures on them, and you fit the blocks together to make them?'

'That's right. This particular set has six fairy tales on it. Thought it might look pretty good in one of the cabinets.'

'Brilliant. It's really exciting, isn't it? Do you mind if I come as well – to the auction? I've never been to one before, but I'm always happy to find things that match the tea room décor.'

'Or don't match,' Locryn had teased. 'Mismatched is the best.'

'Definitely the best!'

Sorcha smiled now as she remembered that conversation and cast a glance up at the Santa teapot. She thought, actually, it might be nice to bring him down and use him over Christmas in her flat. In her opinion, he had not been designed to be entirely decorative and she felt a bit sorry for him.

She pulled over a chair and climbed up on to it, reaching up to get the teapot. As she grabbed him, the bell went on the door and she twisted around to see a lady who appeared to be in her early forties standing at the entrance. It was a lady she knew by sight and she smiled at her. There was about half an hour left of trading for the day before she closed, and she was sure she could rustle up a mince pie and a coffee for her, if nothing else.

'Hello. Just give me a moment and I'll be down. Just thought I needed to use this little fella before the New Year comes.' She raised the teapot and then climbed down the ladder. 'Now – how can I help?'

'Oh, take your time, don't worry.' The lady smiled. She had beautifully blow-dried and curled ash-blonde hair and light brown, curious eyes. 'I'm just after a cup of tea and a flapjack if you've got any – and I think I ought to introduce myself. I'm Susie – Locryn's aunt.'

'Oh! Susie. Aunt Susie. Hello.' Sorcha blinked. She'd expected Aunt Susie to be much older than this lady – almost parental age, really. 'You don't look anything like I expected you to. Sorry. I thought you'd be ... I thought ...' Her voice petered out, and she felt her cheeks flush as she realised how very rude that might sound.

But the lady – Aunt Susie – just laughed and shook her head. 'It's fine. I'm the youngest out of all my siblings – there's a huge gap between me and Locryn's mum. I think I was the surprise twentieth anniversary gift to my parents. I even have a niece older than me. I suppose I'm closer in age to Locryn than to my eldest brother. Never mind.' She smiled. 'Anyway, I've heard *loads* about you. Locryn's just floating around with a great big smile on his face at the moment, so I thought I'd come and introduce myself to you properly. I've been in here plenty of times, but perhaps I was a little more incognito.'

It was Sorcha's turn to laugh. 'I'm so sorry.' She shook her head. 'I do recognise you, actually, but I never put two and two together.'

'No reason for you to.' Susie shrugged. 'I'm extending my Sunday lunch invitation to you as well as Locryn. I've told him he has to come at least once a month for Sunday lunch to my house now he's living here, and I have to say he's been *more* than once a month, but I don't mind. Next time he comes though, I've told him he has to bring you. Are you free *this* Sunday at all?'

'That's so kind of you. Thank you! And yes, I am. But I don't close until three so I'd have to come after that. Is that okay?'

'It can be Sunday dinner then. No problem at all.'

'Oh, that's splendid! Look – have this one on the house as another "thank you".'

'Not at all. I'm a paying customer and always will be. I know how hard it is to get a business off the ground from what Locryn has told me. Luckily, I've always worked for other people so I've never experienced that. But that's great about Sunday. Now, how much do I owe you?'

Sorcha tried to argue, but Aunt Susie won and handed the money over triumphantly. 'I know it's nearly closing time,' Susie continued. 'But do you want to join me? Have one yourself?'

'Why not?' Sorcha poured herself a coffee and took it over to Susie's table. 'I must say,' she said, sitting down opposite the older woman, 'that painting you gave Locryn is amazing. I assume he's told you all about the history and the connection to Pencradoc?'

'Oh yes. He said you were a big fan of the story as well. I'm not surprised – I was as well, even when I was very small and before I really understood that we were connected to it somehow.'

'Do you know any more about the family history?'

'I've got some stuff my grandfather gave me in my attic. I've never really looked through it – but he used to tell me all the family stories when I was little. I was fascinated by them. If you're interested, then it's a good excuse to make me have another rummage through. And then when you come for dinner on Sunday, I'll hopefully have some exciting things to show you.'

'That would be wonderful. Thank you. I mean, I'd love to know what the baby's called in the painting, for instance, and to know a bit more about Holly and Noel as a couple. Obviously, they aren't *my* relatives, but I kind of want to claim a bit of ownership over them. They're going to be sort of living here for a few days anyway, with the painting being on display, so it would be nice to have a chat to them every now and then.' Sorcha pushed the thought of their ghosts drifting around the place to the back of her mind. She didn't really want to talk to *them*, thank you very much! But she could talk to a painting. That was better!

Sorcha had a sudden idea. She already really liked this lady and wanted to show how grateful she was for the fact she'd given the painting to Locryn and it had ended up here – such a touchstone of Sorcha's happy childhood, all leading back to this old fairy tale tower. Who would have thought it, this time last year, when she was permanently arguing with Martin, that she'd be so completely happy and settled and, yes, at home here this Christmas? Even if, deep down, she knew she was just passing through the place as she had done so many times when she was smaller? Like she'd always maintained, she felt at home at Pencradoc, but it wasn't "home". Rather, it was a springboard for her *coming* home – and that was a little deep for this time on a winter's afternoon.

She shook herself back to reality and spoke again. 'Actually, Susie, do you want to come and see the painting? Have a sneak peek of the exhibition? It's up there, ready and waiting.'

'No – I'm going to wait.' Susie smiled. 'I know that painting like the back of my hand, but I think it'll be different when I see it up there – it'll perhaps have a different feel to it, now it's on display back where they met.'

'Okay. Well, if you change your mind between now and the seventeenth, let me know. You're always welcome for a cuppa here, and I don't mind if you accidentally go up the stairs. You might have to limbo under the rope though – we've got it all closed off at the moment. Just a few days' time, though, and we'll be open. I hope it goes well for Locryn's sake.'

'It *will* go well,' said Susie, confidently. 'I've got a lot of influence in this village – I work at the library, and I've made sure it's well advertised there as well as everywhere else I can think of.'

Sorcha laughed. 'I wondered how all those other posters had appeared in the village! I thought Locryn had just been busy!'

'He has – but I knew he had other things to concentrate on, aside from posters.' Susie raised her tea cup to Sorcha in a kind of toast. 'And now I can see what a good distraction you've been. I was never struck on that Laura girl. I can already tell I much prefer you. You seem good for one another – take it from his old maiden aunt! Now, I'm going to go, and I'll see you Sunday. Don't worry, I'll let Locryn know! See you then.'

'See you then!' replied Sorcha.

She escorted Susie out, and as it was now just after closing time, she locked the door behind her, leaning on it with a huge grin on her face.

She was good for Locryn.

She was apparently making him happy.

This really was going to be a *fantastic* Christmas all round!

Sorcha couldn't wait to start – and the next thing to look forward to, apart from her date with Locryn later, of course – was the exhibition in her beautiful fairy tale tower.

Chapter Twenty-Nine

Christmas 1906

She was sad that he'd gone – of course she was. But, even as Holly sat on the window seat in her nightgown, looking out at the dark gardens of Pencradoc beneath the twinkling stars, she hugged her knees and smiled, knowing that she'd see him soon. And this time, there'd be no Emma lurking in the wings with her sour expression. Pearl had specifically said, over their final coffees of the evening, that she was looking forward to seeing "you people, all of you here, if Clara and Mabel are allowed, and Noel, of course" at their home next week. *No mention of Miss Emma Carew, thank goodness!*

Holly loved Christmas, but this year she acknowledged quietly to herself, that she simply couldn't wait for it to be over. Because that would mean she was closer to seeing Noel.

There was that distinctive rap on the door again that signalled Elsie was outside and expecting to come in, and Holly shook her head in comic despair and scrambled to her feet.

'Come in, Lady Elsie,' she said throwing the door open and standing back. 'I sense I couldn't stop you even if I wanted to.'

'Not at all. Champagne?' Elsie held up a bottle. 'Forgot the glasses. Have to share this. Terrible affair.' She danced into the room and took a great glug of the stuff from the bottle, then handed it to Holly.

Holly took the champagne and shut the door. She

herself took a glug and indicated that Elsie should sit on the window seat. Heading across to join her, she dragged a blanket off the bed and brought it over, then settled it on both their legs. She sensed it would be a long conversation.

'You and champagne don't mix, Elsie. Or do I need to remind you of that? Do I need to get that camera after all?'

Elsie shook her head. 'No. Think I know that well enough myself. Had nothing else to bring except the champagne. So! Tell me! Noel!'

She looked enquiringly at Holly and she couldn't help laughing. 'It just seems like a dream, to be honest.' She looked at the gauzy, blue-green dress she had left hanging outside of the wardrobe; just so that when she caught sight of it out of the corner of her eye, tonight would seem less like a fairy tale and more like real life. 'I think you guessed that Noel and I found an excellent location to hide in during Sardines.'

'Hardly big enough for three sardines. Or even two. Not sure how you fitted.'

Holly smiled teasingly. 'We fitted. Don't worry about that.'

'Minx.' Elsie grinned and claimed the champagne bottle. 'It didn't get past Emma, did it?'

'Not at all.' Holly pulled a face. 'What an awful person. She didn't like me at all.'

'Because Noel *did* like you. Even I could tell that – little self-obsessed me. Sometimes I *do* observe, you know?'

'I know you do. Anyway. We have Pearl's delightful *soiree* to look forward to – but tell me, Elsie Pencradoc, what are you going to do about Louis?'

'Make him suffer. I can't believe he didn't come

because of a rotten cold. I mean, that's just *mean*.' Elsie paused, thoughtful, it seemed, as she processed what she'd just said. 'Mean. *Mean.* Interesting. Anyway.' She took a drink from the bottle and passed it across to Holly. 'Would you like to borrow another dress for the *soirée*? I have plenty.'

Holly fought with her conscience for just a moment. She didn't want to pretend she was something she wasn't – and goodness knew she wasn't in a position to own a wardrobe full of Worths … but, at the end of the day, she was a nineteen-year-old girl who, admittedly, wanted to dress up and look her best if she knew a certain young man would be at the very party she was due to attend.

Holly, therefore, looked at the bottle in her hand, took another drink, and raised it to Elsie.

She blinked as the slightly warm, slightly flat liquid did its job almost too well and went directly to her head.

Oddly, there were two Elsies there now – how amusing it was!

'Two of you. Two Elsies.' She pointed at the Elsies and smiled. 'But yes – yes I would.' She nodded decisively. 'I would very much like to borrow a frock. Thank you, Elsies.'

And then she couldn't really remember very much after that at all.

Aunt Elizabeth and Uncle Percy were surprised, as well they might be, when the carriage pulled up and disgorged a weeping Emma and a resigned Noel.

'Oh my goodness, what happened?' asked Aunt Elizabeth.

'Ask *him*,' squawked Emma and stomped off upstairs in, Noel was amused to note, a most unladylike manner.

She turned after a couple of steps and came back to retrieve her travelling bag.

'Leave it, Ems,' he said with a sigh. 'I'll bring it up.'

'No. I can manage.' And off she went, bouncing the thing up the staircase.

'Emma, darling, can't Mr Jobson help with that, if you won't let Noel?' called her mother. Mr Jobson was the butler and, God bless him, must have been as old as Methuselah – but he continued doing things he'd always done, albeit at slower, more methodical pace. His wife ran the house like a tight ship and they were an indomitable pair

'No! I can *manage.*'

For a girl who usually abandoned any task to the nearest person available rather than do it herself, it was an odd thing. Noel frowned. She'd also packed her bag herself at Pencradoc. Oh well. Maybe she was just in such a foul mood that she wanted to throw things around for a little bit. And who was he to stop her?

Instead, he turned to Aunt Elizabeth and shook his head. 'She said she had a headache. But apparently there were raised voices. I came in at the end of it. After a game of Sardines.'

'Did she get found? She's never been good with losing.' Uncle Percy sighed and shook his head as he ushered them into the drawing room, where the unheralded and rather noisy entrance of his daughter and nephew had apparently disturbed a game of cards. 'Where did everyone hide, Noel? I used to love a game of Sardines in my time. Always curious as to where people find to lay low nowadays.'

Noel paused. 'I was in the nanny's room … apparently.' He did feel a little bad lying, but in a sense he wasn't, was he? "Apparently", that *was* where he had been. The thought made the corners of his lips twitch upwards. 'Not sure where everyone else was, but one girl – Holly – found the linen press. *That* was a pretty good place.' And that was the truth at least.

His aunt, however, was quick. 'Holly, you say? I don't think we know anyone in Emma's set with that name.'

'She goes to that Liberal Arts College with Elsie. Very talented girl – I saw some of her work.'

'Oh! And was she pretty?'

'That's rather a subjective – and *odd* – question, Aunt Elizabeth!'

'You've got a little twinkle in your eye, Noel,' she said, cheeky as an imp. 'I haven't seen that before in you, but I'm not so green as I'm cabbage-looking. You liked her, didn't you – this Holly girl?'

'She was … interesting.' He felt his face flush. 'More my type than some of the girls I keep being introduced to. Lacks pretentions, somewhat.' He tried to shrug nonchalantly. 'We had some interesting conversation.' *And a lot of other time together that was equally interesting.*

'Hmm. That probably added to Emma's headache then. She's never enjoyed not being the centre of attention.' Uncle Percy shook his head. 'Shame to admit it, but there we go. Now – would you like a nightcap, young man? Or have you had enough company for one evening?'

'I think,' replied Noel slowly, 'that if you don't mind, I'll just head up to my room.' He knew exactly what he intended doing when he got to his room, of course. He was going to work on his fairy tale story. Now he had met Holly, he had all the inspiration he needed and could hardly wait to get started. Then he suddenly remembered his manners. 'Oh – I suspect I've got a sort of loose invite to an event sometime during the week. Is it all right if I leave here a couple of days early? I'll go to this dinner party, and then head back home. I'll have Christmas with you, of course – then make plans after that. It's a couple who were at the party tonight. We got on well.'

'Oh, of course,' said Aunt Elizabeth. 'We'd love to have you stay for as long as you wish – but if you have a better offer, you should take it! We just didn't want you alone for Christmas.'

'Thank you. I know. I do appreciate you having me here.' He smiled, then leaned down and kissed his aunt on her powdered cheek.

'And is Holly going to be there?' Aunt Elizabeth asked, far too innocently, as she sat down and fluffed her skirts around her, ready to resume her card game.

Noel grinned. 'I have no idea, but do you know something? I hope so.'

'Well, don't worry,' she replied. 'I don't think you'll have to worry about Emma getting one of her headaches there. We had visitors this evening ourselves – one of Percy's associates, Sir George Fleming, and his wife, Lady Enid, are hosting a winter ball. They have a very ambitious son. Young Victor is convinced he is meant for grander things than running his father's estate and I think the two eldest Wheal Mount girls have been invited too, from what dear Enid was saying. It seems as if the hunt is on for a suitable bride for Victor, so I'm sure he and Emma will find plenty to talk about. Emma can go to the Flemings' ball and leave you in peace to attend your dinner party.'

'Once again, Aunt Elizabeth – thank you,' said Noel with a smile. 'I'm sure she'll enjoy that much more.

Goodnight, Aunt. Goodnight, Uncle. I'm not sure if I'll be down for breakfast, so don't worry if I'm not at the table. I'll get something when I'm ready.'

He bowed and hurried out of the room. He couldn't stop the smile from spreading across his face as he took the stairs two at a time, grabbing his travelling bag on the way. Emma would be occupied with preparations for Christmas and this winter ball, so he knew he didn't have to worry about amusing her too much this week – and he had every intention of staying up just as long as he could tonight.

Despite the long evening and the party and the wine, he felt wide awake and his fingers were itching to unpack his notebook and his pen, to sit down at the small desk in the corner of his bedroom, and to start to write his story properly.

Chapter Thirty

Christmas Present

Locryn had to laugh when Sorcha told him how Aunt Susie had come to visit the tea room and railroaded them both into Sunday lunch – or dinner, as it turned out.

'Honestly, we don't have to go if you don't want to,' he told Sorcha. 'Aunt Susie can be pretty forceful, but I can put her back in her box if you need me too.'

'Poor Aunt Susie! No, I really liked her. You don't need to put her back in her box – but is it like a formal thing, this dinner, or can I just come in something casual?'

'Come in something with an expandable waistband,' he quipped. 'Aunt Susie thinks I'm still a growing boy and that she needs to feed me up.'

'I like Aunt Susie even more!' Sorcha said. 'I hate not eating much when I'm out for dinner – or feeling like I need a takeaway when I get home.'

'There'll be none of that at Susie's,' he reassured her.

And he hadn't been wrong. Locryn cast a glance over at Sorcha who was sitting on the sofa after Sunday dinner, being crawled all over by Susie's kittens, who had clearly tired of attacking the baubles on the Christmas tree. Sorcha looked happy, relaxed and comfortable, and had made a valiant attempt at clearing her plate. However, the roast beef and all the trimmings had almost finished her off, instead of the other way round – but she'd gamely attacked a piece of hot apple pie and clotted cream afterwards, and now looked fit to burst.

But she smiled over at him and pointed at her leggings

and cosy sweater dress. 'Good idea,' she said, and he grinned over the top of his coffee mug. Even the coffees came in giant sizes at Aunt Susie's. Which was great, because he'd never really seen the sense in a tiny cup of coffee. Unless it was an espresso, it wouldn't wake you up; and that was the prime reason he drank such a huge mug after lunch at Susie's – to stay awake in order to get home.

Aunt Susie had vanished upstairs to get something that she promised was 'really exciting, so just sit there and I'll get it.'

Locryn had felt he perhaps needed to point out he couldn't do much else *except* sit there, thanks to the huge dinner in his tummy, but he didn't.

Before too long, Susie came back downstairs with a cardboard box and a big smile on her face. 'Here we go. One or two things that you might find quite nice. Not a lot, really, relating to Noel and Holly in there. I suspect their things are scattered around the wider family, but I've got some of their letters and postcards, and something really special for when you've looked at those.'

Susie handed Locryn a few papers and he got up and went to sit next to Sorcha. 'Let's look together,' he said and moved a kitten gently out of the way as it began crawling across his knee, its bright little eyes fixed on the letters he held.

The first thing he unfolded was a letter between Lady Pearl Elton – one of the guests in Elsie's Visitors' Book – and Holly:

Dear Mrs Andrews,
I can't get used to calling you that! It makes me laugh quite loudly when I think of it, and I'm sure everyone

thinks I'm crazy when I do that! How was the
honeymoon? Good, I hope!

I'm writing to ask you and Noel to do us the
honour of being godparents to our new little one – I
know we have a few months to go before he/she
arrives, but you know me. I love to be organised!
Anyway, let me tell you what I've done to the gardens
since the last time you were here ...

The letter went on to describe some landscaping that
had taken place in Elton Lacy, and the fact that Pearl
had called on the services of the famous Arts and Crafts
garden designer Edwin Lutyens to help her with her
vision, and that she'd read a book by Thomas Mawson,
which had apparently made her want to get the whole
thing done and completed as quickly as possible. It was
a sweet little letter, and confirmed what Merryn had said
about Noel and Holly being close to the Eltons and being
godparents to one of their children.

'That's lovely!' said Sorcha. 'Merryn was right. She'll
be so happy to know it's true.'

'And just look at this one,' Locryn said. 'It's a letter
from someone called Marion to Noel – his sister,
apparently. And it mentions someone else from that party
– Emma Carew.' He read the date out loud: 'January
20th, 1907.'

My dearest brother Noel,
Italy is still splendid! I could almost imagine myself
in the Villa Diodati with Lord Byron writing stories
in a storm. Great Aunt Rachel sends her love – she
says she's enjoying revisiting the places of her youth
and I'm the best pupil she could hope for. I had a very

excitable letter from Emma – Miss Carew is, it seems,
betrothed to Lord Victor Fleming ... and on such
a short acquaintance as well! A matter of weeks, I
think? Emma was rather cagey about the incident you
told me about – she will not admit it fully, will she?
But it seems you did not spill the beans to Uncle Percy
so I must applaud you for that. I suspect being in love
with Holly Sawyer has made you soft!

Also, it did not take long for Ems to get her claws
into a titled gentleman, did it? I am willing to bet that
you are pleased her affections now lie elsewhere. She
is our cousin, but I could not possibly tolerate her as
a sister if you married her, so I am happy on many
accounts!

Much love to you. We are heading to Venice before
we come home. I am half promising myself I shall
purchase some Venetian lace and have it made into
a splendid gown for your wedding to Miss Sawyer.
All right, I am teasing – but I think I will buy some
anyway!

Your devoted sister,
Marion.

There were a few more letters – social invitations and
postcards, all with small tastes of the life Holly and Noel
had shared. One sweet memento was a hand-painted
birth announcement; possibly, Sorcha suggested, done as
a tester before sending out to family and friends, as there
were marks on the edge of the paper where Holly must
have been trying out her colours to get the baby's skin
tone correct. It announced the birth of "our cherished
first child, Joe", in July 1911.

'I wonder if that was the baby in the crib?' Sorcha asked.

'If we could find out when Noel's book was published,' said Locryn, 'it might tell us.'

He pulled his phone out, fully intending to Google it, but then Susie jumped into the conversation. 'Ah-ha! No need to do that, Locryn!' she said. 'I think I can help you.' She smiled, quite triumphantly, and dived into the box.

She pulled out a book – a very old-looking book – with gold-blocked lettering and a *very* familiar illustration on the front.

'*The Enchanted Princess*!' cried Sorcha. 'It is, isn't it?'

'It is.' Susie held it out and Sorcha took it from her very gently.

Her eyes widened as she carefully opened it and she looked at Locryn, clearly stunned. 'It's a first edition,' she almost whispered. 'Published 1910. And it's signed! By them both!'

She handed the book over to Locryn and he looked where she'd indicated. 'Wow. So it is. Noel Andrews and Holly Andrews. And it looks as if the dates mean that baby Joe is the one in the crib, bless him. Susie, how come I never saw this before?'

'Probably because it was in a box of old books Gramps left to me, along with the family history. It was with a load of local history and some other books he was particularly fond of. Gramps could never get rid of a book – his house had them tucked everywhere – but there was one special bookcase where he kept all his favourites. He kept saying to me, "one day, Susie, they'll all be yours." He knew I'd always loved books, I guess that's part of the reason I've worked in libraries and bookshops and things. He said I must have inherited Noel and Holly's affection for them, even though I can't write a story for toffee, and can't daw to save my life.' She grinned. 'So he finally gave me his most precious books. And *The Enchanted Princess* was clearly one of them. I feel so bad that it's taken me this long to find it.' She shook her head. 'If I'd known, you could have seen it long before now.'

'No – no, that's fine.' Locryn looked at Sorcha and smiled. 'I think that today has been the perfect day for us to discover it. I don't think I would have appreciated it as much if we hadn't done all the prep for this exhibition and found out so much about Holly and Noel on the way. I think it's been just the right time to find it.'

'I agree,' Sorcha said. She looked at Locryn. 'It's all absolutely perfect timing.'

And he knew that she meant so much more with those words than the simple discovery of such a precious book.

Chapter Thirty-One

Christmas 1906

Holly woke up to a bright, frosty morning with the faint thudding of a headache just behind her temples. Images of the previous evening came back to her, and she pulled the bedcovers over her head as she recoiled in horror, remembering the bottle of champagne she and Elsie had finished off.

But then she remembered meeting Noel and recalled that first kiss in the linen press, and she huddled deeper into the cosy bed, her room warmed by the fire that someone had kindly set going for her sometime in the early hours, and enjoyed thinking about him for a little longer.

However, she had to get up eventually. She needed to get the train further south today, to get home to her family and enjoy Christmas with them – and then she'd be back up here later this week to stay at Elton Lacy, and then after that she'd be back in London at college. And this would all, quite possibly, seem like a dream – that she'd been living in a fairy tale of beautiful gowns and social events and mad waltzes, where she whirled around and around the floor with Noel ... not that she'd experienced any mad waltzes, and she wasn't sure that Elton Lacy would provide the experience ... but a girl could dream. Even a girl who couldn't really dance.

And, to be fair, the way her head had been spinning when she laid it on the pillow last night might well reflect how it would feel to whirl around and around a dancefloor.

Not to worry.

She hauled herself out of bed and sat for a moment on the edge of it, then heard the rap on her door. It was a fainter, more cautious rap this time, and she padded over and opened it to Elsie.

'Champagne. Damnation. Dammit all to hell. Hellish champagne,' was the greeting.

'I did try to remind you.'

'Try harder next time,' Elsie scolded. Then she pointed to the floor outside the room. 'Breakfast on a tray – everyone's got one this morning. I arranged it last night when you were all playing Sardines. And this. Your next ballgown, Lady Holly.'

Elsie lifted up a dusky pink confection, with panels of gold flowers stitched on it running upwards from the hem and onto the bodice, with small gold sleeves and a frill of gold material running diagonally from the neckline to the bust, backed with white lace.

It was utterly divine.

'Really? Honestly? I can borrow this? It's beautiful!'

'And it'll look all the more beautiful on you. This colour rather washes me out, so you may as well keep it. I shan't be wearing it again.'

'Oh Elsie, you're far too kind.'

'Not at all. Here – take it. Shake it out. Make sure it's suitable. And I'll fetch breakfast in.' Elsie handed the precious dress to Holly and then picked the tray up. She headed into the room and placed it on a small table by the fire.

'It is absolutely gorgeous, honestly it is, and I know I was completely in agreement last night, but that was the champagne talking. Don't you think I'm giving everyone the wrong impression if I wear this as well? They'll all think I have an endless supply of these things, and then they'll see me in my own clothes and the illusion will be shattered. I had best be myself for Pearl's party.'

She held the dress out to Elsie, meaning to return it, but her friend gave her an extremely odd look.

'Holly, my darling, that's the sort of thing someone would do in a book. They'd be all holier-than-thou and appear at the next event in their drab old clothes, hoping the Prince would recognise them by shoving a glass slipper on their shivering little cinder-covered foot, and expecting to live happily ever after.' She shook her head decisively. 'This isn't a book, and you aren't holier-than-thou, so you'll be taking the damn dress and wearing it. Understood?'

Holly couldn't help but laugh. 'Elsie! You're terrible!'

'I am. But you're keeping the dress. It's a Christmas gift and it would be rude to return it.'

'Well, if you put it like that – perhaps you're right.'

'I know I'm right. Now. Have breakfast and I'll help you pack, and by then everyone should be downstairs and we can say our farewells.'

And that was what happened – over breakfast, Elsie and Holly packed up all of Holly's belongings, and Elsie laid Holly's portfolio grandly on the top of her trunk then closed the lid with a flourish. 'I'll have this loaded onto the carriage and you'll all be ready to go. We'll see Pearl and Ernie and Clara and Mabel to say goodbye to – but sadly not Noel, and delightfully not Emma. And you can start the second part of your Christmas holidays. Are you looking forward to going home?'

'Oh absolutely. But,' and she couldn't help but smile widely and throw her arms around Elsie, 'I'm very much looking forward to coming back too.'

*

He'd stayed up most of the night, as he'd suspected he would, scratching away at his story. In his mind, the Enchanted Princess was the absolute image of Holly – even down to her silvery-blonde hair and pretty grey eyes.

By five in the morning, he could do no more. He wasn't sure who was the most surprised – the little maid who crept in ever so quietly to lay his fire (Mrs Jobson insisted some things were done just as they were in "the big houses", and his aunt and uncle didn't object), or he himself as he heard the door click open to admit her. He took the basket of kindling and crumpled papers from the girl, ushered her out with a great deal of thanks, then fell into bed fully clothed – with the fire still unmade – and slept without moving for four hours.

Noel awoke to ice on the inside of the window and a perfect blue sky framing the frosty landscape, his head filled with even more ideas for his story as Holly's smile stayed imprinted on his memory. It all seemed like a dream today though. Had it only been last night he'd met her? It seemed incredible to think that.

But first – he shivered as he sat up – he needed to lay that fire.

He got out of bed and headed over to the fireplace, wincing as he felt the cold air on his face. He tossed a few sticks into the grate, and then grabbed a few pieces of paper to ball up and tuck into the gaps. He struck a match and held it to the pile, ready to throw some coal in from the scuttle. The fire wasn't quite catching in the corner, so he took hold of another piece of newspaper, and started to ball it up...

Then he saw it.

Crumpled up with the newspapers was a thicker type

of paper all together. Something made him take hold of it and look at it properly by the firelight, and his heart began to pound – and not in a good way.

The paper was covered in marks and colour. He smoothed it out carefully and swore. It was a watercolour painting, in a style that was already familiar to him, even though he'd just experienced it for the first time last night.

The artwork was very much like an Arthur Rackham. The signature on the bottom right – *H. Sawyer*.

Noel swore again and rummaged through the rest of the basket. There were five more paintings, all Holly's work, hidden in the basket. 'Emma. You little witch!' he exploded.

He jumped to his feet and threw open his door, running along the corridor until he reached Emma's room.

He pounded on the door relentlessly, until she opened it and stared up at him. '*What* do you want?'

'Do you want to explain *this*?' he growled. He waved the paintings at her, and she had the grace to flush.

'I have no idea what you mean.'

'I mean that you're the only person who could have brought these paintings back here. And definitely the only person who would have taken them down to the kitchens to put in the kindling basket. When did you do it? Did you steal them when you were roaming around Pencradoc? Then bring them here and unpack them with your bag last night? And sneak them downstairs when everyone was asleep? Emma, you are deplorable.'

'It's just not fair, all right?' Emma's cheeks turned an even brighter red and she screwed up her face. 'That girl. That Holly. She has *everything*. I hated her last night. She was pretty and everybody liked her. You liked her, Noel!

You ignored me to spend time with her, and I hated that too. And she has a title! And she's at art school. With Elsie! Can you *imagine* how much fun that would be? My life is nothing like hers, and I thought if you were an Honourable you might marry me and I'd get a title eventually, but you spent all night with *her* when you were meant to be escorting *me*!'

'Emma, I'm your cousin. I'm never going to marry you and I don't believe you even *want* to marry me! The only reason you think it might be a good idea to be with me is because of Grandfather's ridiculous title. You are shallow, Emma. Shallow and ambitious, and it's not a good combination. If you continue to behave like that, nobody will *ever* like you and this is just the icing on a very nasty cake.' He shook the pictures angrily and tears sprang into Emma's eyes – she was being told some long overdue home truths and she clearly didn't like it one bit. 'I'm guessing your justification is jealousy – pure and simple. Again, a very abhorrent trait in a person's character. Now – tell me the damn truth. How many of these did you steal?'

Emma's mouth worked hopelessly as she quite possibly tried to come up with another excuse. But she gave up and burst into tears. 'Six of them. Six of the horrible things. They're just stupid. Stupid little doodles. Copies of paintings. They're stupid.'

'They're not copies. They are, I'd guess, a year's worth of work from Holly and the things she needs to submit to her tutors to pass her course.' He looked at Emma and couldn't stop his lip from curling with disgust. 'Emma. This is underhand and downright nasty. I'd tell Uncle Percy about it, but I have far more important things to do right now. I'll think about it later – and it might just make *him* think twice about letting you attend Victor Fleming's party this week. I hear he's in the market for a wife and he'll have a *genuine* title to play with. Now fancy that.'

He turned on his heel, ignoring Emma's sudden howls of despair, and knew there was only one place he needed to be that morning. *Please God, let me make it in time.*

It was jolly cold on that platform – fortunately, Holly was inside the waiting room, which was smartly decorated for Christmas and hosted a huge roaring fire. Now Holly's head felt better, she was fantasising about toasting crumpets over it and eating them with butter dripping down her chin ...

Oh well – in the absence of crumpets, she was sure there'd be a lovely dinner waiting for her at home, and it would be so nice to be with her family again. She wound her scarf around her neck more tightly and pulled her gloves on more firmly and cast a glance at the clock. Fifteen minutes to go.

Elsie had offered to come with her and stay until the train came, but even though Pearl and Ernie had left soon after the late breakfasts, Clara and Mabel were still at Pencradoc, awaiting their parents and the rest of Elsie's enormous family – including Biscuit, of course – to come up from Wheal Mount. So Holly had sworn she'd be very happy to wait on her own ... which made it all the more surprising when she heard a voice drifting through the windows calling her name.

'Holly! Holly Sawyer – Holly! Are you here? Holly!'

'Noel?' she cried and jumped off the bench to run outside and see if she was correct. Or maybe dreaming. What on earth would Noel be doing here, at the station, shouting her name?

And good heavens, if he *was* here, here *she* was dressed

in her horrible, drab travelling clothes, and there were smuts on her coat from the coal fire in the waiting room, and Biscuit-hairs all over her skirt because he'd obviously had a good old roll on the chair in her room before she'd arrived at Pencradoc, and she'd tossed her skirt unthinkingly onto it so the hairs had stuck to the dark flannel fabric ... and her hair! Goodness gracious, what would he think of her hair? – all pulled into a rough plait with bits escaping everywhere from beneath her hat and surely needing a good old comb through it ...

'*Noel*!' She wasn't dreaming at all; here he was. And he was wearing, if she wasn't mistaken, his clothes from last night beneath a big, grey, warm-looking frock coat. The buttons, her sharp artist's gaze noticed, were fastened up in the wrong places, not meeting at all correctly – which was how she spotted his clothing – and his hair was also all over the place. He had huge dark circles under his eyes and he looked immensely worried. In his hand, he carried a sheaf of papers with a spiderweb of creases running through them. Oddly, he looked incredible – even better, she thought wryly, than he had done the previous night when he was all brushed and groomed.

And suddenly, the coal smuts and the Biscuit-hairs and the unkempt plait didn't seem to matter one jot. He was Noel and she was Holly and, by the look in his eyes as they fixed on her, that was all that mattered.

'Holly!' He hurried over. 'Oh God, I'm so pleased I caught you. Poor Uncle Percy's horse – I don't think he's used to scorching that fast any more. What I would have given to have Ernie's car! It's a miracle I didn't lose these on the way. Thank goodness for saddle bags. It was either that or bringing my Gladstone bag, and I didn't have time—' He took hold of her shoulders and stared into her eyes. Her heart started beating wildly and she blinked, trying to break the spell.

'I have fifteen minutes before my train – what are you doing here?' she managed to ask.

'I had to bring you these. I mean, I could have waited until we saw each other in a few days, like any sensible person might have done. Instead of footling around you here, talking nonsense like an old buffer. Good God. Holly! I can't – I absolutely *can't* just see you standing there before me without doing this though.' And he leant down and kissed her ever so passionately on the lips. He pulled away and flushed. 'Sorry. Sorry. Should have given you these first. Emma … stole them, I think. God! I'm unfit.' He handed the sheaf of papers over to Holly and bent double. 'Stitch in the side!' he qualified, and then stood up. 'Sorry. I knew you'd be here and wanted to get them to you. Wanted to see you. Before you left. Good excuse anyway.' He ducked down again briefly. '*Damn* stitch!'

Holly shook her head, still dazed at the kiss, and with slightly shaking hands, separated the pages he had presented to her as he stood upright again and stretched.

'These are mine! My paintings. From my *portfolio* …' She looked up at Noel, horror dawning. 'Emma *took* them? She really *took* them?' Holly had half a mind to take Uncle Percy's old horse and race him back from whence he came to challenge the hideous girl.

'It's a nasty jar all right,' said Noel. 'An awful situation – but you need to get your train today and I'm just pleased I rescued them.'

'Rescued them from *where*?' asked Holly, torn between fury at Emma, relief she had her precious things back, and overwhelming joy and attraction at the sight of the man who stood inches from her.

'Oh, just from her luggage.' Noel shifted position. 'She decided it would be fun to hide them, just to cause a fuss and a bother. Then when she and Mabes had that disagreement last night, she stormed off and brought them to me this morning. Full of remorse. Sorry she'd crumpled them. Yes. Quite.'

'Noel Andrews. I don't believe you for one minute.' Holly waved the paintings at him. 'I believe she took them, but that in itself wouldn't have made you scorch down here on that poor animal. One day, you can tell me the truth. And not embroider it up in a fairy tale. But whatever the reason – thank you. Thank you so much. I would have panicked dreadfully when I got home and thought I'd lost them. My portfolio – it was in my room. When we saw her, she must have been heading that way then. I knew it! I *knew* it! Didn't I say – didn't I—'

But her hysterically rising voice was silenced by another kiss, Noel's lips pressed hard against hers. All thoughts of Emma temporarily drifted away and Holly gave herself up to the moment.

'Sorry – couldn't waste the time. It's a long time until I see you again.' Noel grinned. 'A few days at least. Not certain how I'll survive. Anyway. Hope you can straighten them out.' He frowned and nodded at the paintings.

Holly sighed. 'I'll manage. I'll press them in a heavy old book or something. But thank you. Thank you so much.'

'You're very welcome.'

They stood there, Holly horribly aware that the train would be at the platform before she knew it. In fact, she could already see the steam coming over the buildings and hear the *chug chug chug* of the engine as it made its way to the station.

'Noel – I have to say something. Before I jump on

that fire-breathing dragon and get whisked away for Christmas. What you just did there – you stole *another* kiss from an Enchanted Princess. You really did.'

'I did.' Noel nodded. 'Should I be sorry about that?' He didn't seem sorry in the least.

Holly smiled and reached up, smoothing his hair down. It bounced straight back up again into uncombed disarray. 'No. Not really. But you have to understand that this particular Princess thinks that if she allows you to steal a kiss, the only way to rectify it is if she steals it back, just as soon as she's able.'

'I'll willingly let her steal it – and more besides.' He took her face in his hands and stared down at her, his eyes dark and soft and twinkling and hungry. 'I offer her my heart and my life. And my love. My eternal, undying love.'

Dramatically, he removed one hand from her cheek and placed it on his heart, and she giggled. 'That will do for now,' she said. And she leaned up to him and let him steal another kiss … just as the dragon-train breathed more fire into the air and bore down on her, ready to swallow her up for Christmas.

But Holly knew that, at that moment, she was happier than any princess in a fairy tale, because even as she boarded and sat down before looking out of the grimy old window as the porter loaded all the travellers' bags onto the train, she saw her very own dishevelled, yet extraordinarily handsome Prince waving at her from the platform.

She watched him waving until he was out of sight, then she sat back in the seat clutching her precious paintings, and had the oddest feeling that she had been looking back at her future.

And it was as perfect as the most perfect fairy tale ever written.

Chapter Thirty-Two

Christmas Present
17th December

The Tower Tea Room looked incredible, even if Sorcha said so herself. It was the first night of Locryn's exhibition, and Merryn was just upstairs making sure everything was tip-top before they officially opened. Sorcha and Locryn were waiting as the last few minutes ticked away before they could finally open the door.

'The tea sets really make it, don't they?' she asked Locryn, for the umpteenth time. 'Thanks again for letting me use them. Do you really think I've made enough rum truffles?' She peered across at a large Edwardian serving dish, full of plump truffles, each one covered in real chocolate vermicelli sugar strands and decorated with tiny marzipan holly leaves. The idea was that guests would be able to nibble a truffle and indulge in some mulled wine as a welcome before they headed up to the top of the tower; then they'd come back downstairs for more substantial nibbles and Cordy's ghost stories after they'd admired "The Spirit of Christmas Past" exhibition.

Indeed, the building was wreathed in the scents of Sorcha's festive baking, and there was an antique punch bowl full of mulled wine and some bottles of traditional ginger beer for those who chose to stay a little more sober on the opening night.

Trays of bite-size stollen, gingerbread stars and buttery shortbread graced the kitchen counters, along with some turkey and cranberry rolls, finger sandwiches, miniature stuffing balls and individual Yorkshire pudding canapés, ready to be served up afterwards – hopefully when people were mingling and chatting happily. The nibbles would soon be brought through, along with mini mince pies, the peppermint slices so beloved of Merryn and some tiny squares of Christmas cake, and all set out on the vintage plates in preparation for visitors coming down for tea. Sorcha had also managed to source some Christmas pudding coffee, which was warm and delicious, and some Christmas loose leaf tea, which was a festive, more spicy version of the mouth-watering Earl Grey tea people were more familiar with.

'I really think you've made enough. And thank you again for doing this.' Locryn gathered her up in his arms and she snuggled in happily as they looked at the room, ready to receive the visitors. 'But I don't mind telling you, I'm a little nervous.' He grinned and released her, smoothing back his hair. 'What if nobody decides to come? It's dark, it's cold, and I swear it's going to snow!'

'Let it snow. We don't have far to walk home – and you can always stay at mine if you *really* don't want to walk home.' She knew she was being mischievous – they lived at opposite sides of the village, but the distance still wasn't that far. 'Anyway. It's unlikely they'll not come.' Sorcha nodded towards the door. 'What with Coren's press releases and my flyers, and your posters all over the village.' She nudged him. 'And Aunt Susie's posters as well. And, to be honest, the copy of Holly's picture on all that publicity stuff would be enough to attract anyone, I think – but I'm pleased they didn't reveal your family connection. That would have overshadowed your whole exhibition and they need to see you as *you*. Just wait – the visitors will be barging in any time soon.'

'Let's hope so.'

'Well – it's time to see, isn't it?' She nodded to the clock on the wall, which had a cheeky robin decoration stood firmly on top of it. 'Merryn!' she bellowed up the stairs. 'We're good to go down here.'

'Fabulous.' Merryn appeared, her boots clattering on the spiral staircase as she descended to the tea room. 'It's looking brilliant up there.' She smiled. 'Cordy's over at the house getting her sparkly frock on so she'll head over in half an hour or so. I've set the music playing near the gramophone so we've got some Christmas carols going on, and it's all ready and welcoming. Good luck with it all, Locryn. Would you like to open the door, or shall I do the honours?'

'You can, I think.' He suddenly looked a little uncomfortable. 'There might be a speech or something required.'

'No speeches. But I can tell you we sold the maximum number of tickets – so be prepared for the onslaught of fifty excitable visitors. Just as well you've got Steph and Josh coming, I think, Sorcha.' Steph was Sorcha's niece who sometimes helped out in the tea room, and Josh was her boyfriend, who basically came because Steph did, but was also a very keen milk-frother. Merryn took a deep breath and smiled, then she headed over to the door and took hold of the handle. 'Ready or not, here we go …'

Locryn was stunned at the steady stream of people who came into the tea room, accepted a glass of wine and a truffle, exclaimed in delight at the fact they were here at Pencradoc after hours, and trotted upstairs to see the exhibition. Aunt Susie was right near the front. She squeezed Locryn's hand as she walked in and whispered to him, 'Well done. This is the right thing to do, you know? You've brought them back. I love the fact you've put the book with the exhibits as well. My gramps would be ecstatic. I love Pencradoc, and I love our connection to Noel and Holly Andrews – and I've always suspected it was those two who fell in love here. I'm very happy right now, Locryn! And I'm the most superest-proudest aunt ever.'

'Thanks Aunt Susie! And I'm pretty sure we got it right with Noel and Holly,' he whispered back with a grin. Little did Susie know they'd also had pretty concrete proof that Noel and Holly had been at Pencradoc one particular Christmas, even before they'd known about it from Elsie's Visitors' Book.

Once Locryn had welcomed everyone, he followed the guests up the stairs and was delighted to see the smiling faces and hear the exclamations of delight as they looked at the treasures he'd brought to Pencradoc – *or perhaps back to Pencradoc*, he thought with a smile as he saw a couple admiring the Visitors' Book.

'Noel Andrews! Goodness me. I loved *The Enchanted Princess*. My copy is almost dropping to bits. That copy is so perfect, I can't believe it's a signed first edition. It must have been well looked after to be in such good condition. Imagine the fact that Noel Andrews was actually here. That's his signature in the Visitors' Book as well! Unbelievable.' The woman's nose was practically on top of the glass cabinet as she spoke in awed tones about Noel.

Locryn hid another smile. Part of him was desperate to share the real family connection he had to Noel and Holly, but he didn't feel it was something he should just spring upon these people. Instead, he walked up next to them and spoke, 'Hi. Yes, we've got an original illustration based on the book as well, from Holly – just over there. It's been in their family a long time, so we're really lucky we've been allowed to share it with you guys today.' He glanced across at Aunt Susie who was looking proudly at the picture. She turned and looked back at him and blew him a little kiss, then gave him a thumbs up sign. He was glad she approved. He hoped they all would – Holly and Noel and, yes, even Elsie, whose precious Visitors' Book and hand-painted Christmas notelets, containing festive greetings to her family at Wheal Mount, were displayed alongside each other.

'Oh my! You're so lucky to have these things all together in one place. Actually, we're the lucky ones being able to see it as well. This is incredible. Thank you. It's making me feel so festive.' The lady indicated the room. 'Those little Christmas cards are so pretty as well. I love the angels on them. I'd love to have something like that to frame. Are they for sale?'

'Yes – yes, everything's going back to the shop after this, so it's all for sale, and I've got more of them back there too. Well, I *say* everything's for sale – everything's for sale apart from the Visitors' Book, Elsie's notecards, the first edition and the Holly Andrews' painting, of course.'

'Of course.' The lady smiled. 'Well, I know where I'll be tomorrow! I'll bring my friend and we'll have a good old rummage. I've walked past the shop but haven't been in yet. That is going to change now I know the sort of things you sell. And with the connections to Pencradoc, as well as *The Enchanted Princess*! Wonderful.'

'I look forward to seeing you. And enjoy your tea – I can recommend the Christmas cake squares. Well, I can recommend everything, actually!'

'Thank you. It's so nice to do something a little different, isn't it? This is perfect. My friend is desperate for some vintage tree decorations as well. I'll tell her about those ones over there, the silver ones, and she can see if you've got anything similar in stock. Like I say. Perfect.'

Locryn couldn't agree more, but he simply smiled and thanked the lady again and looked up as someone else waved him over. This time it was a gentleman, who was highly interested in the seasonal artwork he was displaying: prints of Christmassy scenes, snowy landscapes, pretty, wintry engravings. The man had a gallery, apparently, and was looking for some new stock for his own exhibitions. Soon, Locryn had a firm commitment from him as well that he'd visit the shop and see what he could acquire.

All in all, "The Spirit of Christmas Past" was a huge success and, as the visitors drifted away to indulge in Sorcha's incredible baking and settle down for their ghost stories, Locryn was left alone in the tower room, standing silently in front of Holly's watercolour.

It was incredible to think that their story, this story in fact, had started right here at Pencradoc, at a Christmas party over a century ago. And now – now Holly and Noel were back here, the early days of their romance brought back to life in the watercolour and the Visitors' Book. If he held his breath and stood very still, he could almost hear the rustle of a gown, the breathy laugh from so many years ago. The whispered, teasing promises seemed to carry through the wintry evening air to him.

'I offer her my heart and my life. And my love. My eternal, undying love.'

'Eternal and undying. Nice one, Noel,' murmured

Locryn, studying the beautiful woman in the painting and the man who looked so similar to himself.

'Eternal and undying what?' Sorcha's voice was close to him, her footsteps soft on the old floorboards as she came up to him and put her arms around his waist, resting her head on his shoulder and peeking over it at the painting.

Perhaps it had been her clothes he had heard rustling ... but perhaps not.

'Love.' He nodded at Holly and Noel, and traced his finger over the cradle. 'I can't quite believe they're my family when I look at this. And that if it hadn't been for one particular Christmas at Pencradoc, we might not be here now.'

'We would have been.' Sorcha sounded confident. 'We all would have found ourselves eventually. I firmly believe that.'

'Me too, actually.' Locryn smiled and turned around so he was facing her and she was in his arms. 'How's it going downstairs?'

'Splendidly. Everyone's happily clearing their plates, Cordy's here, Aunt Susie has told me I have to come for tea tomorrow to recuperate, and Steph and Josh are doing a grand job holding the fort. I wanted to come up and see how you were. See whether it's all been worth it. Whether Christmas is just a little bit more magical this year – a bit more like a fairy tale come true?'

'A fairy tale come true? Well – yes. Yes, I think it is, actually. They do love their happy ever afters in those things, don't they?'

'They do.' She nodded, quite seriously. 'I'm hoping that kind of happens here. For us. You know?'

'I know.' He drew her towards him and leaned his

forehead against hers, looking into her eyes, seeing excitement and magic and just a little bit of danger in there. The best sort of fairy tale anyone could ever write, in fact. And here he was, living it, at Pencradoc, certain that the spirits of Holly and Noel were urging them on to take the next step in their, as yet unwritten, adventures. But he kind of knew where it would end. And he was very much looking forward to the journey.

'I like happy ever afters,' he said.

'Me too,' she said.

Then, in the shadow of Holly and Noel's love, they kissed.

And just outside, it started snowing again, a gentle little flurry that wouldn't lie for very long – but there was enough, had anyone been looking, to make out two shapes forming out of the sparkling crystals: the final secret in this particular fairy tale. One figure, a girl with long, silvery hair was sitting on a fallen tree trunk, and the other, a tall, fair-haired man, was placing a glistening slipper on her foot. Then he stood up and offered his hand, inviting her into his waiting arms.

'And the Fairy Princess stood, and she walked on the snow in her slippers made of moonlight, and they lived happily ever after ...'

Thank You

Thank you so much for reading, and hopefully enjoying, *Holly's Christmas Secret*. It's the third book in the Pencradoc Cornish Secrets series and I loved writing about Sorcha and Locryn, and Holly and Noel. You might remember Sorcha from *Lily's Secret* – she seemed to be the perfect fit for a Pencradoc Christmas book, the writing of which was fuelled almost entirely by mince pies!

However, authors need to know they are doing the right thing, and keeping our readers happy is a huge part of the job. So it would be wonderful if you could find a moment just to write a quick review on the website where you bought to book to let me know that you enjoyed it. Thank you once again, and do feel free to contact me at any time on Facebook, Twitter, through my website or through my lovely publishers Choc Lit.

Much love to you all,

Kirsty

xxx

About the Author

Kirsty Ferry is from the North East of England and lives there with her husband and son. She won the English Heritage/Belsay Hall National Creative Writing competition in 2009 and has had articles and short stories published in various magazines. Her work also appears in several anthologies, incorporating such diverse themes as vampires, crime, angels and more.

Kirsty loves writing ghostly mysteries and interweaving fact and fiction. The research is almost as much fun as writing the book itself, and if she can add a wonderful setting and a dollop of history, that's even better.

Her day job involves sharing a building with an eclectic collection of ghosts, which can often prove rather interesting.

For more information on Kirsty visit:
Twitter: www.twitter.com/kirsty_ferry
Facebook: www.facebook.com/kirsty.ferry.author/

More Choc Lit

From Kirsty Ferry

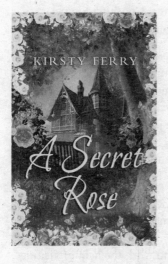

A Secret Rose

Book 1 in the Cornish Secrets series

"Wherever you go, I will follow …"

Merryn Burton is excited to travel down to Cornwall to start her first big job for the London art dealers she works for. But as soon as she arrives at Pencradoc, a beautiful old mansion, she realises this will be no ordinary commission.

Not only is Pencradoc filled with fascinating, and possibly valuable artwork, it is also owned by the Penhaligon brothers – and Merryn's instant connection with Kit Penhaligon could be another reason why her trip suddenly becomes a whole lot more interesting.

But the longer Merryn stays at Pencradoc the more obvious it is that the house has a secret, and a long-forgotten Rose might just hold the key …

Visit www.choc-lit.com for details.

Lily's Secret

Book 2 in the Cornish Secrets series

'There's nothing logical about Pencradoc!'

Aspiring actress Cordelia Beaumont is fed up of spending summer in the city. So, when the opportunity presents itself, she jumps straight on a train to pay a visit to Pencradoc – the beautiful Cornish estate where her friend Merryn works.

But far from the relaxing break Cordy imagined, she soon finds herself immersed in the glamorous yet mysterious world of Victorian theatre sensation, Lily Valentine. Lily was once a guest at Pencradoc and, with the help of visiting artist Matt Harker, Cordy comes to discover that the actress left far more than memories at the old house. She also left a scandalous secret …

Summer's Secret Marigold

Book 4 in the Cornish Secrets series

Can a summer secret from the past allow a new future to bloom?

For two people who run competing arts centres in Cornwall, Sybill Helyer and Coren Penhaligon get on rather well. So well in fact that Sybill often wishes the owner of Pencradoc Arts Centre would look up from his spreadsheets for a minute and notice her. Unfortunately, even that's too much to ask from workaholic Coren.

However, when the pair join forces to run an exhibition on the wild and wonderful life of Elsie Pencradoc, a talented artist who lived at Coren's estate in the early twentieth century, they're in for a surprise. How will a secret sketchbook and an exquisite gothic dress from a long-ago midsummer costume ball lead them to the scandalous truth about Elsie – and perhaps encourage them to reveal a few long-kept secrets of their own?

Visit www.choc-lit.com for details.

Christmas of New Beginnings

Book 1 in the Padcock
Village series

**Not all festive wishes come
true right away – sometimes
it takes five Christmases …**

Folk singer Cerys Davies
left Wales for the South
Downs village of Padcock
at Christmas, desperate for
a new beginning. And she
ends up having plenty of
those: opening a new craft shop-tea room, helping set up
the village's first festive craft fair, and, of course, falling
desperately in love with Lovely Sam, the owner of the local
pub. It's just too bad he's firmly in the clutches of Awful
Belinda …

Perhaps Cerys has to learn that some new beginnings take a
while to … well, begin! But with a bit of patience, some mild
espionage, a generous sprinkling of festive magic and a flock
of pub-crashing sheep, could her fifth Christmas in Padcock
lead to her best new beginning yet?

Visit www.rubyfiction.com for details.

Edie's Summer of New Beginnings

Book 2 in the Padcock Village series

Can Edie rediscover her artistic mojo and become a 'Watercolour Wonder'?

Edie Brinkley went from rising star on the London art scene to hiding out at her gran's cottage in the little village of Padcock after a series of unfortunate circumstances leave her almost too panicky to pick up a paintbrush.

When celebrity artist Ninian Chambers rocks up in the village to film Watercolour Wonders, a new TV art competition, Edie is horrified – especially as he played no small part in her decision to leave London.

But, with the support of the Padcock community, and one very special fellow contestant, could Ninian's show ultimately offer a fresh start for Edie and her art career? Or will Annabel the sixties' style stealer, along with make-up artist Tallulah and her 'Caravan of Hell', sabotage her summer of new beginnings?

Visit www.rubyfiction.com for details.

The Schubert Series

A series of quirky romcoms set in Edinburgh and featuring a big black cat called Schubert!

**Every Witch Way
– Book 1**

**A Christmas Secret
– Book 2**

**It Started
With a Giggle
– Book 3**

**It Started
With a Pirate
– Book 4**

**It Started
With a Wedding
– Book 5**

Visit www.choc-lit.com for more details.

Introducing Choc Lit

The Tempest Sisters Series

Cosy contemporary romances set in Scotland and on the North East coast.

Christmas on the Isle of Skye
– Book 4

Summer at Carrick Park
– Book 3

Jessie's Little Bookshop by the Sea – Book 2

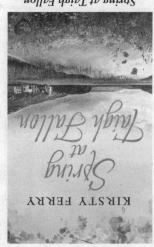

Spring at Taigh Fallon
– Book 1

The Rossetti Mysteries

A series of compelling time-slip romances set in
the art world in Yorkshire and London.

Some Veil Did Fall
– Book 1

The Girl in the Painting
– Book 2

The Girl in the Photograph –
Book 3

A Little Bit of Christmas
Magic – Book 4

Visit www.choc-lit.com for more details.

The Hartsford Mysteries

A series of atmospheric time-slip romances, all set in the same beautiful mansion house in Suffolk.

Watch for Me by Moonlight
– Book 1

Watch for Me by Candlelight
– Book 2

Watch for Me by Twilight
– Book 3

Watch for Me at Christmas
– Book 4

Visit www.choc-lit.com for more details.